Cat's Eyewitness

Cat's Eyewitness

RITA MAE BROWN

& SNEAKY PIE BROWN

ILLUSTRATIONS BY MICHAEL GELLATLY

DOUBLEDAY LARGE PRINT HOME LIBRARY EDITION

BANTAM BOOKS

NEW YORK • TORONTO • LONDON • SYDNEY • AUCKLAND

This Large Print Edition, prepared especially for Doubleday Large Print Home Library, contains the complete, unabridged text of the original Publisher's Edition.

CAT'S EYEWITNESS
A Bantam Book / February 2005

Published by
Bantam Dell
A Division of Random House, Inc.
New York, New York

Quote from the *Book of Common Prayer* (contains Bible passages) of the Episcopal Church of USA, 1928, amended 1952.

Bantam Books is a registered trademark of Random House, Inc., and the colophon is a trademark of Random House, Inc.

ISBN 0-7394-5063-8

Printed in the United States of America
Published simultaneously in Canada

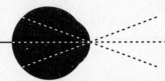

This Large Print Book carries the Seal of Approval of N.A.V.H.

Dedicated to
The Almost Home Pet Adoption Center
of Nelson County

Cast of Characters

Mary Minor "Harry" Haristeen The postmistress of Crozet, Virginia, is curious, sometimes bull-headed, and often in the midst of trouble. Her life is changing and she's struggling to change with it.

Mrs. Murphy Harry's tiger cat accepts change better than her human does. She's tough, smart, and ready for action, and she'll always take a little catnip, too.

Tee Tucker Harry's corgi bubbles with happiness and bravery in equal measure. She loves Harry as only a dog can love.

Pewter Harry's gray cat affects aloofness but underneath it all, she does care. What irritates her are comments about her plumpness and her hunting abilities.

Mrs. Miranda Hogendobber Miranda observes a great deal but keeps most of it to herself. A widow, she's a surrogate mother to Harry and the relationship means a great deal to both women.

Susan Tucker Harry's best friend has been putting up with Harry's curiosity and attraction to danger since they were children. They have their ups and downs like most friends but they stick together.

Ned Tucker Susan's husband and a lawyer who is now running for political office.

Fair Haristeen, D.V.M. Once Harry's childhood sweetheart and then her husband, he hopes to be her husband again. He has a good mind, a stout heart, and the patience to put up with her.

Olivia Craycroft "BoomBoom" Once Harry's nemesis, the two have settled into a slightly strained rapprochement. BoomBoom is quite beautiful, a fact never lost on men.

Alicia Palmer A former resident of Crozet, she keeps an estate there. She conquered Hollywood as an actress and now in her mid-fifties, she's come home. She's retained all of her glamour while losing most of her illusions.

Rev. Herbert C. Jones Beloved, humorous, fond of fishing, all of Crozet knows that when the chips are down, "The Rev" will come through.

Marilyn Sanburne "Big Mim" The queen of Crozet exerts her social power with whatever force is needed to accomplish her task. She can be a snob but she's fair in her own fashion and believes strongly in justice.

Jim Sanburne As the mayor of Crozet, he presides over the town, which is easier to do sometimes than to be Big Mim's husband.

Marilyn Sanburne, Jr. "Little Mim" She is emerging from her mother's influence. She's a contemporary of Harry, Susan, and BoomBoom but she's always been set apart by her family's wealth. She is the vice-mayor of Crozet and a Republican, which is quite interesting since her father is a Democrat.

Deputy Cynthia Cooper A young, bright officer in the Sheriff's Department, she likes law enforcement but wonders if it keeps romance at bay. She's become a buddy of Harry's, and the cats and dog like her, too.

Sheriff Rick Shaw There are days now when Rick is tired of criminals, tired of their lies, tired of pressing the county commissioners for more funds. But when a murder occurs, he focuses his sharp mind to bring the pieces of the puzzle together—if only that damned Harry and her pets would get out of the way.

Tazio Chappars A young architect, she gets men's hearts racing. She's a rather serious sort of woman but kind and considerate.

Paul de Silva Big Mim's new stable manager is handsome, efficient, and a little bit shy. He's crazy about Tazio.

Brother Handle The Prior of Mt. Carmel Monastery is hard-headed and focused on saving his order in an increasingly secularized world. Events at the monastery shake him to his core.

Brother Prescott The second-in-command, he humors Brother Handle while trying to keep peace among the brothers.

Brother Frank The dour, mistrustful and hard-working treasurer. Others can indulge in flights of fancy, he has to pay the bills.

Brother Thomas Susan Tucker's great-uncle. Kind, patient, fond of good cognac, he is the oldest monk at eighty-two.

Brother Mark He never met a substance he didn't try to ingest. He woke up one bitter winter night in the middle of Beverly St. in Staunton and found Jesus. He's the emotional type.

Nordy Elliott A young, handsome, conceited newscaster at Channel 29. He has an eye for the main chance and when it comes, he makes the most of it.

Brother Andrew A physician at the monastery who bends the rules when he feels justified in doing so.

Brother John Also a doctor, goes along with bending those rules.

Bo and Nancy Newell They own and run Mountain Area Realty in Nellysford.

Pete Osborne The program director at Channel 29, he gives Nordy Elliott his big break and deeply repents unleashing that fulsome ego of his. Soon he has cause for other worries.

Mt. Carmel A monastery founded in 1866 modeled on the Carmelite order.

Cat's Eyewitness

A thin trickle of water zigzagged over the Virgin Mary's cold face. She gazed westward from her home on top of the Blue Ridge Mountains, between Afton Gap and Humpback Mountain. Her elevation approached two thousand two hundred feet. The fertile expanse of the Shenandoah Valley spread below, rolling westward to the Allegheny Mountains. The Valley, made immortal by the military genius of Stonewall Jackson, had been beloved of the Native Americans long before the European immigrants, refugees, and mountebanks ever beheld its calming beauty.

Had the Blessed Virgin Mother been able to turn her head and look east, undulating hills traversed with ravines and ridges stopping at the Southwest Range would have delighted her eyes. The last spur of the Appalachian Mountain chain, the Southwest Range gives way on its eastern slopes to land with a gentle roll. These rich fields and forests drop until the Fall Line, the true geographic boundary between low country and up-country, between sandy soils, red clay, and loam mixtures. This line also divided the Iroquois-speaking peoples from the Sioux-speaking peoples. Neither side liked the other much, warfare and raids occurring with savage regularity. Into this political hot zone trooped the English, the first surviving colony founded in 1607. Those that lived, learned.

The conclusion of the Revolutionary War in 1781, one hundred and seventy-four years after Jamestown was founded, unleashed an exuberance of trade, exploration, birthrate, and optimism. Even the fierce Monocan tribe and their allies, who had kept the whites from building safe communities ever westward of the Fall Line, couldn't hold them back.

The land on which Mary stood was settled in 1794 by Catholics more comfortable on the crest of the mountains than walking among their hustling Protestant neighbors in Richmond or the Tidewater. They built a log chapel. The land and altitude were good for apples. Orchards flourished. After the Constitutional Convention, the new Constitution made crystal clear the separation between church and state. Many of the apple-growing Catholics moved down the mountain into Nelson and Albemarle Counties on the eastern slopes, Augusta County on the western slopes. Nestled in the valleys, the temperature warmer, the winds less fierce than on the mountaintop, the former religious refugees prospered.

The hard-core mountain people, many of them distillers of clear liquor—the mountain streams being wonderful for such endeavors—stayed in the hollows. They didn't want to live on a mountaintop.

Finally in 1866 a war-weary Confederate captain founded a monastic order based on the Carmelites. He called it Mt. Carmel after the original in Palestine. Carmelite orders were being founded in the north after the War Between the States. Captain Ainsly was defiant and remained independent of the international monastic order even though he followed their rules. Instead of being known as Whitefriars, the monks on Afton Mountain were called Greyfriars because of their gray wool robes, an echo of their uniform color.

The monastery itself was not open to the public. The dairy, the chandler's building, the food building with honey and jams, and the ironmonger's forge were open, though, as were the exquisite gardens. The products were made by the monks themselves. Applejack was their biggest seller. Made on the grounds from apples grown in the old orchards, the brothers took special care with their distillery. Folks said Greyfriars' applejack could kick one harder than a mule.

The Virgin Mary stood on the highest point of land, the spring gardens nestled below her. She was carved from native soapstone by another Confederate veteran sick of war and worldly corruption. The Blessed Virgin Mother radiated a sorrow, a forgiveness that touched many who looked upon her. The stones leading to her, worn concave from many feet, bore testimony to her grace and power.

On this day, November 24, Thanksgiving, snow settled in the folds of her raiment. It covered the earth down to a thousand feet above sea level. Below that, freezing rain pelted farm and forest.

Mary Minor "Harry" Haristeen had driven up before the rain reached the eastern meadows. But as she squinted upward into a leaden sky, she knew getting down Afton Mountain would take a steady hand and a steady foot, no jamming on the brakes.

Her three dearest companions—Mrs. Murphy, a tiger cat, Pewter, a gray cat, and Tee Tucker, a brave corgi—had smelled the shift in the weather before their human friend knew it was coming. Confident in her driving ability, Harry wouldn't have turned back even if she had foreseen the change. She was determined to spend an hour on the mountain, alone and in thought, before plunging into Thanksgiving cheer. She'd quit her job as postmistress after sixteen years because the U.S. Postal Service was building a large, modern post office in Crozet by the railroad track. In this fit of im- provement, the bigwigs decided that Mrs. Murphy, Pewter, and Tucker could no longer "work" with her. How could she live without the cats and dog? How could millions of Americans sit in windowless cubicles with- out even a bird to keep them connected to real life? Harry couldn't live like that. Not yet forty, she felt a disquieting alienation from so-called modern life. What seemed vital to others, like wading through their e-mail, seemed fake to her. Harry was at a crossroads, not sure which way to jump.

The dear older woman she worked with, Miranda Hogendobber, walked out when she did. But Miranda had her deceased husband's retirement to draw upon; she'd been frugal and was in good shape.

Harry wasn't in good shape financially. Taxes crept upward like kudzu threatening to choke her small farm profits, in particular, and ultimately free enterprise, in general. Services became ever more expensive and gas prices bounced up and down like a basketball in an NBA game.

On top of those worries was her ex-husband, Fair Haristeen, who still loved her and had made significant amends for what Harry saw as bad behavior. Fair had grown up and wanted her back, wanted a mature bond. He was handsome. Harry had a weak spot for a handsome man. Fair qualified at six five, blond hair, all muscle. An equine veterinarian, he specialized in reproduction. They both shared a profound love of horses.

Harry, at last, had made peace with the bombshell Fair had dallied with four years back when their marriage blew up. Olivia "BoomBoom" Craycroft slew men the way longhaired Samson slew his enemies. BoomBoom had enjoyed Fair's impressive physique and his Virginia gentleman ways, but she bored easily, soon dismissing him. "Think of this as recess from class," were her exact words. For all of BoomBoom's heartlessness with men where romance was concerned, she loved animals, was a good athlete, and demonstrated great community spirit. In a word, she was fabulous, until you slept with her or if you were the woman left in the dust by your boyfriend or husband.

As Harry stared up at the unearthly face of the Virgin, she shivered. Tucker, at her feet, shook off the thickening snow.

"She's beautiful," the corgi said.

Harry bent down, patting the glossy head. "Bet you think I'm crazy standing out here. Probably am."

Tucker lifted her nose, breathed deeply. *"Susan."* The little dog took off toward the enticing scent, skidding to a halt about forty yards away where a curved stone bench overlooked The Valley. The bench, situated on a winding path below the statue, was hidden from view if one was standing in front of the Virgin Mary.

The Valley was usually colder than the eastern slopes. Snow was falling there, a patchwork quilt of white, beige, and corn stubble two thousand feet below.

"Tucker," Susan said, surprised. "Where's Mom?"

Harry, pursuing her dog, slipped along the walkway between tall magnificent English boxwoods, only to be equally surprised when she saw her best friend. "Susan, what are you doing here?"

"I could ask you the same thing," Susan replied, smiling.

Harry brushed off the snow to sit next to Susan. Tucker wedged between them. "I'm here because I, well, I need help. I know the Blessed Virgin Mother has always been reputed to have powers—the statue, I mean. Miranda says whenever times get tough she comes up here and talks with Mary."

"Girl talk." Susan smiled, her auburn hair peeking out from underneath her lad's cap.

"Wish she could talk. I'd like to hear that Jesus wasn't perfect." Harry sighed. "It's too hard having perfect Gods—you know, God the Father, God the Son, and I have no idea who or what the Holy Ghost is. I mean it," she said as Susan laughed. "You went to Bible school in the summers, same as I did; we suffered through two years of catechism together. We only made Confirmation because Reverend Jones took pity on us. I can recite the Nicene Creed but I still can't tell you why I'm supposed to care about it. What is the Holy Ghost?" She threw up her hands, red gloves bright against the gloom. "But I understand Mary, the Blessed Virgin Mother. She's one of us; oh, better, but still, she's one of us."

"Yes." Susan reached for her friend's hand, her tan glove twining with the red. "I talk to her, too. Questions. Life. Big questions. Little questions." Susan shrugged.

"The questions get bigger as we get older, don't you think?"

"I do."

Harry took a deep breath, the air scouring her lungs. "I'm here because I don't know what I'm doing. I feel dumb and maybe I really am dumb. And Fair asked me to marry him again."

"Ah." Susan smiled.

"That means you think it's a good idea."

"I'm glad he loves you. You're worth loving." She squeezed Harry's hand.

"Susan." Tears filled Harry's eyes, for kindness and praise affected her more deeply than criticism or meanness. She could stand up to that.

"You are, dear heart. You're my best friend and you know you can tell me anything."

"Tell you? Susan, all I've done for the last three months is bitch and moan."

"Oh, you have not. Anyone in your position is bound to be anxious. No money is coming in and you have to be careful. At least the farm is free and clear and so is the equipment."

"There's the dually payment." Harry mentioned the big one-ton Ford truck with the double wheels that she bought at a great price from Art Bushey, Jr., the Ford dealer and a good friend. His sense of humor was as twisted as hers, so of course they adored each other.

"Four hundred something a month."

"Yes. The feed bill, the gas and electric. I mean, I'm okay, but I've got to do something here pretty soon."

"You're still investigating growing grapes, aren't you? Sounds like a good idea." Susan was encouraging.

"I need to bring money in while I study that. I can't afford to get started anytime soon, since the capital outlay is outrageous. Patricia Kluge said she'd sit down with me. Her vineyards are a booming success. Felicia Rogan, who really revived the whole wine industry in Virginia, said she'd talk to me, too. Still, I need to do something, just get some money coming in. Fair said I could work with him as a vet tech. I know the drill but it's not a great idea. I mean, not until I come to a decision, and I've dragged it out far too long. I'm such a chicken." She brightened a moment. "What I understand, know like the back of my hand, is hay. I'm thinking I could become a hay dealer, not just grow it but buy it from the Midwest, Pennsylvania, and Canada, then sell it. As I do that I could keep learning about grape stuff and see if I could add another string to my bow."

"Sounds like a good plan to me."

"Except I need a paycheck now."

"Pug would take you back in the post office." Susan mentioned the federal employee in charge of postal services for the area.

"No."

"Pride goeth before a fall."

"It's not pride. I'm not working without my babies."

"Where are Mrs. Murphy and Pewter?"

"In the truck, steaming up the windows." Harry leaned toward Susan. "Why are you here?"

Susan quietly looked over the Shenandoah Valley. "It's really coming down. Let's hope by the time we drive down Route 250 it's snowing on our side."

"Susan." Harry knew her friend inside and out.

"Ned and I are drifting apart."

Harry's face registered shock. "How? You seem close to me."

"He's distant. He doesn't much want sex anymore. He's all wrapped up in being our newly elected senator to Richmond. He's spending more time in the apartment he just rented there than at home."

"Mmm, the sex part is disturbing."

"Tell me."

"He's got a lot to learn about the job."

Harry hoped this would help Susan push upsetting thoughts about Ned aside.

"Brooks graduates from high school this year. Danny loves Cornell. The house will soon be empty. He's starting a whole new life. I feel like my life, or at least my usefulness, is vanishing, ending."

Harry leaned into Tucker as Susan did, too. "All of this is a big change for both of you. He's handling it differently than you, that's all."

"I hope so." Tears now ran down Susan's face. "You know I'm not cut out to be a political wife. I'm no good at it." She wiped away a tear. "Ned is handsome. I've heard all those stories about politicians and pretty interns."

Harry wrapped an arm around Susan's shoulders. "Oh, honey, don't cry."

"I remember when it happened to you."

"Fair and Ned are different kinds of men. I knew, like a little seismic rumble underneath, that Fair thought he was missing something marrying his high-school sweetheart. He"—she paused—"well, he just jumped out of the paddock."

Susan cried harder. "I feel so awful. I know now how you felt."

"You were good to me." Harry hugged her.

"But I didn't really know how you felt. I do now."

Harry hugged her again, then straightened up. "Know who can help us?" Susan shook her head, so Harry continued, "Boom-Boom. She's got the best radar for men of any of us. If he's up to no good, she'll figure it out. And really, Susan, I don't think he is."

Susan considered this as she again wiped away her tears, the soft leather of the glove cool against her colder skin. "Think she would?"

"Help? Sure."

"Well—"

"Let's call her on my cell in the truck. If she's free we can go down the mountain and meet her. It will ease your mind."

"I can't right this minute," Susan replied. "I came here to think but also to pick up Great-Uncle Thomas for Thanksgiving dinner. He's eighty-two now. Hard to believe. Anyway," she paused, "it's quite strange, really. He said to me, 'Susan, my time is near. I'd like to spend Thanksgiving with you.' He's healthy as a horse. I told him he was a long way from death's door."

"Some people know. Like animals know." Harry considered what Thomas had told Susan.

"Don't you start." Susan frowned for a moment. "People get older and anytime something happens to them they attribute it to age. I'm telling you, G-Uncle"—Susan called him "G" for "great"—"will outlive most of the brothers of this order."

"Already has." Harry laughed.

"That's true." Susan shook a snowflake from her nose. "He was a chatterbox. He went on about how he loves his work here. He repairs the plumbing, he keeps the fountains in the gardens going. He gardens. It was really touching to hear him." Susan paused. "He brought up the legend of the Blessed Virgin Mother's statue. How she cried in 1914, and then in 1941 after Pearl Harbor was attacked. He said he'd like to believe it, to see her tears, but if he did, it would herald a dreadful crisis, so he supposed he would die without seeing the tears. He believes she works miracles for those who believe. He really is touching."

"Wonder if it's true?" Harry was skeptical. "A stain of runny bird poop could look like tears."

"Harry, you are awful!"

"Says you," Harry laughed.

Susan stood up, linked her arm through Harry's as Tucker jumped off the bench, dashing in front of them. "Come on, I'll walk you to the statue, then I'll go fetch G-Uncle. He should be ready by now."

Tucker, senses sharper, wanted to protect the humans whose senses—except for their eyes—weren't as keen. She'd race ahead, stop, sniff, swivel her ears. The coast was clear, so she'd look back at the humans, wait for them to approach, then scout ahead. Tucker reached the base of the Virgin Mary's statue, where she waited for the two friends.

As they reached the tall statue, both reflexively looked up at her face.

"My God!" Susan exclaimed.

Harry's hand went to her heart. "She's crying blood."

2

Brother Prescott, hands tucked into the thick gray wool sleeves of his robe, watched the Virgin Mary's face intently. His large, watery blue eyes never wavered from her face. "Hmm."

A trickle of fading pink slid down her cheeks.

"It was blood when we left her." Harry felt slightly foolish.

"There certainly seems to be something, but—" He stood on his tiptoes. The statue towered above him on the large boulder on which she was securely replaced after being removed and repaired during the summer.

"I'm sorry to have you come out in this

cold. The mercury's diving." Susan shivered.

"Oh, that's all right. After all, there could be red veins deep inside the stone. She was quarried from Nelson County, you know, over in Schuyler." His voice carried a note of pride.

"Yes, she's one of the treasures of the Blue Ridge." Harry, her art history background from Smith College serving her well, appreciated the artistry of the statue.

"The Blessed Virgin works miracles. The visions at Lourdes get all the attention even to this day, but the Blessed Virgin Mary works miracles every day all over the world. Her love surpasses understanding," Brother Prescott, second in command at the monastery, said.

Harry opened her mouth but nothing came out. A large white snowflake touched her tongue, melting. She intended to say something skeptical, but the words escaped her. Better to allow Brother Prescott—as well as Brother Thomas, standing silently beside him—his belief. She didn't know what she believed about the Virgin Mary except she was glad there was a woman in the holy hierarchy. Her pastor,

the Rev. Herbert Jones, a wise and com-
passionate man, sidestepped dogma, the
dogma of any church including his own,
which was Lutheran. He preferred to con-
centrate on the emotional and spiritual well-
being of his flock. He'd often said that
Mary's fortunes throughout the centuries reflected the status of woman.

Harry wanted to call him.

"Herb?" Susan whispered to Harry.

"How'd you know what I was thinking?"
Harry whispered back as they walked away
from the statue. Brother Thomas hurried to
his room to pick up a few odds and ends to
contribute to dinner. Brother Prescott bid
them good-bye, following Brother Thomas.

Susan raised her eyebrows. "Harry, I usually know what you're thinking."

"You do, don't you?" They held on to
each other as they slipped and slid down
the sloping, winding path to the first parking
lot where Susan's Audi wagon sat, windshield covered with snow.

"*Mom!*" Owen, Susan's corgi, brother to
Tucker, greeted her with delight.

"*I'm here.*" Tucker announced with glee.

Susan opened the door, and sister and
brother rapturously touched noses and

wagged nonexistent tails, as Harry wiped off the passenger side of the windshield and Susan cleaned the driver's side.

"Too bad this machine doesn't have a creep gear." Susan sighed, mentioning first gear in vehicles such as the Wrangler, which allows the driver to go slowly without stalling out. She thought a moment. "G-Uncle was overwhelmed by the fading tears. He couldn't speak."

Harry replied. "Yeah. I hope this doesn't presage disaster."

Harry left Susan as she warmed up her car. By the time she reached her old Ford F-150 truck, the bottoms of her jeans were soaked.

She opened the door.

"I hate you!" Mrs. Murphy jumped off the seat onto the snow, instantly regretting it.

Harry, Tucker, and Pewter giggled as the sleek tiger cat laid her ears back, shaking each paw in turn.

"Fuss." Harry leaned over, picked up the beautiful animal, wiped off her paws, and set her back on the front seat next to Pewter, who didn't budge. She wasn't going to get *her* paws cold and wet. Harry reached in, turned on the ignition as she de-

pressed the clutch. She had parked in gear, also, putting the brake on. The truck was a manual shift with over 160,000 miles on the speedometer. She preferred manual transmission; she felt it gave her much better control of the vehicle. As this was a 1978 Ford half ton, she was right. The new trucks with automatic contained a computer chip that sensed when gears needed shifting better than most humans could. Having an automatic wasn't such a bad thing in the new F-150s.

The powerful eight-cylinder engine turned over despite the cold, the low rumble music to Harry's ears. If it had an engine in it, she loved it. She put the gear in neutral, pulled on the emergency brake. She yanked out a long-handled brush from behind the bench seat covered with an old Baker blanket. After wiping off the snow on the windshield, she manually turned the hubcap centers on the front wheels to four-wheel drive, locking them.

"I told you not to leave the truck," Pewter smugly said as Mrs. Murphy licked her paws. *"Where would you run, anyway? All that does is put her in a bad mood. No cat-nip."*

"Thought I'd run back up the hill, make her huff and puff." The tiger cat bit a tiny piece of ice from between her toes. *"Grooming takes so much time."*

"You go overboard," Tucker, who was still outside, called up. Harry picked her up, putting her next to the cats.

"You're a sloppy pig." Mrs. Murphy's mood could use a lift.

"Crab. Because you're such a crab I'm not going to tell you what I saw."

Repenting instantly, Mrs. Murphy, hind leg still in midair, looked over. *"What? I'm really not in a bad mood. This little ice bit irritates me, that's all,"* she fibbed.

"Tell, Tucker. I'll let you play with my catnip mousie." Pewter, so easy to bribe, thought she could do the same to the corgi.

"That old thing." Tucker enjoyed her moment of glory as exhaust belched from the new tailpipe Harry had installed last summer.

Harry backed out, shifting the gears into four-wheel drive.

As Harry carefully drove along the Skyline Drive to the turnoff for Route 250 East, Tucker excitedly told the cats about the Virgin Mary crying blood.

"*But that's a statue,*" Pewter sensibly replied.

"*Was it truly blood?*" Mrs. Murphy wondered.

"*I don't rightly know. It was the color of blood, the consistency, but I couldn't smell it. She's high and it's too cold. By the time the blood reached her heart it washed away.*"

"*Blood carries a powerful scent, almost metallic.*" Mrs. Murphy knew the odor well.

"*By the time we returned with Brother Prescott and Brother Thomas, she was weeping pale pink. The tears were slowing down. Probably something to do with the temperature.*"

"*Did Mom say prayers?*" Pewter, curious as to human religious impulses, asked.

"*She was thoughtful and still before we saw the tears. I smelled Susan, so I ran down to her. Mom followed. The statue cried when Susan and Mom walked back up to it. Susan's upset.*"

"*Why?*" both cats said in unison.

Mrs. Murphy quickly yelled, "*Jigs for tuna!*"

Pewter, long whiskers swept forward, grumbled, "*You win.*"

In the South, if two people say the same

thing at the same time, the first person to say, "Jigs for _____" gets whatever they ask for—in this case, tuna. Pewter, ever solicitous of her stomach, would have to share a morsel of flaky tuna.

"Susan is afraid her marriage is getting stale." Tucker gave her opinion of the conversation. *"Maybe tempted by young women in Richmond."*

"Ooo," Pewter crooned.

"Oh, boy, there will be hell to pay if he doesn't resist temptation." Mrs. Murphy considered monogamy one of those peculiar human concepts. They tried, but it was against their nature. Some could do it but most couldn't, and she thought the idea nothing but misery.

"Glad Mom put snow tires on this truck last week," Pewter noted appreciatively.

"Yeah." Mrs. Murphy, hind paws on the seat, leaned forward so her front paws rested on the dash. *"Coming down thick now. We're lucky the temperature dropped so it's not raining anymore. That's the worst."*

"Spring is so far away." Tucker hoped ice wasn't underneath the new-fallen snow.

Harry didn't punch in BoomBoom's number until she was safely down Afton Mountain. "Boom, Harry."

"Where are you?"

"Foot of Afton Mountain."

"Getting rough out there," the statuesque blonde said.

"Could I stop by for a minute, unless you're in the midst of cooking?"

"Come on. Alicia's here. We're going to the club later for Thanksgiving dinner. We've plenty of time."

"Fifteen minutes," Harry succinctly replied. They'd grown up together so could employ shorthand without offending.

Alicia Palmer, in her mid-fifties, had been a huge star in film. She retired in her middle forties, having married well on a few occasions; divorcing well, too. But the great love of Alicia's life had been Mary Pat Reines, a kind, generous, and fabulously wealthy woman who'd died when Alicia was in her mid-twenties. Alicia had inherited Mary Pat's estate. Over the years she'd visit the place once or twice a year, but she finally came home from Santa Barbara to settle in last year. She wondered why it took her so long to return to Virginia, only realizing once she came home that she had never laid

Mary Pat's ghost to rest. Once this emotional milestone was crossed, Alicia's heart lightened.

BoomBoom, an avid golfer and rider, found Alicia a warm and understanding friend. As both women were stunning beauties, they had spent their lives fending off men or, in BoomBoom's case, toying with them. Alicia didn't do that. She had tried to love her two husbands. The strain proved more than she could bear as she never felt deeply close or connected to either man.

When BoomBoom hung up the phone she turned to Alicia, who was throwing cherry wood on the fire in the huge kitchen fireplace.

"Harry is stopping by."

"Good. She's a tonic, that one." Alicia smiled her dazzling smile.

Older people said she looked like Hedy Lamarr, younger people said she looked like Catherine Zeta-Jones, but, really, Alicia looked like Alicia.

"Wonder what's going on? Not like Harry." BoomBoom had heard a note of urgency in Harry's voice.

"You two have made up."

"Pretty much." BoomBoom, blond hair

curling around her shoulders, inhaled. "I was an ass. I could have slept with a lot of men. I didn't have to pick her husband, even though they were separated."

"He's uncommonly handsome. And nice. Fair is a genuinely nice man."

"Six months is my limit." BoomBoom tossed this off as she confronted the enormous espresso machine. "Espresso with cream and a curl of orange rind would be perfect on a day like this. You know, I need an engineering degree to work this thing."

"Mocha latte with lots of cream." Alicia watched as BoomBoom's two rescue kittens charged into the kitchen, tumbling over each other. "Cream. I swear they know the word."

The two women laughed as BoomBoom knelt down to scratch the cats' ears, one black and white and the other a red tabby.

"Hard to believe they came from the same litter."

"I know." BoomBoom again faced the espresso machine. "Since I can work this, I have full confidence I could work for NASA. Have you ever seen anything so complicated in your life?"

"Yes, the iDrive on the seven-series BMW.

Worst piece of you-know-what to come down the pike. And that ugly sawed-off truck lid—the designers have lost their minds, screwing up a fabulous machine like that."

"Heard BMW has gotten so many complaints they'll simplify the iDrive soon."

"Not soon enough. The unflattering design has now carried over into the five-series, the five-series!" Alicia threw up her hands, the large diamond on her ring finger catching the light. "How could they?"

Both women were motorheads, as was Harry, and the three could blab for hours about cars, trucks, and tractors. Boom-Boom didn't like the changes made by BMW either so instead of trading in her four-year-old 7-series for a new one, she traded it for a Mercedes S600.

Alicia drove a Porsche C4 911 in good weather. She also owned a Land Cruiser, a spanking-new F-150, and an older F-350 dually. With her wealth she should have just bought a dealership.

The deep-throated rumble of the old Ford truck alerted them and the kittens that Harry had arrived.

"This isn't the day, but we'll have to get

Harry in a corner about the redesigned F-150. You know she'll know everything about it." BoomBoom peeled rind off an orange as Alicia set out large mugs.

"I could make my famous chicken potpie. Given the weather I'm not sure I want to drive over to the club. I can live without turkey and sweet potato pie."

"Doubt she'll stay that long," BoomBoom replied.

"Actually, I shouldn't, either. I'd better get home before it turns pitch black." Alicia noted the ever-darkening skies.

BoomBoom, walking toward the mudroom where the back door was located, stopped and surprised herself by turning to Alicia and saying, "I miss you when we're not together."

"BoomBoom, that's the greatest compliment you could give me." Alicia beamed at her.

"Knock, knock." Harry opened the back door a crack.

"Come on in." BoomBoom peered out into the snow. "Bring in the kids. They won't want to sit in the truck."

"You don't mind? I heard you found two kittens." Harry loved kittens better than anything on earth and had just spied the black and white one, four legs spread out, looking up at her from under a kitchen chair.

"Lucy and Desi will have to get used to other animals. Yours are so well behaved."

"Most times."

Within seconds Mrs. Murphy, Pewter, and Tucker marched through the mudroom into the kitchen, the delicious smells curling into their nostrils.

Desi, the black and white kitten, and Lucy, the red tabby, puffed up like blowfish.

Tucker ignored them as they spit at her.

"Worms," Pewter said.

"Oh, Pewts, they're scared enough."

As the kittens crouched low and crept forward toward the visiting animals, Harry sat down and took a sip of her espresso, whipped cream swaying on top. "God, this is fabulous." She then relayed Susan's fears.

"She could ask him," Alicia kindly said.

"Susan won't. She's kind of paralyzed," Harry observed. "Also, she doesn't want to hear a lie."

"She's feeling left out. Overreacting. Right now he can't spend a lot of time with her," BoomBoom remarked. "And he never flirted with me. She has nothing to worry about."

"That puts him in a special class." Alicia ate some of her whipped cream with the small demitasse spoon. "I don't know Ned as you all do, but, without intending to stray, people do fall into one another's arms." Alicia turned to Harry, who never could get used to looking into those fabulous violet-tinged eyes. "And Susan is ninety miles away, beginning to worry about turning forty, I expect. I'm not saying Ned is having an affair, but sometimes it just . . . happens."

"It never happened to me."

BoomBoom couldn't resist. "Put on a little makeup, hike up your boobs in a lace lift-and-separate bra, and, Harry, it will happen."

The two women laughed as Harry, face red, looked deeply into her cup. "I can read whipped cream. Did you all know that? Other fortune-tellers read tea leaves or tarot cards, but I read whipped cream, and this whipped cream tells me there are two bad girls tormenting a saint. Karma! Beware of karma." As they laughed, Harry's mind flashed back to the statue. Since she had grown up with BoomBoom, she knew the blonde was accustomed to her hopping from subject to subject. "Susan and I saw the Virgin Mary cry blood! Today. Weird. Scary, actually."

Harry filled in BoomBoom and Alicia about this strange event as well as why both she and Susan were at the monastery grounds.

The kittens became emboldened enough to slink toward the grown cats.

Little Lucy, belly flat on the heart-pine floor, reached out and batted Pewter's fat, fluffy tail.

"Hey." Pewter flicked her tail.

"It's alive!" Lucy shrieked, jumping back.

Desi, rocking back and forth, eyes wide, couldn't believe Pewter's tail.

"It's too short. Now, my tail is the proper length for my body." Mrs. Murphy slyly thrashed her tail a bit.

"My tail is not too short. It's full. I have Russian blue blood. My bones are big."

"Oh, la." Mrs. Murphy rolled her lustrous eyes.

"What's a Russian blue?" Desi squeaked.

"A figment of her ever-active imagina-

tion." Mrs. Murphy rolled over, displaying a creamy beige tummy.

Pewter turned her back on Mrs. Murphy. *"Alley cat."*

"Oh, bull, Pewter, we're all alley cats. This is America. Even the humans are alley cats."

"Am I an alley cat?" Little Lucy softly came up to Mrs. Murphy, who rolled over to look the tiny bundle of red fur in the eye.

"You are."

"Are you my mommy?" Lucy asked.

"Ha!" Pewter hooted.

Desi padded up to Mrs. Murphy. He squeezed tight against his sister. *"We don't remember our mommy very well. She didn't come home one night."*

"Where were you?" Tucker joined with the cats.

At first the kittens puffed up, then calmed down when Tucker, who seemed very big, smiled at them reassuringly.

"We lived in a washing machine down in the ravine."

"Ah." None of the adults said anything after that, since all knew their mother had been killed in some fashion.

"How did you find BoomBoom?" Mrs. Murphy inquired.

"She and the other pretty lady were riding and we screamed. She got off her horse and we were really scared, but she kept talking to us and we were so hungry. Then she picked us up and put us in her jacket and we felt warm. We were cold. She's a nice lady."

"She fed us," Desi chimed in. He wasn't as talkative as his sister.

"And then," Lucy's voice rose, *"the next day she took us to a man with a beard who gave us pills and shots. That was awful."*

"But necessary." Tucker's brown eyes sparkled.

"I'm not going back there," Desi boasted.

"That's what we all say." Tucker laughed.

"I saw a dog with hair the color of Boom-Boom's at the vet's," Lucy remarked. *"Are they related?"*

At this, the grown-up cats and dog laughed so hard the humans noticed.

"Isn't that sweet? Mrs. Murphy is grooming Lucy." Alicia smiled broadly.

"She has a maternal streak," Harry commented.

"Oh, I am going to throw up." Pewter pretended to gag.

"Roundworms," Mrs. Murphy said sar-

castically as she pushed Pewter with her front paw.

Pewter pushed back. This escalated into a boxing match, then Pewter took off, Mrs. Murphy in hot pursuit.

Desi's jaw dropped. *"Gosh."*

"Mental." Tucker touched noses with the little guy. *"If one says apples, the other says bananas. They live to disagree."* She sighed, then added, *"But that's cats for you."*

"We're cats." Lucy blinked, her eyes still blue.

"Don't get me wrong. Cats are very fine." Tucker sounded very worldly. *"But dogs are much more logical, especially corgis."*

"Don't believe a word of it." Mrs. Murphy, having heard everything, soared over all the seated animals in a dazzling display of athletic ability.

Pewter cleared the kittens, only to land smack on Tucker, who took it with her usual sense of humor.

As the cat and dog rolled over each other, the humans laughed and refilled their cups while trying to sort out Susan's dilemma.

"Why don't I discreetly poke around?" BoomBoom turned her attention for a second to the TV, which was on but muted. It was the start of the news report.

"Susan's upset. It surprises me. I mean, her imagining something unproven. If Susan gets upset it's about an event or someone being ill. It's not in her head." Although not much of a coffee drinker, Harry found the espresso delicious, especially after the biting cold up on Afton Mountain.

"People respond to different situations in ways even they don't understand." Boom-Boom again checked the TV.

Harry crossed one leg over the other. "Isn't it odd how we don't know ourselves? We think we do, but if life is a circle of three hundred sixty degrees, has there ever been any human being who experienced all three hundred sixty degrees? We'll never know everything about ourselves."

"Then how can we know about anyone else?" BoomBoom asked.

"Because it's easier to look out than to look in," Alicia briskly replied. "Don't you think?"

"I don't know," BoomBoom honestly answered.

"I'm not sure I do, either." Harry smiled.

"I guess we spend our lives finding out." BoomBoom laughed.

"I'd rather work on my tractor or fix the barn roof." Harry shook her head. "The interior stuff is too much for me."

"You have a good mind for solving problems. The interior stuff, as you call it, is a different kind of problem." BoomBoom complimented her, then blinked her eyes, a slight jerk to her head as a handsome young man appeared on the TV. She rose to turn on the sound.

Wearing a deep-green silk tie against an ecru shirt, and an expensive tweed jacket over that, Nordy Elliott smiled the biggest, phoniest smile he could muster at the petite redhead sitting beside him. "So, Jessica, how's it look for football? And what about travel tonight? A lot of people are on the road on turkey day."

"Nordy, a low pressure system is—"

BoomBoom, who had brought the remote back to the table, clicked off the sound. "Nordy Elliott is like sand in my eye, a major irritant. I can't stand the note of false urgency in his voice, which is always the same whether he's interviewing shoppers at the mall or covering a car wreck."

"He irritates you because he pesters you." Alicia reached down to entice one of the cats to come over.

"He doesn't listen." BoomBoom turned to Harry. "I told him over and over—I mean, I tell him every time I see him or he calls that I am taking a year's vacation from dating. So he calls each week and says"—she imitated his delivery—"one more week bites the dust. Twenty more to go!"

"Give him credit for persistence." Alicia laughed.

Ruefully, BoomBoom shrugged. "Yes and no. I hate it when men don't listen."

"Sometimes they can't." Harry offered an unexpected insight. "Their bodies trump their minds. When most men look at either one of you, the blood heads south."

"Harry, you flatter me," Alicia demurred.

"True, though." BoomBoom exhaled. "Men fall in love with their eyes."

"For us, the true hook is, 'Honey, I'll take care of it.' " Harry's mouth turned up as the other two laughed, since that, too, was true.

"A sweeter sound coming from a man than 'I love you.' " Alicia reached over and touched Harry's forearm.

" 'I love you' is too easy. Fixing the dead

battery in your car or doing your taxes—
that's love." BoomBoom's laughter sounded
like perfect crystal when struck. It filled the
room.

"I can do all that," Harry boasted.

"Can't we all?" Alicia said. "But how
wonderful when a man does it."

"Sometimes." BoomBoom pointed toward
Harry's cup and Harry indicated she'd had
enough. "But sometimes I'd rather get my
hands dirty. Is it just me? Maybe it is, but I
feel constrained around a man and I don't
want to feel I owe him something."

"You're beautiful, Boom. A man wants to
keep you to himself. I suppose that feels,
um, restrictive?" Alicia replied.

"You're the most beautiful woman I've
ever seen, Alicia. It doesn't happen to you?"
BoomBoom's large, expressive eyes seemed
even larger.

"Yes."

"Constrained is an interesting word."
Harry wiggled her toes in her boots. "I don't
want a man telling me what to do. I don't
want anyone telling me what to do, including the damned government. I can make my
own decisions. If I make a mistake, it's my
mistake."

"Hear, hear," Alicia agreed.

"Oh, call the Duncans." BoomBoom changed the subject, mentioning the couple, Fred and Doris, who ran Alicia's farm. They were wonderful people. "You can stay here, safe and sound. We'll sit by the fire and tell stories."

Alicia didn't reply to that directly. "When this storm clears, let's go up to see the Virgin Mary."

"Speaking of going, I'd better hit the road. Sun's set and it's looking like a real storm." Harry checked outside the window, then back to the TV screen as the news cut frequently to Jessica, the weatherwoman.

BoomBoom also watched. "Snuck up on us, this one. Alicia, we'd better bag going to the country club."

"That's what makes it so exciting living at the foot of the mountains," Alicia said as she rose. "I'd better head home, too."

┌─────────┐
│   3   │
└─────────┘

The red taillights of Alicia's Land Cruiser disappeared in the gathering snow. From the paned glass windows in her elegant living room, BoomBoom watched the two ruby dots become swallowed up.

She folded her arms across the ample chest for which she earned her nickname. The soft three-ply cashmere felt glorious against her skin.

Lucy and Desi, perched on top of an overstuffed chair, watched BoomBoom watching Alicia.

"If she'd take off that sweater and put it on the floor we could sleep on it." Desi had fallen in love with the sweater when Boom-Boom had picked him up to pet and kiss him. He loved that, too.

"Drawers," Lucy replied.

"Huh?"

"Drawers. She puts her clothes in drawers. The boxes that slide in the big box in the bedroom."

"How do you know that's what they're called?" Desi admired his sister's acumen.

"When she showed Alicia the sweater she bought from that expensive store in New York, whatever New York is, Alicia was impressed. She said, 'Paul Stuart.' Then BoomBoom said how they ought to go to New York." Lucy pricked her ears as the wind rattled the outside shutters. *"And she said, 'I keep all the sweaters in the drawers.' "*

BoomBoom exhaled through her nostrils, a mark of discontent, a touch of the blues. She walked over to the kittens, petting each. "If she were a man she would have stayed." This was followed by a silence. "What am I thinking?"

The tall blonde strode into her den, a high-tech, bright space very unlike the rest of the house. She sat down at her bloodred enamel curving desk with the heavy inlaid glass top. On the left side of the curve rested her computer. In the middle of the curve was the gleaming glass inlay where she could handwrite letters on stationery printed by Tiffany's. On the right side of this exquisite creation rested a small pile of tan, green, or red leather-bound foxhunting books from the eighteenth century.

BoomBoom ran her deceased husband's quarry and business. A keen mind and one that rejoiced in profit, she proved better at this than Kelly had been. She imported marble from Italy as well as from Barre, Vermont. She specialized in the stones for fencing. Her quarry also carried every grade of gravel needed in construction. Twice-washed sand for riding rings, for masonry, was also a lucrative product. BoomBoom enjoyed a business that could change its selling methods, change the speed of delivery, upgrade customer services, but the actual process of building a stone fence, cutting marble for a fireplace, or putting down number-five stone on a farm road would never change. For this, she was exceedingly grateful.

She was also grateful that the men who worked at Craycroft Quarry remained loyal to her. Once she'd proved she knew what she was doing and those Christmas bonuses fattened, the teamwork only got better and better.

Each day she'd stop by the office. She always checked a job. She listened to her customers; she listened to her staff. She couldn't work a nine-to-five job, but many days she worked from five in the morning until eleven at night. It was her business and she loved it. Often she could schedule her hobbies—foxhunting in fall and winter, golf in spring and summer—around work. She lived a fabulous life and she knew it, except for one thing: she had no partner, no true love.

BoomBoom checked addresses on her computer, writing down those people to whom she could speak discreetly about Ned. Since BoomBoom gave generously to the Democratic Party, she had many strings to pull.

"Damned Republicans," she said out loud, which caused Lucy to try and crawl up her leg to see what this outburst was all about. "Come on, you little girl. You, too, Desi!" She placed them on the desk. Both were mesmerized by the computer as she switched it to the pattern of shifting, different-colored shapes. "Here are the desk rules. You can come up here anytime you like once you're big enough to get up on your own. But you can never pee here or anywhere but your dirt box. You can't chew my papers. I don't care if you play with the computer, but you can't chew the wires or pull them out of the back. You can't press the phone buttons and, oh, yes, this is the most important thing, no biting or chewing my old leather-bound books. See this book right here?" She held up a large tome, dark green with gilt lettering "Notitia Venatica." "This cost me three hundred seventy-five dollars. Three hundred seventy-five dollars!"

"What's three hundred seventy-five dollars?" Lucy cocked her head.

"Must be important." Desi noted Boom-Boom's stern tone.

"Follow the rules and we'll have a wonderful life." She kissed their soft tiny heads, right between their ears. "We already have a wonderful life."

"I can catch mice." Desi puffed out his white chest. Set against his black body, he looked like he was wearing a tuxedo.

"You can not." Lucy giggled.

"Can, too." He swatted her and she swatted back.

"You two may be the cutest little kittens God has put on earth." BoomBoom laughed, then punched in numbers on her thin, flat phone. "You're home. I was so worried about you."

A laugh, clear, greeted her concern. "Honey chile, I was driving before you were born."

"Oh, you were not."

"Pretty close to it." Alicia replied. "You're sweet not to think I'm old. As I recall you're thirty-seven," she paused, "just a sprig, a green sapling and such a pretty one at that."

BoomBoom laughed. "Are you flirting with me, Alicia? I'm not used to these things."

"Do you expect me to believe that? Beauty is a magnet."

"Look who's talking." She paused. "But, no, women have not flirted with me, or if they have, it's gone right over my head, like the Blue Angels." She made a jet sound, which startled the kittens, who had fallen asleep on the desk.

"Silly girls." Alicia's voice, part of her outrageous allure, sounded exactly as it did on the big screen.

BoomBoom experienced an uncustomary flutter; she stuttered for a second, then caught herself. "Well, I'm so glad you're home safe and sound."

"Once the weather clears, let's go up to Greyfriars'. You wanted to go, right?" Alicia asked.

"Can't wait," BoomBoom responded. "I look to Mary for light. Not that I'm in danger of being a good Catholic, mind you."

"Actually, sugar, I'm a bad Christian, but it's too late to be a good anything else." Alicia laughed.

As the two women bid their good-byes with promises to call first thing in the morning, high on top of the Blue Ridge Mountains, the Virgin Mary was again crying tears of blood, quickly freezing in the cold.

4

"What do you think of that?" A puff of air streamed from Harry's lips as she spoke on her cell phone, a gift from Fair on her birthday.

The horses, including the brood mares, munched in their stalls. The minute Harry reached home she had brought in the horses, thrown them flakes of hay, and topped off their water. She turned them out during the day unless the ground was covered in ice. Horses that spend most of their times outdoors, grazing and playing, are far happier than horses stuck in stalls.

She wore a tiny earpiece, phone tucked in her belt, as she swept out the aisles. Although the mercury would drop into the twenties, she knew the inside of the barn wouldn't get below freezing. The outside air would have to stay in the teens or below for the water buckets to freeze inside. Some of this was due to the good construction of the barn, well built but still airy. A tight barn is bad for equine breathing. The warmth of those large thousand-plus-pound bodies did the rest, so the barn stayed reasonably warm—if one considers the high thirties or the low forties warm.

"The Lord moves in mysterious ways His wonders to perform," Miranda Hogendobber replied, as Harry had been telling her about the Virgin Mary.

"Oh, Miranda, you don't believe it's a miracle, do you?"

"Does it matter? Does it matter if it can be explained by natural causes or if she truly cries blood? If this helps someone, provides light in a dark world, then it's a miracle."

Harry stopped, propped the broom against Tomahawk's stall. "I never thought of it that way."

"You don't think of a lot of things," Miranda said with warmth, not rancor.

Harry moaned, "Fair says I'm more of a guy than he is, in the mind. Actually, everyone says that. Even my mother used to say that. Irritates the hell out of me."

"I'm not saying that." Miranda thought of Harry as a daughter, since she herself had not been blessed with children. "I'm saying you seek practical solutions. From time to time, you need to sit quietly, or take a walk, allow your spirit to roam. God's love will find you."

"You're right. I suppose I'd say, 'Take time to smell the roses.' "

"I am never closer to the Good Lord than when I'm in my garden." Miranda, a gifted gardener, engaged in hot competition with Mim Sanburne, not nearly as gifted but tremendously rich. "You know Tazio and I are drawing up plans for my dream garden shed." She mentioned a young friend and architect.

"Speaking of gardens, when I visited the monastery gardens, I found Susan there, too. I've never seen Susan so blue. She thinks Ned is drifting away from her. She's questioning the marriage."

"She needs her friends." Miranda, not prone to gossip, was always prepared to assist a friend. "I'll ask her to tea. This is about Ned's getting elected to the state senate. It's changing her whole life. For one thing, Susan is going to be on display, and that requires a great deal of discipline as well as an extensive wardrobe."

"Expensive and extensive."

"Yes. Political wives are judged rather harshly, you know."

"Thank heaven Fair doesn't have the political bug."

"So you *are* going to remarry him?"

"That's why I visited the monastery. I prayed for answers. There's something about that statue of the Virgin Mary that settles my mind." She paused a moment, then picked up the broom. "I can't believe you didn't ask me why I was there in the first place."

"You'd get around to it," Miranda chuckled.

"You know me too well."

"I watched you grow up, sweetie pie. Takes you awhile to get to the point, especially if the point is emotional."

"Funny, isn't it, and Fair wears his heart on his sleeve."

"He trusts himself."

"Oh." This had never occurred to Harry.

"Did the Blessed Virgin Mary answer your prayers?"

"Not yet. I talked to her about money, too. Am I going down the right path? I even talked to her about the meaning of life. Sounds ridiculous coming from me, but am I here to pay bills? Am I here to farm? Am I here to serve on the St. Luke's vestry board, which I enjoy, actually. I asked so many deep questions I made myself dizzy."

"The answers will come."

Harry exhaled, real emotion in her voice because she trusted Miranda completely. "I hope so, Miranda. I do. Sometimes I wake up in the middle of the night and I'm scared to death. My heart is racing. I don't know if I can pay my feed bills, I don't know if I can afford to fill up the diesel gas pumps." She mentioned the large outdoor pumps with underground tanks that she used for the tractor. "I can't afford dress-up clothes, and I know I embarrass Susan, BoomBoom, Big Mim. I probably embarrass Fair, too, but he's too much of a gentleman to say that."

"Now, honey, you listen to me. I can't speak for the Blessed Virgin Mother, but I can speak as someone who loves you. You're pretty even without doing one thing to yourself. Yes, you do need some frocks. But there's no point fretting over it until money starts coming in again. Let it go. You're researching growing grapes. That takes time, soil, and sun tests. Maybe you can find a temporary job to get a paycheck for your electric and phone bill."

"I've been racking my brain."

"What about Fair's offer of working with him?"

"I don't want to be with him twenty-four hours a day. I don't love him that much."

Miranda exploded with laughter. "To tell you the truth, much as I loved George, I didn't want to be with him around the clock, either. Now, Tracy is a different story." She mentioned her current boyfriend, an athletic man who had been her high-school boy-friend and who moved back to Crozet two years ago after his wife died.

"Two peas in a pod."

"Sometimes I wonder what life would have been like if I had married Tracy out of high school," Miranda mused. "Well, I have no complaints."

"If you want to ruin a relationship, get married," Harry said teasingly with a hint of seriousness.

"Now, Harry, you don't mean that."

"People get married and think they own

each other. It's the unspoken expectations that get you. Once a woman becomes a wife, society expects things of her even if her husband doesn't. I can be a friend, a lover, a pal, but I'm not much of a wife. Fair makes a better wife than I do, all six feet five inches of him. And you make a good wife. Not me."

Miranda thought for a moment. "Wife. Husband. Those are words and the meaning changes with the times, but marriage is a sacrament. It's a vow before God and man. Do I think marriage can keep people together? No. But mind your mouth about this. People are peculiar."

"Hypocritical is more like it."

"That, too," Miranda agreed.

As they were chatting, Fair drove to the barn. He cracked open the large sliding doors and slipped in, closing them behind him.

"Fair, we were just talking about you." Harry kissed him on the cheek. "Your other girlfriend wants to say hello."

Pewter, in the warm tackroom, which had electric heat, pricked up her ears. She heard the mice behind the paneled walls. Mrs. Murphy had climbed into the hayloft to visit the possum, Simon. Pewter could climb the ladder, which was flat against the wall, nailed to it, but she preferred the warmth. Anyway, Simon, a kleptomaniac, had to show his most recent treasures, which bored the gray cat mightily. Tucker stuck close to Harry. Pewter liked Tucker but thought dogs so slavish. She closed her eyes, then opened one. The mice were singing, *"The old gray mare."* As she was gray, she knew this was directed at her.

Pewter roused herself from the toasty sheepskin saddle pad to creep over to the small opening shrewdly hidden behind the tack trunk.

"You aren't nearly as funny as you think you are," she growled.

A tiny set of dark gray whiskers appeared in the mouse doorway, then a little head stuck out. *"You scared me half to death,"* came the insolent reply.

"Your day will come," Pewter warned. *"But you'd better shut up. If Harry comes in here and hears you, we're all in trouble. A deal is a deal."*

The deal was that the barn mice wouldn't get into the grain bins, chew tack, or steal the hard candies that Harry kept in a bowl

on the old desk. In return they could have all the grain the horses dropped from their buckets, which was plenty. The cats wouldn't kill them. If any human, Harry or a visitor, left food out, unwrapped, the mice could have it.

"She's in the center aisle," the head mouse replied.

"Fair walked in and they'll both be back in here in a minute, and don't tell me humans don't have good ears, because Harry hears almost as well as we do. It's her sharpest sense. Kind of odd."

"Okay, okay," the head mouse grumbled, then called back to the group. *"Cut it."*

Later that Thursday night, at the monastery, the temperature was ten degrees colder than down below. The wind whipped through the conifers, intensifying the howling sound. Snow swirled around.

Curiosity got the better of Brother Prescott. He trudged through the darkness, a strong-beamed flashlight in hand. He was followed by Brother Mark, a young man who had nearly killed himself on drugs when at Michigan State but now gave himself wholeheartedly to Jesus, to the discipline of the order. Brother Frank, a middle-aged, sensible man who was the treasurer, also accompanied them.

No one said anything as each man concentrated on keeping his footing. Their long sleeves and long robes furled outward, with the winds dragging them backward at times.

Finally they reached the Virgin Mary.

Brother Prescott shone the beam on her face, snow so thick he had to squint, shielding his eyes with his left hand.

The wind abated for a second.

"Holy Mary, Mother of Our Lord, Christ Jesus." Brother Mark fell to his knees, then prostrated himself in the snow.

Brother Frank, not given to gusts of emotion, took a step back.

Brother Prescott crossed himself. "Hail Mary, full of grace, the Lord is with thee, blessed art thou amongst women."

"She's bleeding for our sins. She's crying tears of blood to save mankind." When Brother Mark lifted his face from the snow, he, too, was crying, the tears cold on his rosy cheeks.

"Up." Brother Frank reached down,

grabbed the young man's hand, and pulled him up.

"She's exhorting us to save mankind," Brother Mark sobbed, sides heaving.

"You save mankind one man, one woman, one child at a time," Brother Prescott evenly replied, but he, too, was moved deeply by the sight of frozen blood, which had coursed down Mary's cheeks and spilled onto the upper folds of her robe.

"Don't jump to conclusions," Brother Frank, face framed by the hood of his robe, admonished. "We don't know what's going on here. It looks like tears, it looks like blood, but we don't know and we won't know in the middle of this snowstorm. So I advise each of us to keep his mouth shut."

"She's speaking to us, Brother Frank, she's speaking to us through her tears. We can't keep quiet."

"For a day or two." The older man held to his opinion. "Brother Prescott, you say two women came to you? And you and Brother Thomas followed them up here?"

"Harry Haristeen and Susan Tucker." Brother Prescott knew them, not well, but in passing, as did Brother Frank.

"Won't stay a secret, then." Brother Frank

pinched his lips together. "Women can't keep secrets."

"Men can't, either." Brother Prescott bridled at Brother Frank's sexism.

"We have to tell the other brothers. We have to tell Brother Handle," added Brother Mark. The young man's eyes widened.

"It can wait until morning. I need to think about this." Brother Frank took the icy cold flashlight from Brother Prescott's hand, stepped forward, and peered intently up at the beatific face, winds renewing their assault. "Forgive me, Blessed Mother, I am a skeptic and must investigate," he said matter-of-factly.

Brother Prescott shouted, for the wind was now a steady roar, "This could be the best thing to happen to us. You're the treasurer, you know that."

"It could also be the worst," came the measured reply, as Brother Frank wondered not only what was happening but what to do about it.

5

"What a beautiful color, rich with depth." Susan commented on the cranberry sauce as she handed it to Brooks on her right.

"You look good in this color, Mom."

"Sweet thing." Susan beamed at her daughter. "I could hold the sauce up to my face."

"I remember when you were tiny, Susan, you spilled more food than made it to your mouth." Brother Thomas accepted the cranberry sauce when Brooks handed it to him. He glanced at the window. "Look at that."

Ned, at the head of the table, watched the snow whirl by the old-paned, hand-blown glass windows. "We've had an early winter and a hard one. I'm crossing my fingers for the January thaw."

"Might be the March thaw this year." The thin old fellow smiled. "When does Danny come home for Christmas vacation?"

"December eleventh. I miss him at Thanksgiving, but it's such a long way from Ithaca, New York, to here. He's spending Christmas with the Wadsworths, just outside Cazenovia. He's made so many friends up there. They all fight to have him," Susan bragged.

"Brooks, what are you thinking about college?" her great-great-uncle asked her.

She simply addressed him as "Uncle." "Uncle Thomas, I'd like to go to Stanford. It's real expensive, though."

Susan and Ned looked at each other but said nothing.

"Saw California when I was in the service." Brother Thomas gleefully cut into the juicy turkey slices on his plate. "Guess I wouldn't recognize it now, but, oh, it was beautiful. I couldn't get used to the days being hot and the nights being so cold." He laughed.

"I like Mary Baldwin, too, even though it's

real different from Stanford," Brooks added as an afterthought.

The dinner continued with talk of the future, what Ned hoped to accomplish in Richmond, Susan's determination to finally make the A team in golf at the country club.

Outside, the snow piled up, making it cozier to be inside.

After their feast they retired to the small den, which Susan had smothered in chintz. She couldn't help herself.

Ned and Brother Thomas talked about whether Ned could continue his legal practice. Susan and Brooks cleaned up before joining them, bringing in yet another round of desserts and hot coffee.

The fire crackled as Brother Thomas reached for a small shortbread cookie dipped in bitter chocolate. "If only we ate like this at Afton."

"You'd all be fat as ticks." Susan laughed.

He replied with assurance, "The Bland Wades don't get fat."

"Well, I take after the other side of the family," Susan groaned.

"Now, Susan, your father's people weren't fat." He paused a minute. "Come to think of it, Minnie was big as a house. Remember Minnie?"

"Those polka-dot dresses!" Susan's eyes brightened, then she said to Brooks, "Honey, I'm sorry you didn't know my father's Aunt Minnie. She died long before you were born. She had a sweet tooth but she was funny."

"Your father put on a little weight in his fifties," Ned remarked, immediately wishing he hadn't brought that up.

"At least he didn't blow up like Aunt Minnie." Susan snuggled into the overstuffed chair, a needlepoint pillow behind her back.

"What a blessing that we could have a quiet Thanksgiving together." Brother Thomas leaned back into his own overstuffed chair, reveling in the comfort. "You know, the contemplative life is fading. Few young people are called these days. In fact, anyone desiring to dedicate themselves to work, prayer, abstinence, and good works, if possible, is considered mentally ill." He waved his hand. "It's all going. Two thousand years of spiritual life, going. Each year our prior struggles to make ends meet with less. It's aging him. Brother Frank, too. There really isn't anyone to whom they can pass the torch."

Brooks, having been raised properly as a Virginia lady, knew that since her great-great-uncle was their special guest, he must be the center of attention. "Don't you think it's possible some young people will turn to a contemplative life? I mean, don't you think some people will find success—what we call success—empty?"

He smiled at her, this lovely young girl, embarking on life as he was disembarking. "Ah, I hope so, but for contemplative life to be valued, to flourish, spiritual life must be paramount. If you think about it, the so-called Dark Ages and then the Middle Ages were a fertile ground for this kind of a life." The fire illuminated his face as he continued. "When Henry the Eighth dissolved the monasteries in England, that was the true beginning of the rise of secular life. Each century has witnessed a further erosion of spiritual values as the center of individual life and community life. Oh, there are revivals, spasms of religious energy, but truthfully, it's over. That time has passed, never to return in a way central to civilization. That's how I read history. And with each passing century, the concept of a whole community's relationship to God, the concept of one's relationship to God, has eroded. It's one's relationship to the dollar today." He shrugged his bony shoulders. "Which isn't to say people weren't interested in money in the Middle Ages; they were, but they put it in a different perspective."

"More dreadful events might bring people back to monasteries," Ned thought out loud. "Not that I wish for them."

"I don't think so." Brother Thomas tasted the rich coffee. "Susan, this is quite something."

"My husband bought me a coffeemaker for my birthday that cost more than my monthly car payment. I love coffee and I love Ned." She smiled a touch nervously at her husband, who smiled back.

"Ah." Brother Thomas loved Susan as he had loved her mother and her grandmother before her. When he looked at Susan he could see three generations reflected in her face. "Well, Ned, you made all the right choices." He placed the bone-china cup on the side table, then folded his hands. "I've lived a long time. I don't know if I've done much good in this life, but I hope I haven't done harm. The war—" He stopped. "I did harm in the war, for which I ask God's forgiveness. I put the desires of my government before the tenets of God. 'Thou shalt not kill,' and I killed."

Susan interrupted, "If you hadn't gone to war, Uncle Thomas, we might not be here today."

"Perhaps." He smiled at her. "I won't be here next Thanksgiving. I feel fine, but I feel my time on earth is nearly over. I really do feel fine. Poor Brother Sidney, only sixty-two, has to get transfusions of blood to keep going. And here I am, no obvious problems. Yet, I feel I will soon be called to our Lord. I want you to know, Susan, that I have arranged for the Bland Wade land, those fifteen hundred acres that wrap behind Tally Urquhart's over to the edge of the Minor place"—he used Harry's maiden name—"to go to you. There's not much else that I have of value. I thought for years about what to do about the land. As our numbers dwindled I knew the monastery couldn't manage the Bland Wade tract, and I can't bear the thought of it begin broken up and sold. So few large tracts these days. A great pity. Land is the ultimate wealth, you know." He paused again, took a deep breath. "All the pastures are over-grown, second-growth timber on them pretty much. I can't tell you what to do, but if I were a young man, I'd restore the pas-tures, because the soil is good. And I wouldn't harvest the hardwoods, although I'd thin them. Whatever you do, Susan, and you, too, Brooks, don't sell the land. I as-sume some day the Bland Wade tract will pass to you and Danny. No matter how great the temptation, don't sell that land. It's one of the last land grants intact. Land is a breathing thing."

A silence followed this, then Susan, over-come, said, "Uncle, I never expected any-thing like this. I promise we will cherish the land, and I promise Ned will create ease-ments so it can't be subdivided."

"Just leave me room to build a house, Dad," Brooks blurted out.

Ned, with gravity, stood up, walked over, and shook the old man's hand, inhaling as he did so the odor of lanolin from the virgin wool of Brother Thomas's robe. "This is a great blessing to our family. I don't think I can properly express my gratitude."

Brother Thomas smiled, squeezing Ned's hand. "Care for the land, Ned; she is under all of us." Then he laughed. "Since not one of you is a good Catholic, I can't exhort you there." He laughed again. "A Lutheran, Susan. I could have died from mortification when your mother became a Lutheran before her marriage." He paused a moment. "But then, the years have taught me perhaps that the denomination isn't as important as I once thought, so long as one fears and loves God."

Brooks didn't take to the fear part, but she kept that to herself. "Uncle Thomas, how do I know God loves me?"

He blinked, then replied with a depth of feeling that reached each of them. "Every time you behold the Blue Ridge Mountains, every time you feel a snowflake on your eyelashes, every time you see a frog on a lily pad, every time a friend gives you his hand, Brooks, God loves you. You're surrounded by His love. We look for it in all the wrong places as we pray for worldly success. We say that must be proof of God's love. Some people pray not for material success but for an easy life." He shook his head. "No, even our pains are a sign of His love, for they will lead you to the right path, if you'll only listen." He opened his eyes wide, touching his fingertips together. "Ah, well, I'm not much of a preacher. I didn't mean to go on. I spend so much time in prayer or fixing pipes or both," he laughed, "or with Brother Mark, my apprentice. This summer when we repaired the statue of the Blessed Virgin Mother he asked so many questions he made me dizzy. He's still a chatterbox around me." His eyes twinkled. "Sometimes I forget how to carry on a true conversation."

"We will never forget what you've said," Ned replied.

"Well, you're kind. I'm an old man with an audience. That's more intoxicating than wine." He laughed at himself. "Or cognac?" He lifted his white eyebrows.

Ned rose, returning with three brands of cognac—each expensive—and four snifters, all on a silver tray. He placed them before Brother Thomas, pointing to one brand. "I think this was first made by monks." Ned wasn't sure that the precious liquid had been created in a monastery, but the possibility shouldn't be overlooked.

"Yes. Well, I mustn't disappoint my brethren. I'll try just a taste of each of these to see if the spiritual life improved the product."

Ned poured Hennessy Paradis for Susan and a little drop of Rémy Martin Louis XIII for Brooks after he poured Uncle Thomas's Hors d'Age No. 9. "Ladies." He then poured some of the amber liquid into his own snifter, holding it high. "To Brother Thomas, a man of love and a man of light."

They toasted Brother Thomas and he acknowledged the accolade, savored his cognac, then held up his glass for Ned to fill it with another brand. He tasted that. "Hmm, the distiller may not have been a monk, but I'm certain he was a Christian." He took another sip. "A very good Christian."

6

Driving slowly through the fast-falling snow, Fair kept his eyes on the road.

"Can't see the center line." Harry squinted.

"It's the side I'm worried about. Damn, it's easy to slide off. We'd be sitting in a snowbank until morning."

"Well, at least we'd be well fed. Miranda knocked herself out."

Fair smiled. "And who would have thought that a big, tough Korean vet like Tracy could bake? I still can't believe he made the pumpkin pie." His shoulders dropped a bit as he could just make out the sign to the farm. "Whew."

As he turned his truck off the road, the wheels sank deep into the snow. He geared down.

"Glad I put the snow blade on the tractor. It must be snowing two inches per hour. Jeez, I'll be out on the tractor all day," Harry exclaimed. "Any scheduled calls?"

"A full book, but it's exams and X rays; can be rescheduled if need be. It's the emergency calls that worry me."

"Maybe I'd better plow the drive tonight. Still be covered with snow tomorrow but not as deep." She turned to look at him as the bed of the truck slowly swung right.

He corrected the slide but didn't breathe normally until he pulled up by the back porch door. "Thank God."

They hurried inside, Harry carrying a take-out bag. "Aunt Miranda made Thanksgiving dinner for you all."

She picked up their bowls, putting in giblets, gravy, and some dressing.

"Hooray," the three cheered in unison as they pounced when the food was placed on the floor.

"Honey, don't plow. It's late. Let's trust to luck. If I get an emergency call we can worry about it."

"Sure?"

"Sure. Let's sit in front of the fire and re-member Thanksgivings past." He walked into the living room, removed the fire screen, and began placing hardwood—oak, walnut, one precious pear log on top—in a square.

Harry picked up the bowls, instantly licked clean. She rinsed them in the sink.

"Is a saint bigger than the Blessed Virgin Mother?" Tucker thought for a second.

"No. The BVM is the Big Cheese." Mrs. Murphy cleaned her whiskers.

"Think any human has ever made a statue to cheese?" Pewter thought honoring food with a statue not a bad idea.

"Not that I know of." Mrs. Murphy intended to join Harry, who had just walked into the living room, but her belly was full and the distance seemed too great.

Harry inhaled. "Pear wood smells fabulous."

Fair smiled, holding out his hand.

She took it and he led her to the sofa. They put their feet on the coffee table, continuing to hold hands.

"Remember the other Thanksgiving when it snowed so much? Not that common. We were in junior high."

"Yeah. Dad had to put chains on the tires."

The fire crackled and glowed. The two cats were fast asleep in the large basket filled with old towels that Harry saved. They were in the kitchen. Tucker managed to totter to the hearth before conking out.

"I remember digging Mrs. Clark out of that big snow. So many of our teachers are gone now. Mrs. Clark died back in 1989. Liver disease, and she never even drank."

"An entire generation is leaving us. Funny how fast time goes." He squeezed Harry's hand. "I don't have anything else to say about what I did, what I learned, where I am at this exact moment. You've heard it all. I want to marry you. I won't ask again. I know making a big decision is very hard for you. You can be so good in a crisis, but you don't like change, and life *is* change."

"I'm trying. I'm studying viticulture, other ways to make money," she softly replied.

"I know. Skeezits, give me an answer by Christmas Eve."

"This is an ultimatum?" She liked ultimatums about as much as she liked change.

"I guess it is, but I don't think about it quite like that. There's a lot of life left to me. I'm staring at forty. I want to love a true partner. I want a family. I love you." He took a deep breath. "But if I'm not really the man for you, I have to move on. It will kill me, but I have to go. I can't live in limbo."

Harry heard him in her heart, yet she feared making the same mistake twice. And it was true, she feared change. She'd adjusted to single life. She liked it. No, it wasn't as fulfilling as a deep partnership, but could she be that partner?

"Fair, you'll have your answer by Christmas Eve." She paused. "And whatever it is, I do love you."

Tucker, ears sharp, eyes closed, heard every word.

7

The long, slanting rays of the rising sun reached the statue of the Virgin Mary at 7:02 A.M., Friday. The back of her snow-covered robes shone pale pink, then deepened to crimson. The frozen blood on her cheeks glowed dark in the blue light for she faced west and it would be hours before the sun would climb high enough to warm her face.

Brother Mark, trembling in the biting air, again threw himself in the snow. He wept, he wailed, he prayed.

He pulled himself to his knees, his hands bright red from cold. He clasped them together, his face upturned to that most perfect of faces.

"Blessed Virgin Mother, forgive me, for I have sinned. Forgive me for the hours I have wasted, for the destructive things I did. Forgive me for being weak." A persistent memory of himself lying comatose at three in the morning in the middle of Beverly Street, Staunton, crept into his head. He had nearly died from a speedball overdose. "I come to you. I come to your Son. I give my life to this life, to your wishes. Make me your vessel."

He prayed dramatically, fervently. He seemed not to hear footsteps coming up behind him.

"Brother Mark, you'll catch your death," Brother Frank said gruffly.

"My life is of no importance."

Brother Frank was about to say, "Your history confirms that attitude," but instead he said, "Your life matters to our Blessed Virgin Mother, otherwise you wouldn't be on your knees before her. You must stay strong and become wise, Brother Mark. There is much to do and fewer and fewer young men to do it."

A radiance washed over the young man's face at this. He clasped his hands tighter. "Yes, yes, of course. I must be strong. We must bind the wounds of the world."

"What we can." Brother Frank long ago gave up on improving the world. He'd even given up improving himself. "Now, please, Brother, on your feet and come back inside."

"Isn't she beautiful?" Brother Mark couldn't tear his eyes away from that face.

"Yes." Brother Frank remembered only too well the beauty of women. He felt he had been led astray by women. Perhaps he had, but then again, blaming women for one's own weakness was a central part of Judaism and Christianity, starting with Adam and Eve.

As the two men, one middle-aged, stout, the other younger, slight, carefully walked back to the main section of the old stone buildings, Brother Mark alternated between tears and euphoria.

"This sign must be shared. I know it. In my heart."

"Not yet," Brother Frank chided.

"We have to tell the world."

"No. The world is, well, a world away. This is our world now, Brother Mark. We need to think this through before, like Pandora, we open the box."

"Our Lady will overcome all obstacles, including the evils of man."

"Why make her task more difficult?"

"Two women already know. Why should we remain silent?"

"Brother Mark, give me one day. You're a fully stoked furnace and, I confess, I'm embers. But the years give one perspective. Announce this prematurely, and our haven will be overrun, and not just by those coming to worship or coming to Mary for her intercession. The media, the mountebanks, will turn this into a circus, a degenerate entertainment." He drew in his breath, the cold air filling his lungs, painful to inhale. "She deserves better."

Unconvinced, Brother Mark did promise. "Twenty-four hours."

People visited the grounds, the various shops. This was the only mark of the outside world on the Greyfriars. The products the monks made barely kept the order in the black. Some monks had more contact with the outside world than others due to their special skills. All of the brothers, whether totally withdrawn or more "worldly," would feel the impact of people flocking to see the miracle.

The lures of the Internet disturbed the older brothers greatly, partly because the temptations therein could so easily be hidden from others. Each shop contained a computer to keep accounts of their wares, the candles, goat's milk soap, jellies and jams, iron trinkets, flowers, and potent applejack, their best seller. The order sold every kind of apple product, including even dried apples for decoration. Every Christmas the brothers wove huge wreaths, some as costly as five hundred dollars, filled with gleaming red apples and other dried tidbits, wide flat gold and red ribbons adorning the soft pine needles of the wreath itself.

Brother Frank walked down the long, cold corridor to his office. The job of treasurer suited him. He had hoped to find a successor among the few younger men in the order, but no one seemed suitable.

As treasurer, he used a computer for business purposes. He used the telephone sparingly. He found the hidden costs for both on-line and phone service infuriating. He checked his file, then dialed.

Harry, in the barn, heard the silly "Jingle Bells" ring on her cell phone. Fair had programmed it for Christmas. She pulled the tiny cell phone out of her belt.

"Hello."

"Mrs. Haristeen, it's Brother Frank."

Harry sensed Brother Frank did not like women, despite his good manners. "Hello, Brother Frank, how are you this crisp morning?"

"Crisp? It's cold as ice. But I'm well and thank you for asking. How about you?"

"I love the snow."

"Well, at least one of us does. I'm calling to ask you a favor. You beheld an unusual occurrence yesterday, I believe."

"The statue. Yes." She dropped her voice slightly. "Very strange."

"Indeed it is, and I don't want to jump to conclusions. Would you mind keeping quiet about this? Now, I'm sure you've told a few friends. May I rely on you to ask them to also remain silent as a favor to the brotherhood? I'm afraid a premature announcement could send people here looking for, well, miracles, perhaps. We need more information first."

"Yes, I understand. Of course, I'll do what I can. Luckily, no one will want to drive the icy roads up the mountain today; you'll be alone."

"I appreciate that. God bless you."

"You, too, Brother Frank."

Harry called Susan first, since they had

seen the tears together, and filled her in on the conversation.

"Not an unreasonable request." She reached for an ashtray. "What a time Ned had last night getting G-Uncle back to the monastery. We wanted him to spend the night, but he pleaded to go back up. He's a little obsessed with the statue—and perhaps a little dotty, too. Then again, I don't trust my own judgment these days. Maybe I'm dotty."

Susan was sneaking a cigarette, letting out a loud exhale. A recent gain of ten pounds had driven her back to her blue menthol Marlboros. Her worry over Ned accentuated her fretting over her weight. She thought her kitchen needed an overhaul and she was falling behind in the decor department. She was nervous about so many things.

"You're not losing it." Harry paused. "Something's wrong up there on the mountain."

"Harry, you're always looking for a mystery." Susan laughed, then coughed.

"I told you smoking isn't a good way to lose weight. Help me muck stalls or go to the gym. ACAC is really good." She mentioned a local gym.

"Who said I was smoking?"

"Susan."

"Oh, all right! One."

"Well, if you're going to lose weight, then one isn't going to do it, is it? Either light up or hit the gym. So there."

"You're a big help."

"What do you want me to say? I think you look great. You're the one who complains that your thighs rub together when you walk."

"Must you be so graphic?"

Harry giggled. "You look good. You and Brooks could be sisters."

"Liar."

"No. That's true. I'll forgo a lecture about smoking. It's your body. But back to this Virgin Mary thing. My sixth sense tells me something's not right."

"Your sixth sense has gotten us both into one mess after another. I wish you'd turn it off."

Harry was right, though. Brother Mark proved unable to contain his deep emotions. He snuck into the chandler shop when Brother Michael, a nearsighted man, was helping a customer. Since he'd grown up with the computer, using one was natural to him. Brother Mark fired off an e-mail to Pete Osborne, an executive at the Charlottesville NBC affiliate, Channel 29. Whenever he could he'd watch the local channel, since Nordy Elliott, his college friend, anchored the news. He'd learned who was who at Channel 29.

When Pete, a witty man, read the e-mail, he blinked and read it twice.

Pete, the Blessed Virgin Mother who overlooks us all from the top of the Blue Ridge Mountains is crying tears of blood. These are shed for the sins of the world. I have seen her weep with my own eyes. Some of the other brothers don't want people to know. They are afraid of what might happen. How can they be afraid of a miracle? A miracle from Our Lady, who is love and only love! The world should know that Our Blessed Mother is speaking to them. Brother Mark (Mark Croydon)

Pete reread the message, sat at his desk for a moment, tapping a yellow pencil against a large white coffee cup. True. Mark Croydon had scrambled his brains. Pete had met him once last year when the station ran a spring special on the apple blossoms in the orchard. He thought the young man quite peculiar. However, it would cost only one reporter two hours and a quarter tank of gas to drive to the top of Afton Mountain, then turn north for a mile to the iron-gated entrance to Mt. Carmel. Okay, maybe half a tank, because they'd need an SUV.

He stood up, flung open the door to his office, and strode down to the newsroom. "Nordy!"

8

"So, there you have it." Harry threw up her hands in quasidefeat as Mrs. Murphy, Tucker, and Pewter looked on along with BoomBoom, Alicia, Susan, Miranda, Big Mim, and Little Mim.

An impromptu gathering had occurred at Alicia's farm. Harry called around, and BoomBoom informed her that the state roads were plowed. Alicia's farm wasn't far off Route 250, so they gathered there.

The living-room walls, painted eggshell cream, and the woodwork, trimmed out in linen white, bespoke quiet elegance and warmth, like Alicia herself. Although she regularly visited the farm she had inherited, over the decades she'd changed it little from Mary Pat's taste. Once it was finally home, Alicia began to exert her own tastes, which proved bolder than Mary Pat's. Alicia, much as she loved sporting art and the great masters, wasn't afraid of modern art. Nor was she afraid of a splash of bright color here and there, like magenta silk moiré pillows on the mustard-colored Sheraton couch.

Big Mim, arbiter of taste in Crozet, at first was shocked at Alicia's "statements," as she called them. Gradually, the controlling doyenne warmed to the color and airiness of the place. Her daughter, Little Mim, a contemporary of Harry's, reveled in Alicia's palette, style, cleverness. Little Mim, ever keen to differentiate herself from her mother, even painted her bedroom pale lavender, inspired by Alicia.

The women ate chicken sandwiches, a thin veneer of herbed mayonnaise on them, the bread freshly baked. Alicia, ever a thoughtful hostess, put out crisp vegetables to nibble on, a wide variety of cheeses, and an array of drinks, including a yerba maté tea that gave the girls a buzz. As a joke, she placed a tiny card with the calorie count by each item.

"No wonder you stay so trim," Big Mim,

in her sixties and in excellent shape herself,
noted.

"Work out, walk, ride horses, and stop
eating before you're full." Alicia smiled her
incredible smile, a bit crooked, which added
to her high-octane allure. Even sitting there
in men's Levi's 501s, a crisp white Brooks
Brothers' shirt, a farmer's red hanky tied
around her throat, and wide gold Tiffany
hoops in her ears, Alicia couldn't be anything but a movie star.

"Good genes." Big Mim reached for a
raw carrot. "Good for the eyes, you know."

"Maybe that's why the horses like them
so much," Harry replied. "What do you
make of all this?"

Susan reached for her second sandwich.
Her willpower, not her strongest feature,
had faltered during the holidays—hence the
cigarettes. Harry teased her that the real
reason she visited the top of the mountain
on November 24 was that it was Thanksgiving and she was praying she wouldn't eat
too much.

"What do you make of Brother Frank's
call?"

Big Mim spoke first, her custom. "Until he
can ascertain whether this is something in

the stone, something explainable, his request for a news blackout, if you will, is sensible. This so-called miracle could become terribly embarrassing."

"All God's work." Miranda smiled. "Whether it's explainable or not."

"Of course it is, Miranda"—Big Mim and Miranda were contemporaries, so Mim couldn't sway her friend by hauteur—"but if the monastery advertises the Miracle of the Blue Ridge, which is subsequently discovered to be nothing more than a vein of iron deep in the soapstone, the order will appear in a less than holy light."

"Can it be worse than priests molesting boys?" Alicia replied with a hint of sarcasm.

"And covering it up!" Little Mim smacked her sandwich on the plate. "You know what else? I think they're still covering it up."

"Why boys?" BoomBoom shrugged. "Are they all gay? For the last two thousand years we've been herded and prodded by a bunch of pederasts. Does that ever explain a lot—think about it."

"This isn't to say you wished they'd molested girls, dear." Big Mim coolly drank some piping hot yerba maté tea. "But it is most peculiar, as is the response from the Vatican."

"In keeping." Alicia took a restorative sip of the bitter brew herself. "Pope Pius the Twelfth knew perfectly well what was going on in Nazi Germany. Not a word. Politics is politics. The Vatican is about power, not about saving souls."

"You don't find God in a building with a cross on it, you find God in your heart and in the hearts of others," Miranda, who was devout, agreed. "But that doesn't mean we rejoice in the sorrows of the Catholic Church. We're enduring a little contretemps in the Church of the Holy Light." She mentioned her church, a charismatic Baptist one, where she sang in the choir. "All about money."

"Always is. When I served on the vestry board I nearly went bald from tearing my hair out." Susan laughed. "Now Harry's taken my spot. And you were thrilled when you were elected."

"Oh, it's not so bad, but you have to sit there while everyone shoots off their mouth. Time-consuming. Once we settled the issue of new carpets, things calmed down." She reached for a gooey brownie. "But I swear what was running down the face of Mary's statue wasn't rust."

"She's right. It really did look like blood: the color, the consistency. I tell you, it was eerie." Susan shook her head.

"Why don't we go up there when the ice is off the roads?" Big Mim suggested, unaware that, with the exception of her daughter, the others had agreed to this.

Miranda nodded. "If we see it with our own eyes, we'll know more."

That settled, Harry changed the subject. "Doing my grape research. Grape expectations." Everyone groaned. She plugged on. "Virginia is home to eighty wineries, which bring in five-hundred thousand tourists a year and put ninety-five million dollars into the state economy. Read it in the *Daily Progress.*" She named the local newspaper, which paid its staff a pittance, but since they were dedicated newspeople they did a bang-up job, anyway, out of pride, pure pride in their craft.

"Well and good, but let us not forget that the horse industry brings over one point five billion dollars annually to this state, and as Colonial Downs gets better and better, if we can finally convince the legislature to authorize more offtrack-betting sites, you will see that double in five years. I *promise* you." Big Mim bred Thoroughbreds, mostly for steeplechase racing, some for foxhunting, but she kept a keen eye on the overall equine picture.

"The equine industry should be one of our most protected industries. As tobacco slides, it will be horses that make up lost revenue, if the state is smart enough to offer generous incentives." Little Mim, vice-mayor of Crozet, supported her mother one hundred percent in that area.

"You never know down there in Richmond." Harry laughed. "Are they smoking tobacco, weed, or opium? When you look at some of their decisions, you have to wonder."

"Harry, you're a rebel underneath it all." Alicia smiled at her with warmth. "Any state has its share of blistering idiots elected to public office, but this state has a solid government. If you want to observe entrenched corruption, watch Massachusetts; the reason they were the only state not to vote for Nixon was because the voters could spot a crook before anyone else." She paused. "Ah, but you're too young to remember all that, and I'm sounding like sour grapes. Let's go back to your grapes."

"Just doing my research. Good soil, rainfall, and sunshine for whites I've got. Maybe I can put in a row or two to see how they turn out. One good thing our legislature did was pass that Farm Wineries Act in 1990, which taxes wineries like farms, not like commercial businesses. That shows some foresight. But for now I'll stick to hay and timber."

"What about ginseng?" Big Mim kept up with the agricultural market.

"Down by the creek I might could grow some." Harry looked around the room. "You know, here I am talking about myself and my little world. I'm lucky you put up with me. I'm even luckier that you all help me."

"Harry, we're all family here." Miranda meant that. "We circle the wagons when we need to do so."

"Or open them up." Little Mim's face was flushed.

"Yes?" Big Mim pushed her glasses down on her nose, looking over the top.

"Nothing, Mother, just adding to the conversation." Little Mim didn't fib; she was merely withholding the major news that

Blair Bainbridge had proposed to her after Thanksgiving dinner. As her mother and father were herding the guests toward what Big Mim referred to as the "just desserts room," Blair had taken her by the hand and trotted her to the den. She thought the big question might be coming. She answered yes with blazing speed. They kissed, then joined the others, deciding to tell her mother and father in private when it seemed propitious.

"Let's see what the weather holds. If we're going to climb the mountain we might as well make our plans now." Alicia clicked on the large flat TV screen mounted on the wall in her den.

"You can do that from here? From the living room?" Miranda was incredulous.

Alicia held up a small remote. "I can turn on the radio, the TV, the security system, I can specify the rooms. Easy."

"She's so high-tech." BoomBoom was impressed. "I thought I was cutting edge, but Alicia is way ahead of me. Do you know she even had a computer built to her own specifications?"

"Don't be too impressed. Most of making a film is sitting in a chair trying not to wear off your makeup or crinkle your wardrobe. I had plenty of time to learn from the techies. I liked it.

"Why don't we take our tea into the den and see what the report is? Dessert, too, if anyone would like more."

Susan's eyes fell on the brownies next to the small lemon-curd pastries. Lust filled her. "I can't."

"Susan, honest to God, you make me miserable by denying yourself," Harry complained.

"I don't deny myself enough."

They filed into the den, a large room painted lobster bisque with creamy white trim. History, military history, and natural-science books filled the shelves. Alicia, an avid reader, skipped through a book every two or three days. In Hollywood she'd kept her brains to herself, which only proved how very smart she was.

The tail end of the news finished just as they found seats. The weather report came on.

"Should be good tomorrow. Mid-forties. You never know." Big Mim, like most residents of central Virginia, was continually surprised, even enchanted, by the change-able weather.

The news returned after ads for carpet cleaner, aspirin, the Dodge Durango, and pet food.

"Hey!" Harry shouted, which caused her pets to run into the room followed by Alicia's steady, placid, and terribly handsome Gordon setter, Maxwell.

A close-up of the Virgin Mary's face, bloody tears still frozen, filled the screen. The camera pulled away to reveal the entire statue, with Nordy Elliott at the base, look-ing dapper in his navy winter coat, tan gloves, and red plaid cashmere scarf.

"The monks discovered this unusual phe-nomenon Thanksgiving morning." No broth-ers were in sight as Nordy spoke, great puffs of air coming from his mouth like car-toon captions. "At this point no one can say just what is happening, but it appears the statue is crying tears of blood."

As he continued, the women erupted, all talking at once.

"Hear, hear." Big Mim finally called them to order.

"Liar!" Harry's cheeks burned. "Brother

Frank lied through his hat or his tonsure or whatever!"

"Don't jump to conclusions," BoomBoom sternly advised. "He's a cold fish, but he's not a liar. Someone else has let the cat out of the bag."

"Why do people say that?" Pewter wondered.

"To irritate you." Mrs. Murphy giggled.

9

"Norton "Nordy" Elliott reveled in his good fortune. Pete Osborne called him "Nerdy" to his face, but on this night, Nerdy/Nordy was a star. Even Pete had to give him that.

The scandals in the Catholic Church, while creating profound misery for the victims, the church hierarchy, and those priests still trying to do God's work, were a boon to the media. A church steeple needed repair. Made the news. One nun in the entire nation left a convent to become a lap dancer. Big news. A priest and a nun found love, rescinded their vows to marry. News. The image of blood on the Virgin Mary's cheeks was picked up as a feed by NBC affiliates throughout the U.S.

Although Pete regarded Nordy as little

more than a talking Ken doll, he was not averse to the attention this brought Channel 29.

The switchboard lit up after the first airing, the one the ladies had watched in the early afternoon. By the six o'clock news the switchboard twinkled like Christmas lights. For the eleven o'clock news the station took on a carnival atmosphere. E-mails jammed the system.

Nordy pushed the story. His next planned foray would be interviewing the brothers. As Prior, Brother Handle had sternly declined to give an interview or to have anyone else talk to the reporter. Pete allowed Nordy use of whatever equipment he needed. Nordy was in heaven.

The response proved the opposite at the monastery.

Brother Handle, in his late fifties and feeling it this evening, angrily clicked off the TV, one of two on the grounds, the other one in Brother Frank's office. First he called Brother Frank and Brother Prescott into his office. After a fulsome discussion in which each man pledged complete agreement with the Prior, he called in Brother Mark. Brother Handle's patience, already wafer-thin, wore through to threadbare. He finally ordered the young man to shut up and get out. Seeing Brother Mark slink away made him feel even angrier. Brother Handle never could bear emotional types. He then attended a choral practice.

When the eleven o'clock news aired, the brothers were still singing in the chapel. At eleven-thirty, Brother Handle ended the musical contemplation, as he liked to call it. The chapel, usually chilly, seemed even colder.

"At midnight we shall begin penance and silence. Two hours of private prayer will be followed by a return to your quarters. At five, we will again convene for Mass, followed by breakfast. You shall each go about your tasks in silence. The gates will be locked. No one is allowed onto the grounds and no one shall leave. If anyone speaks before I lift this rigorous rite of prayer and cleansing, a severe penance will be enforced." He turned on his heel, sandal squeaking against the stone, and strode down the center aisle, the gray folds of his raw wool robe swirling outward, the white cape slightly lifting up behind his shoulders.

He said under his breath, "Silence, prayer, work, abstinence, austerity, seclusion."

Twenty minutes remained wherein brothers could speak, but as the men filed out, no one did.

Once out of the chapel, Brother Frank motioned to Brother Prescott.

Whispering, Brother Prescott intoned, "Runs a tight ship, our Brother Handle."

"Our tight ship has sprung a leak," Brother Frank whispered back, as both men smiled at the double entendre.

10

"I knew I shouldn't have listened to you." Susan mournfully looked out the window of Harry's 1978 Ford F-150.

Although in four-wheel drive with snow tires, the truck, even in second gear, struggled for traction on the steep climb up Afton Mountain, the fog increasing in density with each ten feet of altitude.

"You always say that." Harry peered ahead, scanning for red taillights.

Mrs. Murphy and Pewter watched the road intently. Tucker sat on Susan's lap.

"Pea soup."

"The mountain wears its mantle of fog all too often." Harry remembered the time a pileup of over thirty cars closed down Interstate 64.

She kept to Route 250. She could swing onto it easily from Crozet. Since it was a two-lane highway, the opportunities to speed remained limited to whatever vehicle chugged along in front of you. At least, that's what she told herself as she kept her foot steadily on the accelerator, her hands moving the steering wheel in the direction of the skid, then back straight again.

"I wish we'd never seen those tears."

"Will you stop being morose? We're almost there. Relax." She coasted under the overpass, turned south onto the Skyline Drive. The fog was almost impenetrable. The Skyline Drive had been plowed out. Often, when weather became treacherous, the Skyline Drive shut down, since far too many people thought they could drive in ice and snow but events proved otherwise. The drop from sections of this extraordinary roadway sheared away at hundreds of feet. The height at the turn onto the Skyline Drive from Afton Mountain was about 1,800 feet.

Harry couldn't see a thing as she passed the Inn at Afton Mountain, its lights diffused to yellow circles in the gray fog. She missed the mobile unit from Channel 29, but they couldn't see her, either. Had they been outside the unit, they would have heard the deep rumble of the big eight-cylinder engine.

She checked her speedometer. The monastery was just a half mile from the inn.

"The icicles are blue." Susan noted the ice covering the rock outcroppings. "True ice blue." She folded her hands on Tucker's back. "I really am crazy to listen to you."

"Hey, takes your mind off your troubles." Harry's concentration was intense, although it did flit through her mind that she had not told her best friend of Fair's latest proposal and deadline.

Seemingly out of nowhere, the great iron gates loomed. Harry wisely did not hit the brakes but slowly applied pressure. The truck skidded slightly to the left, toward the drop side of the road. Susan gasped, reaching for the Jesus strap hanging over the window of the passenger door. Harry calmly corrected, slowly stopping.

She got out as Susan, grumbling, also stepped into the snow, a foot deep now.

"Dammit!" Susan stomped her feet, her Montrail boots leaving a distinct tread print.

"Calm down, Susan. God, you're edgy these days." Harry regretted this the second it escaped her lips. "Sorry. Really. I would be, too." She reasoned that in Susan's current state she really ought not to discuss Fair.

Tucker and the two cats jumped into the snow. Each time Mrs. Murphy and Pewter sank in over their heads, they'd fight their way back up, pyramids of snow between their ears. They resembled kitty coolies. Tucker, who was larger, had an easier time of it.

The cats squeezed through the iron gate. The humans remained on the other side. Tucker looked for a way in, since she was too big to squeeze through the bars.

"Girls, don't go far," Harry admonished them.

"We won't," they lied, plowing through the snow.

"If we had a brain in our head we'd have figured out that the brothers would circle the wagons. I don't blame them. It's all rather bizarre."

"Someone else has been here. Three someone elses." Harry pointed to tracks already filling with snow as another squall descended upon them.

"Hmm." Susan knelt down to inspect the

frozen imprint of a boot tread in the compressed snow. "Men or women with big feet."

"We know it wasn't the brothers. They wear sandals despite the weather."

"It doesn't mean squat, Harry. There's nothing wrong with people coming up here. We did. The gates are usually open."

"Yeah, but the news about the statue—" Harry stopped talking mid-sentence as she witnessed her two feline friends disappearing in snow, reemerging, throwing snow everywhere. When the cats would hit a smooth, windblown patch where they didn't sink in, they'd chase each other.

"Can you imagine feeling such joy?" Susan looked at the cats with envy.

"Yes."

Tucker wormed her way under the fence, digging out snow. She finally made it and tore after the cats. *I'll get you.*

Both cats puffed up, standing sideways. *"Die, dog!"* They spit.

Tucker roared past them, a spray of snow splashing both cats in the face. Their whiskers drooped a bit with the debris.

They shook themselves to run after Tucker, though it was harder for them because of the varying snow depths. They persevered.

"Tucker! Mrs. Murphy! Pewter!" Harry called in vain.

"Don't even think about it." Susan put her hand on Harry's forearm, the fabric of her parka crinkling.

"I won't." Harry was considering climbing the fence.

The animals gleefully frolicked. They enjoyed many opportunities to play at home, but Harry's discomfort added to the moment. They paused, hearing buzzards lift up to circle overhead. As it was deer season, a few irresponsible hunters had left carcasses. Most dressed the deer where they dropped. Deer season was feast time for vultures.

Before they knew it, the animals came upon the statue, snow swirling about her, frozen blood on her cheeks. They stopped in their tracks.

There, kneeling in the snow, hands clasped in prayer and resting on the boulder base, no gloves, hood over his head, was one of the brothers.

"*Shh,*" Tucker respectfully ordered the cats.

Mrs. Murphy lifted her nose, followed by Tucker, then Pewter. In the deep cold, the mercury hung at eighteen degrees Fahrenheit; at this altitude, they couldn't smell a thing. That was the problem. A live human at normal body temperature would emanate scent.

The three cautiously crept forward. Tucker sniffed the back of the thick gray robe, white with snow, as white as the wool mantle worn with the robes.

Mrs. Murphy circled around, as did Pewter. Both cats stiffened, jumping back.

The brother's eye sockets were filled with snow. Snow had collected at his neckline, covering halfway up his face. His face, though, remained uplifted to that of the Blessed Virgin Mother, who looked down, her own face lined with snow.

"He's frozen stiff!" Pewter finally could breathe. *"A human frozen fish stick!"*

Mrs. Murphy stepped forward boldly as Tucker came around. *"I can't make out his features."*

"Even if you could, we might not know him. There are many of the brothers we don't see," Tucker spoke quietly. *"The ones*

who work in the shops and talk to us are hand picked."

"Why would anyone come out in bitter cold—and he's been here awhile"—Pewter's dark whiskers swept forward and then back—*"to kneel and pray? This is beyond devotion. Why would the Virgin Mary want someone to suffer like that? No."* The gray cat shook her head, snowflakes flying off like white confetti.

"Maybe he had big sins to expiate." Tucker couldn't believe her eyes.

"Mmm, whatever they were, they had to do with humans. They never pray for forgiveness for what they do to us." A bitter note crept into Mrs. Murphy's voice. *"Humans think only of themselves."*

"Not Mom. Not Fair." Tucker stoutly defended his beloved Harry and her ex-husband.

"That's true," Mrs. Murphy agreed.

Pewter sat in the snow, her fur fluffing up. *"It's hateful cold. Let's go back. There's nothing we can do for this one. Maybe he's found Mother Mary."*

"We ought to check for tracks," Tucker sagely noted. *"In case there's more than one pair."*

The three fanned out, soon returning to the frozen corpse.

"Tucker, there's so much wind and snow this high. The statue's on the highest point here. If there had been someone else, the tracks are covered, which makes me believe he's been here since the middle of the night," Mrs. Murphy said.

"Why did we look for tracks, anyway?" Pewter realized she'd cooperated without putting up a fuss or demanding a reason.

"Maybe he didn't die in prayer," Tucker simply replied.

"Or maybe he died with a little help," Mrs. Murphy added, finding the sight of those snow-filled eyes creepy.

"Absurd. Who would want to kill a praying monk?" Pewter again shook off the snow.

"Maybe I should bark and get someone up here."

"The buildings are down that hill. The brothers can't hear you, and if Mother can, you'll only make her frantic." Mrs. Murphy started down the hill, dropping into deep snow here and there.

Tucker pushed in front of her. *"I'll go first. You and Pewter can follow in my wake."* She put her head down, pressing forward as the wind suddenly gusted out of the northwest.

Pewter grumbled from the rear, *"I still can't imagine going out in the middle of a snowy night to pray in front of a statue, even if she does have blood on her face."*

"On her hands." Mrs. Murphy fired back, then corrected herself. *"No. Not Virgin Mary. She is love."*

"He froze to death in prayer or had a heart attack or something. We've all been around Harry too much. She can't resist a mystery. She's still trying to find out who had Charlie Ashcraft's first illegitimate child almost twenty years ago. She's rubbing off on us." Pewter laughed at her friends and herself.

"You're right. The brothers will eventually find whoever that is, then there will be a burial and prayer service. That will be the end of it." Tucker dropped over snow-covered stones.

"Yeah. Who would want to kill a monk? They don't have anything to steal." Pewter could hear Harry calling faintly in the distance. They'd traveled farther than she remembered.

"Like I said, the service will be in the paper and we'll know who it was and that will

be the end of it." Tucker, too, heard Harry. *"Murph, you're not saying anything."*

"I don't think that will be the end of it. This is the beginning." The tiger felt the snow turn to tiny ice bits between her toes. She wanted to hurry back to the truck. She wished the strange, uneasy sensation washing over her would ebb away, a sensation deepened by the sound of wings passing overhead, the snow so thick she couldn't see the buzzards. *"Buzzards' luck,"* she thought to herself.

"Not necessarily." Rev. Herb Jones's gravelly voice had a hypnotic effect on people.

"I've become a cynic, I fear." Alicia's lustrous eyes, filled with warmth, focused on Herb.

They'd run into each other at Pet Food Discounters. Alicia was buying toys and pigs' ears for Maxwell, while Herb carried flats of special cat food for his two cats. He'd placed them on the counter, then walked to the toy section for some furry fake mice, when he bumped into Alicia.

The subject of the "miracle" came up and Alicia asked if Herb thought this might be a scam.

"Your line of work taught you not to trust." Herb placed his hand on Alicia's shoulder, feeling a pleasurable twinge when he did so. No man was immune to her beauty.

"And your line of work taught you the reverse." She smiled at him.

He reached for the furry mice with pink ears, little black noses, little beady eyes, the tail a dyed bit of thin leather. "I'll ponder that, Alicia. I have learned to trust God in His infinite wisdom, but I don't know that I always trust man—or should I say people?" He blushed. "Words change, you know. I'm beyond being politically correct. I, uh, well, I still think it's proper to open the door for a lady."

"So do I." Her laughter sounded like a harp's glissando. "But, now, Herb, do you think I'm a hard-edged feminist and will take offense if you use 'man' to mean humankind?" His eyebrows raised and she continued. "I won't take offense, but I will take note." Now her eyebrows raised. "So long as 'man' is the measure of all things, women will be shortchanged. I guarantee you that."

"Point well taken." He rubbed the fur on the mousies. "Antonia Fraser wrote a book some years ago. I wish I could remember the title but it was about men being the measure of all things in the seventeenth century, I believe. Quite good. I like her work even if I have forgotten the title."

"I do, too. That's one of the things we share, you know, a love of books." She selected a fake sheepskin doll, a sheepskin bone, and put them in her shopping cart. "Maxwell adores these toys. I tell him, 'Bite the man,' and he runs for the doll. If I say, 'Bite the bone,' he goes and shakes it and then brings it to me. You know, Herb, the love of a dog is the most perfect love in the world."

He chuckled. "Elocution and Cazenovia will disagree with you."

"Your communion cats." She laughed again, because all of Crozet had heard the story of Herb's cats eating the communion wafers, assisted in this desecration by Mrs. Murphy, Pewter, and Tucker.

"They're very religious cats."

At this they both laughed.

He accompanied her as she walked down the aisle, which was stacked with foods, medicines, toys, and new products. How marvelous it was to walk with a woman. His wife had passed away some years ago.

Grief still sat heavy on his shoulders, although he tried not to burden his friends. Only within the last six months could he imagine dating again. Imagining and doing were still worlds apart. He fretted over his age. Was he too old? Was he too set in his ways? Was he too overweight? Yes. Would he go on a diet? Maybe. Food was a comfort. He'd tussle back and forth with himself until he realized he most likely wouldn't do much of anything until he found a woman who caught his eye. Alicia did that. But, then, she knocked everyone for a loop.

As he strolled with her, chatting, reaching up high on shelves for her, placing twenty-five-pound bags of feed in her cart, energy flowed through him. When young, his father and mother had patiently counseled him on the qualities of a good mate, and he'd listened. His wife, very attractive, had been his lover, his friend, his partner. He'd chosen wisely.

He felt empty without a woman, and it wasn't just sex. He loved doing for a woman. He loved picking up the twenty-five-pound bags of dog food for Alicia. She could pick them up herself, but he could do it with such ease. The thousand small attentions a Virginia gentleman pays to a woman made him feel like more of a man. Without a woman to care for, dote over, occasionally fuss with and then kiss and make up, what was life, really?

"I'm so glad to be home. I don't know why I waited so long to come back." Alicia placed the furry mice in Herb's cart.

Herb put in a trial can of cat food that supposedly controlled hairballs. "If you want to get rid of hairballs, shave the cats." He laughed.

"Then you'd have to buy them little mink coats."

They laughed again. The glass front door opened. Harry and Susan swept through, Susan marching in front. She spied Alicia and Herb.

"Herb, say prayers for me. I've lost my marbles. I mean it. Sssst." She indicated that her brain circuits had fried.

Harry caught up, quickly defending herself. "Don't listen to her. She's—"

"No. Wait, let me tell them. First," Susan held up her forefinger, "look out the window. Gray skies, snow falling, not nasty-nasty but not great. So if it's that way down here, imagine what it's like on the mountain. Did I consider that? I did. Did I let my best friend talk me into going back to Afton? I did. Tucker, Mrs. Murphy, and Pewter ran through the iron fence—"

Harry interrupted, "The monks locked the big iron gates."

"And we stood there in the cold—which was worse that high up—snow falling, and we waited for those three little shits to come back. Excuse me for swearing. We had no business being up there in the first place, and you can't see the hand in front of your face. It's a miracle we didn't slide off the face of Afton Mountain."

"The Virgin Mary is working miracles," Alicia said with a straight face, then laughed. Herb couldn't help it; he did, too.

"Herb." Harry stared at him in mock horror.

"I'm a Lutheran minister, not a Catholic. I don't believe in miracles."

"You do, too." Susan's lower lip jutted out.

"I do but not—mmm, how can I put this— let's say that there's a reliquary with the tooth of St. Peter. Do I believe it will cure your ills? No."

"But if you were a dentist it might im-

prove business should you own the reliquary." Alicia leaned on to him for a second.

Even Susan laughed, recovering from her
snit. It worried her that she couldn't control
her bad moods, her anxiety. Harry always
talked her into stupid things. Susan would
bark at her and that would be the end of
it, but lately, every little thing about everyone—including her own self—irritated the
hell out of her.

"Locked the gates?" Alicia folded her
arms together, leaning on the handrail of the
cart. Alicia's pearl necklace, which she wore
often, glowed against her skin, each pearl
the size of a large pea, perfectly shaped.
Her shirt was open just enough to reveal delicious cleavage.

Harry noticed, like most women looking
at another woman. She saw Alicia's beauty
but it had no sexual effect on her. Seeing a
beautiful woman was like seeing a beautiful
horse. She appreciated it.

Susan didn't notice. Herb did, and a
warm glow spread to parts of his anatomy
he thought moribund.

"I wonder what's going on up there?"
Harry hated not knowing things.

"Nothing," Susan said.

"Susan, you saw the statue. How can you say that?" Harry had had enough of Susan's mood.

"I did. I did. It moved me, but that doesn't mean something's going on. We should all let it go."

"Not going to happen," Herb sagely replied. "It's too good a story on many levels. And if it is something we can't explain, so be it. Why must we try and explain everything? How about simply experiencing it and thanking God for the opportunity to experience it?"

"Eloquently put." Alicia nodded in agreement.

"Tell that to Miss Marple." Susan's humor was returning.

"Go ahead and laugh." Harry tossed her head, effecting disdain, which made the others laugh.

Herb glanced at his watch. "I hate to leave such pulchritude, but I told Tazio Chappars I'd meet her at her office today. She's drawn up some preliminary plans for remodeling the meeting room in the annex. Doing a garden shed for Miranda, too. I'd like to see those plans when she's finished."

"Wait one second, Herb." Harry ran to the

toy section, picked out a big shaggy doll, took the tag off, and gave it to Herb. "For Brinkley." She mentioned the special yellow Lab that Tazio rescued last year. "I'll pay for it."

"Oh, that's right. I've got to pay for my things." He looked at the long line. Pet Food Discounters was always jam-packed. He said, "Better put it back. I'll never make the meeting on time."

"Herb, don't give it a second thought. I'll bring the cat food and toys to you this afternoon, if you'll be home," Alicia offered.

"I will." He'd break or move whatever appointment he had. "Let me give you the money." He reached into his pocket.

Alicia put her hand on his wrist. "We can settle up later. You go or you'll miss your meeting. You know Tazio will work her magic. I can't wait to see what she's come up with."

Tazio Chappars was a young architect who had won a big commission from The University to build a new sports complex. From this, other large commissions soon flowed. She kept her office in Crozet. The encroaching fame didn't go to her head. She served on the vestry board with Harry, both women exhibiting a lot of common sense. They worked well together.

Herb kissed each woman on the cheek, then hurried out the door.

"He may be the best man I have ever met." Susan put her hand in her pocket.

"And here comes one of the worst." Harry put her hand on her hip, calling to the curly-haired man who stepped through the door, "You're stalking us!"

Bo Newell, graduate of the U.S. Naval Academy, owner of Mountain Area Realty, grinned as he beheld the ladies. "The Three Amuses. I'm not stalking you, I'm seeking divine inspiration."

"Buying food for the Almost Home Center?" Susan asked, since Bo and his wife, Nancy, along with Bette Grahame, spearheaded a drive to build a no-kill shelter in Nelson County.

"Yes." He put his hands in his pockets. "Thought I'd go up and pray on Afton Mountain for an angel. We need contributions."

"Not today. Another storm is brewing," Susan replied. "And the monks have locked the gates."

His light eyes opened wide. "You're kidding?"

"No," Susan said. "Harry forced me to go up there."

"At gunpoint, I'm sure," he slyly replied.

"Kidnapped," Harry said.

"Held hostage against her will." Alicia picked up on it.

"Is this like the rape of the Sabine women where they were carried off against their will? Harry just carried you off to the mountain?" Bo solemnly asked.

"Well, not with the two of us." Susan's mood was passing. "Murder maybe."

"Me!"

"Harry, it really does occur to me on the odd occasion." Susan nodded.

"Right here in Pet Food Discounters." Bo, voice rising, rubbed his hands. "But really, Susan, the monks have locked the gates?"

"Yes."

"That will keep Nordy out. Jesus, that guy is like a hemorrhoid. He slips down and hangs around." Bo was warming up, his typical outrageous humor in play. He paused, lowered his voice, now sounding achingly sincere. "Actually, I don't have to drive to

Afton Mountain. The Madonna is in front of me." He kissed Alicia's hand.

"Bo, you are so full of it," Harry said.

"Think of me as Divergent Mary," Alicia quipped.

Bo loved a witty woman. "I'll think of you often." He sighed. "Well, ladies, I've got strays to feed. That must be how Nancy thinks of me. Was I lucky or what! I practiced my hangdog look."

"You were lucky." Susan smiled as he waved, heading toward the stacks of fifty-pound chow bags.

Alicia watched Bo for a moment, then turned to the two friends. "My friend Maggie Sheraton will be visiting me next week. I thought I'd give a small dinner party and invite Herb. Maggie lost her husband a few years ago. I think the two of them would get along."

"You mean Margaret Sheraton the actress?" Harry's jaw dropped.

"Yes."

"Didn't she win an Oscar?" Susan rummaged her brain for the film.

"Best Supporting Actress. Um, twelve years ago. She works now and then but, you know, Maggie is in her early sixties. The business ignores actresses who age. It's a sin to grow old in Hollywood. She's still good-looking. A man with Herb's strong character and warmth would appeal to her."

"He's not too fat?" Harry blurted.

"Harry." Susan elbowed her.

"Sorry."

"He is portly. She'll overlook it, but if a spark should fly between them, I bet he gets himself in better shape. He's let himself go."

"Miranda did that after George died," Harry remembered.

"Look at her now. She looks years younger. Lost the weight. Found love—another one of those miracles." Alicia smiled.

"Maybe there's one left over for me," Susan said plaintively.

"Honey, now, everything will be all right. Really. I just know things aren't what you think." Harry hugged Susan. "There's nothing to worry about."

"I hope so." Susan sighed.

Alicia reached for Susan's hand. "Courage. Life calls for courage." She squeezed her hand. "And Harry is right, it will all turn out."

"Think you'll find love again?" Harry

couldn't help herself. She shouldn't have asked this directly and not in a public place.

"Yes," Alicia forthrightly replied. "Love may not make the world go around, but it certainly makes the ride worthwhile."

"I never thought of that." Harry folded her arms across her chest.

"If it has anything to do with emotions, you don't think of it. You're worse than any man I've ever met." Susan rolled her eyes.

"Poop to you. If we weren't in the middle of Pet Food Discounters, I'd say worse."

"You two can't live without each other." Alicia stood up straight.

"I could try." Susan giggled.

"Be bored." Harry giggled, too.

"I have two children, Harry. I don't need a third."

"Let's not talk about me." Harry turned back to Alicia. "Are we too country for you now? When you were here as a young person, you hadn't seen the world. You weren't a big movie star."

"Oh, Harry, I'd rather fall in love with someone country than the president of the largest entertainment group in the world. Trust me. I am so glad to be home, home with real people with real lives. Hollywood gave me many opportunities and a great deal of money. I'm grateful for that, but if you're not careful it can erode your sense of reality and, ultimately, your sense of self. It's a debilitating environment."

"I'm so glad." Susan corrected herself. "Not about a debilitating environment but that you could fall in love with a Virginian, a farmer, a banker, a—" She stopped.

Alicia looked from Susan to Harry, back again to Susan. "I know exactly what you're thinking."

"You do?" they asked in unison.

"Will I fall in love with a man or a woman?" Both women's faces reddened, then Susan nodded that Alicia had hit the nail on the head.

"It's none of our business." Harry picked up the mousies.

"Coming from you?" Susan was incredulous.

Alicia laughed. "Better get some mousies for Mrs. Murphy and Pewter. Since you're interested in my life, let me say one thing: anyone who refuses love is a fool. That may not answer your question, but that is a truth I have learned. Do I know? In a way, I do. While I have loved two men in my life, there was always a part of me on guard. I like being totally relaxed with another human being. Just being myself."

"Ah." Susan understood. "But Alicia, aren't all women on guard with men, even the men they've lived with for decades?"

"Susan, I can't believe you're saying that." Harry's eyes opened wider. "On guard?"

"I am. There's a part of me I keep to myself."

"Is that being on guard?" Harry puzzled. "I don't feel on guard with Fair. I can't say I feel on guard with men, anyway."

"Because you're a man in a woman's body, a beautiful body. I don't mean that as an insult. Harry, you've got bigger balls, forgive the phrase, than most of the men I know," Susan said.

"Oh, come on, that's not true. I'm tired of hearing that. Just because I don't ooh and goo and carry on about what a caretaker I am, ooze love and all that bullcrap, doesn't mean I think like a man. I'm logical. Big deal."

"You two have been having this argument since first grade. I'm heading to the checkout. Susan, I believe you can love a man and not be on guard. The reason I was on guard, even though I loved and was loved, was that I wasn't being true to myself. And, Harry, a good man is in love with you. You won't find anyone better. You all spoke directly to me, I'm speaking directly to you. Susan, drop your guard. Harry, seize love."

As Alicia left, Susan's face looked as though she'd been slapped hard. What the unusual woman said had cut deep down to the bone.

"Susan? Susan, are you all right?" Harry, also affected, touched Susan's face, which burned.

"Huh? Yes. Come on, let's get what we need. Mrs. Murphy, Pewter, and Tucker will shred the truck seat."

Outside in the truck, the three animal friends constantly looked through the windshield for sight of Harry. They had little to say to one another since coming down the mountain. The sight of the frozen monk wasn't grotesque, but it was macabre, startling, and it had sobered all three of them.

12

Bruised air hovered over the friars as they ate in the common room. The meal was so silent, one could hear bread being torn from the freshly baked loaves. Brother Handle ate at a table perpendicular to the others. His scowl, etched on his face, accentuated the general discomfort.

Brother Mark, the youngest, sat with the other younger men—in this case, "younger" being anyone in their forties.

Brother Frank, head full of numbers, counted things. He couldn't help it. He'd count the number of loaves of black bread. He'd count the pencils on Brother Handle's desk, noting those with broken lead, with erasers chewed off. He'd count the number of steps from his cubicle to another cubicle.

He'd count the number of long-needle pines from the large arched door of the main building to the chandler's shop. He'd count the bee boxes at the edge of the meadows. Sitting there, he counted heads. One was missing. He made a mental note to check the infirmary.

Once the meal concluded, prayers and song again given, Brother Frank walked nimbly down the long, cold corridor to the infirmary, the flagstones shooting cold upward through his shins. Brother John and Brother Andrew, both physicians, oversaw the infirmary. Cleaner than most hospitals, it contained the basics for emergencies. Both men kept certain drugs in a locked refrigerator and a locked cabinet. Some blood packets and plasma packets were also in the refrigerator. Brother Sidney needed his transfusion but in the event of a life-threatening emergency, blood types other than O, Brother Sidney's, were on hand. Since keeping blood in such a manner was against the laws, the two doctors felt no need to inform the Prior as to regulations. He assumed they knew what they were doing and they did. The laws about private physicians giving transfusions outside of a hospital or regulated clinic just didn't make sense at two thousand feet above sea level in, say, a bad storm. They needed the blood. Brother Frank knew what those drugs were, since he paid the accounts. Other than the two doctors and Brother Handle, it was assumed no one else knew of these powerful painkillers. A stainless-steel table dominated the center of a small operating room, used for routine sufferings such as stitching a wound. Anything more serious was performed at Augusta Medical Center, with one of the brothers, in scrubs, in attendance. Both men kept their licenses current, which meant they attended medical conferences and did whatever was necessary to stand in good stead in their profession.

Each had left lucrative practices for different reasons, but both were regularly off the monastery grounds to serve the poor at various local clinics.

Brother Frank also attended special conferences, if they addressed new methods of accounting or finance. He picked things up speedily. He could learn from the Internet, although the computer screen in his office hurt his eyes. This irritated him enormously, since a whole new computer system had been purchased just this past summer. Each shop had a terminal and a laser printer. Each computer could talk to every other computer. The cost just about sent Brother Frank over the edge. This expensive purchase did help keep track of sales and accounts, though. Much time was saved in each of the shops. And Brother Frank could keep current with each day's financial activities. That was all to the good, but the screen still hurt his eyes.

Some men retreat to a monastery for a life of contemplation, hoping to find a peace, an understanding, a closeness to God. Brother Frank had arrived out of profound disgust for the world.

As Brother Frank walked from sickroom to sickroom, twenty-five flagstone steps in between, door to door, Brother Andrew entered the infirmary.

Neither man felt compelled to remain silent in the other's presence. Neither would censure the other. Both men respected Brother Handle, his iron rule, but neither especially liked him.

"Can I help you?"

"Brother Andrew. Has anyone been in sick bay?"

"No, but these beds will fill up in the next three weeks as that new flu strain works its way through Virginia."

"Thought you gave us our flu shots?"

"Works for some." Brother Andrew half-smiled.

"I see. Shall we consider the flu a scourge sent from God to punish our sins?" Brother Frank liked probing, finding out what the other person really felt. Despite his cold demeanor, he respected a confidence. He earned the trust the other monks felt for him.

"I don't," Brother Andrew simply replied.

Brother Frank shrugged. "Microbes? Bacteria? Viruses? Haven't you asked what God wants with these tiny monsters?"

"I don't question God, I question man. But as a scientist, I hold that many of these seeming pests have a positive function on the whole."

"Just not positive for man?"

"Precisely. God gave us powers of reason. As a physician, it is my task to use that reason for the good of others. You might say I'm at war with the latest virus, bacteria, even deer ticks."

"Lyme disease."

"It's devastating. People don't realize how dreadful Lyme disease can be." Brother Andrew, relieved to actually be speaking with another intelligent person, sat down, drawing the folds of his robe around his legs. The infirmary wasn't as warm as it might be, although it was warmer than the corridors of the main building.

Brother Frank sat next to him, both men leaning back on the upright wooden school chairs, their sandaled feet stretched out before them.

"What do you make of all this?" Brother Frank turned toward the lean monk.

"The tears of blood?" Brother Andrew held his palms upward. "I didn't see them. And now that we're held here, I expect I won't until tomorrow, Sunday. Surely we can walk the grounds on Sunday?"

"I saw them." Brother Frank crossed his arms, his hands inside the sleeves up to his elbows. "I kept it to myself; four of us saw them and promised to keep it among us for twenty-four hours. Someone didn't."

"But I'd heard the tears were first seen by Harry Haristeen and Susan Tucker. They could have revealed this."

"I called Harry. I asked her to button her

lip." He shrugged. "She probably couldn't do it. Too good a story."

Brother Andrew drew his feet in toward him. "Misogynist."

"My observations lead me to conclude that most women are superficial, emotional, and gossips."

"You're foolish, Brother Frank. Just because one woman wronged you doesn't mean they're all the devil's temptresses. Has it ever occurred to you that you asked for the wrong woman?"

Brother Frank's face darkened. "I gave her everything."

"That's not the point. The point is we often attract our own doom in the form of another person. If it's a woman, if it involves sex, so much the worse. The light by which we seek is the fire by which we shall be consumed."

"If you love women so much, why are you here?"

"One woman." Brother Andrew smiled a slow, sad smile. "Much as I understand a life of contemplation and prayer, I think we would all do ourselves much good by sharing our pasts. We learn from others. I'm a physician, and I couldn't save my wife from cancer. In the end I couldn't even stop the pain." What Brother Andrew did not divulge was that he finally injected a lethal dose of morphine into his wife to end her hideous suffering. He wondered, was he truly a murderer, or did he send to God a soul he loved more than any other, a soul at last free from pain? The monastery was his refuge from his perceived inadequacy.

"I'm sorry," Brother Frank said genuinely.

"I tell myself it was God's will." Brother Andrew put his hands on his knees. "Back to Harry. I see her more than you do when I go out to clinics. I'll stop by Crozet sometimes for fruit or an ice cream, my guilty pleasure. I'll talk to Harry at the post office. She would keep her promise. Someone else has disturbed our peace here. Would the other men have been indiscreet, not kept the promise?"

"I don't know. I can't imagine Brother Prescott doing this. I can, however, imagine Brother Mark, who is convinced this is a miracle, the Miracle of the Blue Ridge, Our Lady of the Blue Ridge." He grumbled, "People will pour through that gate once Brother Handle unlocks it, as he must sooner or later. How can we handle the numbers and the hysteria? Keeping silent, pretending the Blessed Virgin Mother isn't weeping, isn't going to cut it."

"I agree, but perhaps our leader thinks this diffuses the situation among ourselves."

"And perhaps it gives him time to think." A long pause followed. "We could make a great deal of money from this, you know."

"Ah." Brother Andrew nodded appreciatively.

"Will it fatten our coffers without violating our order?" He held up his hand as if in supplication. "As one who wishes to withdraw from the world, I don't like the idea of people beating their breasts, crying, making a spectacle of themselves in front of the Blessed Virgin Mother or, I confess, in front of me."

"She's seen worse," Brother Andrew wryly said.

"Ha." Brother Frank allowed himself a rare laugh, then stood up, his feet feeling slightly numb, tiny little pinpricks of pain slowly awakening them. "At least Brother Handle lets us wear socks with our sandals in winter, but my feet never feel warm. I hate it."

Brother Andrew stretched his feet out again. "I do, too. I think I can pray in here as easily as in my room, and it's a tad warmer." Brother Andrew wiggled his toes to make his point.

Brother Frank replied, a hint of playfulness in his voice, "Best foot forward."

"Quite right."

Brother Frank crossed his arms again, then slipped his hands back up the long folds of his sleeves. "So you haven't treated anyone in the last two days?"

"No. Why?"

"Well, I counted one head missing tonight."

"No, no one's sick that I know of." Brother Andrew now stood up. "Let's check the rooms. If someone was too sick to come to our evening meal I should know about it. It's quite possible in this aura of silence"—he tried not to be sarcastic but was anyway—"that someone is ill and told no one. We're all concentrating so hard on remaining silent, we aren't paying attention to one another. I didn't notice anyone missing."

"Someone is."

"Then I suggest, Brother Frank, that we get to it."

Together the two men walked down the east corridor. All was well there. Then they inspected the west corridor, nodding and smiling as they looked in on each brother. When they reached Brother Thomas's cubicle, it was empty.

"If we ask the other brothers whether they've seen him, we break the vow of silence imposed by Brother Handle," Brother Andrew whispered.

"Let's go to Brother Handle."

The two knew they'd find him in his office, books and papers piled high, his computer screen blinking. If they were lucky maybe the TV would be on. It was turned only to the news. He glanced up, not at all happy to be disturbed from his work—scheduling, which he loathed doing.

"Forgive us, Brother."

Brother Handle glared at Brother Frank. "What is it?"

"We can't locate Brother Thomas."

"Look in the carpenter's shop."

"He wouldn't be there, Brother Handle.

He'd be in the chapel or at private prayer in accordance with your orders."

Remembering his recent order, Brother Handle's expression changed. "Where did you look?"

"In the infirmary. I counted heads at table. Brother Andrew, whom I forced to speak"—for this Brother Frank gained Brother Andrew's favor—"informed me that no one has been there for two days and the only case he or Brother John have seen within the week was a nasty cut on Brother David's forearm."

A long silence followed. "It's not like Brother Thomas to be disobedient or frivolous. He must be here somewhere."

"We can't find him." Brother Andrew spoke at last.

Brother Handle knew that Brother Thomas, despite his strong constitution, would most likely meet his maker before the other monks. Worried, he rose. "Brother Andrew, if he suffered a heart attack but not a fatal one, might he be disoriented?"

"Yes. We must find him."

Brother Handle said to Brother Frank, "Ring the bell, gather the brothers."

Within ten minutes all the brothers sat on

benches in the great hall. Meetings were conducted there, not in the chapel. After lifting the ban on silence, Brother Handle asked if anyone had seen Brother Thomas.

The last time anyone could recall seeing the elderly fellow was the night before at chapel.

"Each of you go to your place of labor. See if, by chance, our brother is there, if he needs assistance. Brother Prescott, divide the remaining brothers into teams, give each a quadrant, and search the grounds. Oh, give them a whistle, too. You know where they are."

Twenty minutes later, those outside in the cold and the dark heard a shrill whistle rise above the stiff wind. All the monks outside hurried to the call.

When they reached the statue of the Virgin Mary, they found Brother Thomas. Brother Prescott had found him first. He had a hunch that the older man might have come to this place, a favorite place of his, so he took this quadrant along with Brother Mark and Brother John. Brother John was ministering to Brother Mark, who had passed out at the sight.

Brother Prescott quietly recited First Corinthians, Chapter 15, Verse 22: "For as in Adam all die, so also in Christ shall all be made alive."

13

"Dead as a doornail," Harry called to Fair as she hung up the phone.

"What?" He stuck his blond head in the tackroom.

"The monks found Brother Thomas dead in front of the statue, which is still crying blood. That was Susan."

"Poor Susan." Fair worried that Susan was on emotional overload.

"She's sad, of course, but he was eighty-two and she said he had a premonition. I think she's okay."

Mrs. Murphy pricked her ears. *"So that's who it was."*

Tucker grimaced. *"Poor fellow. Frozen like that."*

Pewter helpfully remarked, *"Freeze-dried.*

You know, there are people who freeze-dry their pets or deer heads. It's an alternative to taxidermy."

When both Mrs. Murphy and Tucker stared at her, she turned her back and licked her paw.

"Think it hurt to die like that?" Harry wondered aloud.

"How does it feel when you get cold? It stings, throbs. Yes, it hurt, but maybe by the end he was so disoriented he didn't feel much." Fair hoped that was what happened, as he brushed hay off his sleeves. "Why would he go out there in this weather?"

"Because of the tears. He wanted to see it again." Harry finished wiping off a steel bit, the chamois soft in her hands.

"I guess." Fair pulled his leather gloves off, revealing red fingertips.

"I'm going back up there."

"Now?"

"No, daylight. After all, I saw the tears first."

"Stay out of this."

"Aha!"

"What? Aha what?" He blew on his fingertips.

"You think it wasn't a natural death."

He clapped his hands together, the fingers stinging. "For God's sake, Harry."

"You told me to stay out of it. You only say that if I'm, uh . . ." She groped for the word.

"Nosy."

"I prefer curious."

"Call it what you will; you stick your nose in places where it doesn't belong. This is one of them."

"Now, Fair, Susan, and I did see the apparition. The cats and Tucker saw it, too. It was unnerving."

"Couldn't smell, though. Too cold and too high up." Tucker heard that tone in Harry's voice and knew nothing would stop her.

"I'm sure the testimony of Mrs. Murphy, Pewter, and Tucker will comfort the monks greatly. You keep away from Afton. For one thing, Harry, they've suffered a loss, and you don't go snooping in those circumstances."

"There will be a service. They'll have to blast the ground out. Frozen solid. Guess they'll have to thaw him out, too, or bury him in a kneeling position, which isn't so bad."

"Harry, you think of—"

"Practical things." She completed his sentence.

"Graphic."

"Fair, do you think I think like a man?"

Accustomed to these abrupt shifts and the land mines that usually accompanied them, he stalled. There are some questions a woman asks that can't be answered by a man, no matter how he answers them, without a fight or a fulsome discussion. "Why do you ask that?"

"Susan said that to me. Actually, I've heard that since I was a child. You know that."

He rubbed his hands together. "You think logically. That's not specific to gender, despite cultural stereotypes."

She was relieved. "It doesn't bother you that I'm not . . . oh, you know."

"What?"

"I'm not frilly or gushy."

"If it's never bothered me before, why would it bother me now?"

"Good answer." Mrs. Murphy giggled.

"She wants more than that," Pewter wisely noted.

"Well, BoomBoom is feminine. Her body

is very feminine. Mentally she's not really girly. Kind of middle of the road."

"Harry, I'm not going there."

"All right. All right. I will say for Boom-Boom that she's no coward, that's for sure." Harry put another bridle on the four-pronged hook hanging from the ceiling. She rubbed it. "Wonder what it's like for her to have someone in town as beautiful or maybe even more beautiful than she is."

"Alicia?" He placed a bridle on the opposite prong, then reached for a sponge. "There's close to twenty years between them—fifteen or twenty, I guess. They get on like a house on fire. Maybe the age difference lowers Boom's natural competitiveness."

"I really like Alicia."

"I do, too." He smiled. "I liked her when I was in grade school. She didn't put on airs, she spoke to me as if I was an adult."

"I know why you like her," she teased.

"Only you, Skeezits." He called her by her childhood nickname.

"Really?"

"Really." Why did he have to keep proving himself to her? he wondered. But, then, most guys wondered the same thing, so he didn't feel alone.

"Miranda brought over her chicken corn soup. Want some when we finish the chores?"

"Did she bring over corn bread, too?"

"She did."

"Call her and see if she'll come out and have dinner with us; after all, she made it." He laughed.

"Date with Tracy."

"Tell you what, I'll make brownies." He glanced at the old large clock on the wall. "Half an hour."

"That's a deal." She loved brownies— anything chocolate.

The minute Fair left the tackroom, she wiped down a rein with one hand while dialing with the other.

"BoomBoom." Harry proceeded to tell BoomBoom what she'd just heard from Susan. Then she asked her to go to the top of the mountain with her. She knew Boom-Boom would do it.

When she hung up the phone, she was thrilled with herself; she had a partner in crime. Harry liked doing things with people, and BoomBoom suggested that Alicia come, too. Three of them would deflect some of Fair's criticism—not that she'd tell him. Of course, he'd find out, but it might take a day or two.

She hummed to herself as she inhaled the odor of Horsemen's One Step, a whitish paste in a bucket. When she'd strip down her bridles, once a year, she'd wash them with harsh castile soap, rinse with pure water, then dip them in a light oil and hang them outside over a bucket to drip-dry. In the cold she used Horseman's One Step, which kept the leather supple after she cleaned it.

"Don't let me forget to put out candies for Simon," Harry cheerfully instructed her animals.

Simon, the half-tame possum, loved his candies.

Harry would occasionally put out little bits of raw beef for the huge owl in the cupola, but the owl was such a mighty hunter she needed little augmentation; Simon, on the other hand, was lazy as sin.

She chirped and chatted to her pets.

"She's going to get into trouble." Pewter shook her head.

"*Never a good sign when she gets all bubbly like this,*" Tucker agreed.

"*Then we'd better all hope that the Blessed Virgin Mother really can work miracles.*" Mrs. Murphy sighed.

14

BoomBoom sank into a snowdrift up to mid-calf. Shaking off her foot, she gingerly stepped ahead, hoping for more-solid ground. She sank again.

Alicia, also struggling, with a royal blue scarf over her mouth to ward off the bitter cold, couldn't help but laugh.

Harry, head down, pressed forward, slipping on the new powder over the compacted snow, which was like a layer cake with thin sheets of ice between the snow.

Tucker stayed immediately behind Harry. The cats, left at home, would exact their revenge for this slight.

A blush touched the snow. This Monday morning a thin mauve line appeared on the distant eastern horizon.

The three women, accustomed to rising early, rendezvoused at BoomBoom's house, drove to the top of the mountain, and parked BoomBoom's truck at the cleared parking lot of the Inn at Afton Mountain. They were hiking into the monastery the back way, which from the parking lot was only a quarter of a mile. However, the property covered over two thousand acres, and the statue of the Virgin Mary stood a good mile and a half from the property's northernmost edge.

It was a testimony to each woman's spirit that she elected to do this. Then again, Harry could talk a dog off a meat wagon.

The wind blew snow down the back of Alicia's neck, tiny cold crystals working their way behind her scarf. It occurred to her that this adventure prevented them from doing anything about Christmas. She felt overwhelmed at Christmas. When she lived in Hollywood, her staff decorated everything, and her husband—it didn't matter which one—wrote the check. This Christmas she was going to face it with Fred and Doris, who could always lift her spirits.

As the sky lightened in the distance, Mary

was standing as a lone sentinel on the highest part of the mountain.

Harry paused for a moment. The image,
stark against the bare trees, was com-
pelling.

BoomBoom gave a low whistle. The other
two floundered toward her. She'd found a
deer trail snaking down toward the gardens
below Mary as well as to the stone pumphouse that serviced the gardens, the greenhouse, and the garden cottage. They fell in
line, Tucker still right on Harry's heels. The
going was better now.

Native Americans invented the snow-
shoe. Tribes in the Appalachian chain had
need of them. Harry wished she had a pair.

The three women and Tucker arrived at
the statue just as the sun cleared the horizon, a deep-scarlet ball turning oriflamme.

It always amazed Harry how fast the
color of the sun changed, how the world
suffused with light seemed to smile.

Chickadees, goldfinches, cardinals, and
small house wrens tweeted, swooped in
and out of bushes, many heading for the
places where the monks had put out seed.
One bold male cardinal flew to the top of the

Virgin Mary's head. He peered down at the humans and canine.

BoomBoom's gloved hand involuntarily flew to her heart. "My God."

Alicia, without thinking about it, put her arm around BoomBoom's waist, as she, too, stared at the tears on that face, radiant in the sunrise.

Harry, even though she'd seen it before, stood transfixed.

"Is it blood?" the dog asked the cardinal, as birds possess marvelous olfactory powers. The hunters were especially keen, but even a seed-eater like this flaming cardinal had a sense of smell beyond anything a human could imagine.

The cardinal cocked his head, one eye on the intrepid corgi, snow on her long snout. He then cocked it toward the tears, bent over low. *"Yes."*

"Are you sure? Blood has that odd coppery smell."

The cardinal, knowing the corgi wasn't going to chase him, carefully walked toward Mary's brow, the little bits of snow that fell from his pronged feet catching the light, falling as tiny rainbows. He bent over as far as he could. *"I know that, you dim bulb! It's* blood, human blood. I can tell the difference, can you, doggie doodle?" He threw down the challenge.

"Of course I can." Tucker puffed out her white chest, then said, "To humans this is Mary, Mother of Jesus Christ, so she's very holy. Even a statue of her is holy. Her tears set them off. Not these three humans, but other humans."

"Mmm." The cardinal unfurled his brilliant crest as his mate flew onto a tree limb nearby. "I know about her. Jesus, too. You can't live among the monks and not learn their stories. Every species has its stories, I reckon." He puffed out his own plump chest. "The church has cardinals, you know, imitating us, which shows some sense, don't you think?"

"I never thought of that." Tucker had seen a Catholic cardinal, resplendent in his red cassock.

"Oh, yes," the bird confidently replied. "That's why they're called cardinals. They realize that we are closer to God than they are. I can fly nearer, you see. They're stuck on earth."

"Chirpy fellow, isn't he?" Harry whispered.

"Happy." Alicia smiled, pulling her scarf below her mouth.

"Never thought about flying." Tucker pondered the cardinal's remark.

"How could you? You're earthbound, too. I get to see everything."

"Have you seen God up there?" The strong little dog didn't think God sat on the highest tree branch.

"No." The cardinal, crest falling back down slick, lifted one foot from the snow, the tiny sharp claws on the end glistening. *"The great cardinal in the sky is beyond my comprehension."*

"How do you know it isn't a bald eagle?" Tucker had seen quite a few bald eagles in the last four years. The symbol of the United States was making a comeback along the great rivers of Virginia as well as near the incomparable Chesapeake Bay, one of the wonders of the world.

He blew air out of the two tiny beak holes. *"Ha! What do they do but eat fish? Sit in trees, swoop down, and snag a fish. So self-regarding, those eagles. Wouldn't give you a nickel for the lot of them."* He leaned forward a bit, toward the dog. *"If the mature males didn't have that white hood—a little like the true Carmelite monks, you see, white hood over brown—well, you wouldn't look twice at them."*

"They're pretty darn big." Tucker's brown eyes stared upward. Even she found the sight of the bloody tears peculiar.

"Piffle." The cardinal tossed his head and his crest again unfurled, which made his mate laugh. *"Piffle, I say piffle. If I flew next to a bald eagle, you'd look at me first."*

As the women examined the base of the statue, the huge boulder on which it was placed, and the area around it, they couldn't even determine where Brother Thomas's body had been found, because the fierce winds and snow squalls at this altitude swept away any depressions in the snow, depositing yet more snow.

"You say you can see everything when you fly? Did you see Brother Thomas's body?"

"Of course."

His mate lifted off the branch, landing gracefully on Mary's outstretched hand. *"We saw everything,"* she boasted.

"What do you mean?" Tucker's ears pricked up and her mouth opened slightly, revealing strong, big fangs as white as the snow.

"Hour after twilight, and we, well, we live right over there." She indicated a knarled old walnut, big knobs on the sides. *"Dark as pitch, snowing again, and we heard an odd sound, so I looked out and there he was."*

"Came up to pray?" Tucker sat down, the snow cold on her tailless bum.

"I think so," she answered.

"Poor fellow must have had a heart attack, then froze to death." Tucker felt sorry for the old man, although perhaps dying in front of the Blessed Virgin Mother provided a comfort of sorts.

"Oh, no," the cardinal said. *"No. He was praying. We snuggled back down but heard footsteps. Brother Thomas, being human, couldn't hear them in the snow. We roused ourselves in time to see what we could, but the flakes were flying; big ones, too, and thick. Someone snuck up behind him, put his right hand on Brother Thomas's mouth, and held him down with his left hand pressing on Brother Thomas's shoulder."*

"What?" Tucker barked louder than she'd intended.

"It was hard to see; the snow swirled

around. *He bent next to the monk, then sort of arranged him back in his praying posture. Killed him, sure as shooting."*

"Could you see his face?"

"His hood and cowl covered it," the female cardinal, who was a brownish chartreuse color with darker, reddish tinted wings and tail feathers, informed Tucker.

"A monk murdered another monk." Tucker thought this especially horrible.

"A man murders another man." The male cardinal hopped down to sit next to his mate. *"When humans deny their essential natures, they get twisted."*

"Yes, I agree, but I don't think murder is part of their essential nature."

"Ha!" He lifted his head back, emitting a warble. *"They kill deer, they kill pheasants, they kill whales and dolphins, they kill lions and tigers, and they kill one another morning, noon, and night. All they do is kill."*

"My best friend doesn't kill." Tucker stubbornly defended Harry.

"She's a woman. Women don't go about killing things. The men do. I tell you, they live to kill." The cardinal noticed six goldfinches talking with animation to one another down in the old holly bushes.

"I don't believe that." Tucker wasn't rude, but she wasn't going to agree with something she found erroneous or wrong. *"Most of them want to live and let live; the ones who don't cause all the trouble. And I don't see there's much we can do about it."*

"That's true," the female cardinal replied.

"Are there odd things that happen up here? I mean, apart from Brother Thomas being murdered?" Tucker asked.

"Oh, my, yes," the female said, her voice dipping down.

"Not everyone in Holy Orders is holy," the male said. *"They drink and smoke and take drugs."* He opened his wings. *"You'd better get out of here."*

As the birds flew off, Tucker turned and inhaled deeply. Three other humans were coming on up; she could just catch their warm lanolin scent weaving over the frigid air, bright like a ribbon.

Alicia touched Harry's arm. "I don't think we're going to find anything."

BoomBoom spied the Brothers Frank, Andrew, and Mark before Harry saw them.

"Harry," Brother Frank called out.

"Oh, shit," Harry muttered under her breath.

15

The passing of Brother Thomas affected the three monks. It was assumed he died of natural causes. He was, after all, long in the tooth. If the cardinal could have communicated with these men, Brother Andrew would have performed an autopsy. Since the body wasn't embalmed, the deceased was buried quickly, with all the proper rites.

"What are you doing here?" Brother Frank angrily asked Harry as his eyes swept over the other two women.

"I came to see the Blessed Virgin Mother's tears." She told a half truth as Tucker sat protectively on her right foot, never taking her eyes off the three monks.

"Death from the ankles down" was Tucker's motto.

"The front gate is locked. How did you get in here?" Brother Frank's face reddened from emotion and the cold.

"Walked," Harry simply replied.

"Heavy going." Brother Andrew noted that all three women appeared in remarkable glowing health. He half-smiled. "Those media vultures can't come in the back way. 'Course, the camera is heavy, but they aren't up to the trek."

"We're country girls." BoomBoom hoped to defuse the situation. "And we are sorry to disturb you. Harry was the first person to see this phenomenon. We wanted to see for ourselves."

"This is the Miracle of the Blue Ridge." Brother Mark's eyes moistened. "Our Lady sends her love to us and she weeps for us. Her tears will wash away our sins."

"You are in no position to declare miracles," Brother Frank snapped, a wisp of gray hair escaping from under his hood.

"I'm not declaring anything." Brother Mark exhibited a rare streak of defiance. "Our Lady stands before us and we can't deny her tears."

"That's enough." Brother Frank raised his voice, which prompted Brother Andrew to lightly place an ungloved hand on the treasurer's shoulder.

"You're right, Brother, but this is so unusual we are each reacting in our own way." He turned to Brother Mark, smiled kindly at him, and then addressed Alicia, whom he recognized. "It's one thing to come through the snow and cold out of curiosity, but perhaps you have other reasons?"

"Do you know anyone who couldn't benefit from prayer?" Alicia did have her reasons. She was falling in love and not at all certain she wanted to do that, because, in her life, love upended everything.

"No," Brother Andrew warmly replied. He was not immune to her beauty nor to Boom-Boom's.

"We're sorry we disturbed you," Alicia said. "But I must say, the sight of her tears is deeply moving."

"Yes." Brother Andrew smiled again.

"The love of Our Lady is available to anyone who prays to her. These external manifestations are"—Brother Frank searched for the word—"fripperies."

"That's not true!" Brother Mark blurted out, his hand gripping the rope tie at his waist. "This is a sign from—"

Brother Frank held up his hand as if to strike the impertinent pup, but stopped midair. "Haven't we endured enough without your extravagant outbursts?" He then grabbed Brother Mark's sleeve. "There's revelation and there's reason. Try using a little reason. You can't go declaring miracles."

Brother Andrew chimed in. "He's right. I'm not saying that Our Lady isn't reaching out to us, but we must be prudent and responsible in how we share this."

"Why? Channel Twenty-nine has already been here." Brother Mark didn't have the sense to shut up.

Brother Frank raised an eyebrow, stared directly at Harry. Her returning stare told him what he already knew. She'd kept her promise. "Did you really come to see her again?"

"Yes." Harry wavered a second. "Yes, I did, and I thought if we came up through the woods we wouldn't disturb anyone. And, I confess, I know that Brother Thomas was found, frozen, praying in front of this statue."

Brother Andrew sharply jerked his head in her direction. "How did you know that?"

"Susan Tucker. Brother Thomas was her great-uncle on her mother's side, the Bland

Wades. The family was notified of his death. You knew they were related, didn't you?"

"Ah." Brother Frank, in his current state, hadn't remembered Susan.

"He was an old man, a good man. I don't know what we'll do without him. He was teaching Brother Mark how to use all the old tools, how to nurse along old equipment," Brother Andrew said with feeling. "If the boiler blew, Brother Thomas nursed it back to health. If an old joist needed mending, he could fix it using tools from the time this monastery was constructed." This was said with admiration.

"At least he died with Our Lady's face looking down at his." Brother Mark looked about to suffer another paroxysm of emotion.

"Yes, yes," Brother Frank absentmindedly murmured.

"The exertion of walking up here and the bitter cold may have been too much," Brother Andrew announced.

"I'm sorry. Really. I didn't mean to cause trouble, and I cajoled BoomBoom and Alicia into coming up here with me." Harry was contrite.

"Harry, your curiosity—well . . ." Brother Frank shook his head.

A puff of air streamed from her lips. "I know. I'm sorry."

"We are sorry," BoomBoom said. "We'll leave you in peace."

Brother Frank looked up at Mary's face. "As long as she's crying I don't think we will have peace here."

Brother Mark started to say something, but Brother Andrew quickly put his strong hand on the young man's wrist.

As the three women headed down into the ravine, the cardinal flew overhead.

"It was nice talking to you."

"You, too. Keep your eyes open. I'll be back," Tucker said.

"Your human won't be back up after this," the cardinal confidently predicted.

"You don't know Harry."

Following their tracks, which were already beginning to vanish in the blowing snow, the way back proved easier than the way up to the statue, despite a few slips here and there.

Once inside the cab of BoomBoom's truck, Alicia burst into laughter. "I feel like a kid."

BoomBoom laughed, too. "I know. It was like getting caught in school passing notes."

Harry, who sat by the window so Tucker could look out, squinched up tighter against it. "Brother Frank can just trip on his rosary beads. They should be praying to St. Valerian, the saint you invoke against exposure and snowstorms."

"Harry, you're a cynic." Alicia laughed at her. "Let's go into Staunton. We're already on top of the mountain. Take twenty minutes from here to Shorty's Diner. Time for breakfast."

"I second the motion," BoomBoom, jammed up against Alicia, agreed.

"Me, too."

"Me, too," Tucker echoed.

BoomBoom turned on the motor, letting it warm up for a moment. The truck, wired for phone, beeped as the motor cut on. BoomBoom pressed the number 4 on the numbers by the radio.

"Cool." Harry admired all things technical.

"I programmed in the numbers I call most frequently."

"Who is Number One?" Alicia wiggled her toes as they warmed up.

"I'll never tell."

"Her mother, luxuriating in Montecito, California. Bet you." Harry felt a surge of envy. She wanted this phone in her truck. However, her truck was so old the phone system would be worth more than the truck.

"No." BoomBoom smiled coyly, then a woman's voice came over the tiny speaker, built into the roof lining.

"Hello."

"Alicia, Harry, and I will be at Shorty's in half an hour, tops. Come on. I'll buy you breakfast."

"Wait a minute."

The others recognized the voice of Mary O'Brien, a doctor in Staunton.

"She's checking her book." BoomBoom opened her coat, unwound her cashmere scarf.

"I'll see you there." With that, Mary hung up.

As they pulled onto Interstate 64, heading west, BoomBoom stayed extra alert. Within five minutes they dropped down out of the fog that enshrouded the top of Afton Mountain. Below them spread the incomparable Shenandoah Valley, resting under a low gray cloud cover.

"Did you see that chinchilla coat Mary wore last Saturday?" BoomBoom loved clothes.

"Her mother's. Beautiful. You don't see chinchilla much these days." Alicia petted Tucker, who decided attention was better than looking at the Waynesboro exits.

"I always wanted a silver fox." Harry saw the Wendy's sign flash by, a stop for her in the hot weather. She liked the Frosties.

"I didn't know you were interested in furs," BoomBoom said.

"Well," a long pause followed, "I am, kind of, but my fashion sense is limited."

"Not a fashionista." BoomBoom—who was—said this without sarcasm.

"White T-shirt or white shirts, Levi's 501s, my cowboy boots or winter boots, an old cashmere sweater, and Dad's bomber jacket, unless it's hateful cold." Harry listed her wardrobe.

"You wore those two-carat diamond stud earrings at the Hospice Foundation." Alicia liked Harry. "Very becoming."

"Mother's. Kind of like Mary's chinchilla coat."

"Your mother dressed beautifully." Boom-

Boom remembered the elegant, soft-spoken Mrs. Minor, née Hepworth.

"You know that show *Queer Eye for the Straight Guy?*" Harry asked. "I need *Queer Eye for the Straight Girl,* except I don't think those boys would exactly get a country girl."

"They would. You have good bones and a great body," BoomBoom complimented her.

"You noticed." Alicia laughed.

BoomBoom blushed. "Sure. I've noticed since we were in first grade and Harry and I were forever competing in every sport there was. I'd win at some, she'd win the others."

"Then puberty hit. You got the big ta-tas." Harry giggled.

"You don't want bosoms out of proportion to the rest of your body," BoomBoom simply replied.

"Look, if you want a wardrobe overhaul, tell me and I'll go down to Nordstrom's with you, down in Short Pump. I'm not going up to Tyson's Corner. Wild horses couldn't drag me up there, especially now before Christmas, but I'll go to Short Pump after the holidays," Alicia offered.

"Thank you." Harry didn't mention that

she didn't have the money, although the other two knew it.

Alicia, generous to a fault, was thinking to herself how to help Harry without embarrassing her by giving her the money. She'd find a way, just as she'd sent money anonymously to the Almost Home Pet Adoption Center in Nelson County after running into Bo Newell.

"If I took what I spend on clothes each year and put it in the stock market, I'd be a rich woman," BoomBoom mused.

"You're already a rich woman," Alicia corrected her. "You work for it. You might as well spend it. You can't take it with you. Witness Brother Thomas."

"Did he have anything?" BoomBoom asked.

"Yes," Harry informed them. "He inherited the fifteen hundred acres of Bland Wade land. Monks have the right to private property, to income from their labors. Over centuries this has caused abuses. There have been spasms of reform. But Brother Thomas had money. Don't know more than that." Harry paused. "Hmm, I wonder who else knew—about Brother Thomas's financial condition?" Harry stroked Tucker's ear.

"Don't go off on money." BoomBoom laughed.

Once at Shorty's, Tucker had to stay in the truck. Harry brought her sausages, putting them on the floor on paper towels, although BoomBoom didn't really care. Fussy as she could be about her own appearance, BoomBoom wasn't a queen about her truck. She loved animals, accepting the shedding, the little dropped bits of kibble here and there, wet nose smears, and muddy pawprints on the windows.

The three filled in Mary about events on the mountain.

"No autopsy." Harry jabbed at her eggs.

"That's not unusual." Mary drank a strong cup of coffee.

"You're a doctor; don't you think everyone should have an autopsy?" Harry prodded.

"Not until they're dead," Mary dryly replied.

"I read, I think it was in the *Wall Street Journal,* about noninvasive autopsies, kind of like Magnetic Resonance Imaging for corpses," Alicia said. She read five newspapers every day.

"It's so expensive. There's no way the

staff at Augusta Medical is going to put a, shall we say, ripe corpse in the MRI machine and then use it for a live patient. And there's no way the county can afford an MRI for the dead. The price for this procedure on one corpse is about four thousand dollars."

"Four thousand dollars," Harry gasped. "I could put up a three-board fence in one paddock for that!"

"Oak or treated pine?" Mary asked, blue eyes twinkling.

As they were all country women, they were keenly aware of such costs. The fluctuations in lumber prices affected them a great deal.

"But don't you find it odd, no autopsy?"

"No. As a doctor, I would like to know the exact cause of each death, but for many family members, the procedure upsets them. They think it violates their loved ones, and I can understand that although I don't agree. When the soul leaves the body, that's that. Use the body to learn. I see Brother Andrew and Brother John at the Health Co-op"—she named a clinic for the poor—"and they feel the same way. In this case, the autopsy would need to be requested by Susan."

"Susan feels he should rest in peace." Alicia happily ate her eggs, sunny-side up.

"Harry, why are you obsessing about this?" BoomBoom figured she knew the answer but asked anyway.

"Well, what if he didn't die of natural causes?"

"I knew it!" BoomBoom triumphantly said. "Harry, you see a murderer behind every bush, I swear."

16

"Arrogant twit." Pewter, her low opinion of all fowl confirmed, had been listening to Tucker recount her conversation with the cardinal.

Mrs. Murphy listened to the cherry logs crackle in the living-room fireplace as she reposed on the wing chair facing the old mantel with Wedgwood inserts. Pewter faced her in the other wing chair while Tucker had plopped in front of the fire.

Harry, at that moment, was opening a can of asparagus. Since she was in the kitchen she missed the conversation—not that she could have understood any of it, but she did listen when her animals spoke. From time to time, she grasped a bit of what they tried to convey to her. She hadn't gone into the basement or she would have instantly grasped the fury both cats wished to convey. They had turned their spite at being left behind on the fifty-pound bags of thistle and wild birdseed Harry stored there. With the bottoms neatly torn open, the tiny seeds spread over the concrete floor, long tendrils of edibles. Satisfied with the mess, the two returned upstairs to await Harry and Tucker.

"Brother Thomas knocked off his perch," Tucker said.

"Birdbrain," Pewter added.

"Brother Thomas, or are you still referring to the cardinal?" Mrs. Murphy sat up to stretch.

"Both," Pewter succinctly replied.

"That's mean, Pewts," Tucker said. *"Brother Thomas wasn't a birdbrain."*

"Well, he was stupid enough to pray in that bitter cold and blinding snow and then get choked to death or strangled." Pewter, despite her thick gray fur, hated cold.

"He wasn't strangled. The cardinal said a monk put his hand over Brother Thomas's mouth; he saw it through the blowing snow."

"Mmm, if he was strangled it would have shown. Apart from the marks on his neck,

his eyeballs would have been bloodshot." Mrs. Murphy, having killed many a mouse and mole, although never by strangulation, had a sense of what happened according to type of death. And being a cat, she didn't shy from this as a human might.

"Could have covered up the marks with makeup," Pewter thought out loud.

"Not really. There's nothing anyone could have done about his eyeballs. Whatever was done to him worked quickly. Remember, too, he didn't fall over. He stayed kneeling, with his hands resting on the boulder base." Mrs. Murphy was becoming intrigued by this strange death.

"Probably half frozen already," Pewter saucily tossed off.

"Maybe so, maybe so." Tucker moved a foot away from the fire, since she was getting hot.

"Does the cardinal live near the statue?" Mrs. Murphy asked.

"On the ravine side. Lots of bushes and enough open spaces, too, to keep him and his mate happy. That whole place is full of birds."

"Birds stink." Pewter made a face.

"Chickens, turkeys, and ducks stink if

they're in pens. Wild birds aren't so bad,"
Mrs. Murphy replied.

"You can smell them, though," Pewter
replied.

"We can smell them. Humans can't. Humans can only smell a hen house." Tucker
couldn't understand how any animal could
live without a highly developed sense of
smell.

"Smoking," Pewter said.

*"Doesn't help them, but they aren't born
with good noses. Look how tiny their noses
are. Can't warm up air in that."* Tucker
laughed.

*"Yeah, but look how tiny our noses are
and we have excellent olfactory powers."*
Mrs. Murphy gave Tucker pride of place in
the scenting department, but feline powers
were very good. *"It's their receptors—they
don't have many. Nothing they can do
about it."*

"Harry uses her nose a lot for a human."
Tucker studied Harry. *"I think it's because
she pays close attention to what's going
on around her, so even though she doesn't
have the equipment we have, she catches
scent before other humans."*

"She ought to pay attention to what's go-

ing on inside her," Pewter complained, as Tucker had filled in her friends concerning Fair's deadline.

"Not her way." Mrs. Murphy accepted Harry as she was. The cat had learned a long time ago that she couldn't change anyone. She didn't have much desire to change Harry, who was, after all, a less evolved species than herself. If she could change one thing, though, it would be to improve Harry's ability to understand the cats and dog. *"She hasn't told Susan or Miranda about her Thanksgiving talk with Fair. Who knows when she'll work herself up to that?"*

Tucker switched back to the statue. *"The cardinal said the blood smelled coppery, which it does, you know."*

"Very odd." Mrs. Murphy sat straight up with both paws in front of her like an Egyptian cat statue.

"Why kill Brother Thomas?" Tucker hated all this.

"Maybe his murder has something to do with his life before becoming a monk," Pewter sensibly replied.

"Brother Thomas took his vows before most of the other monks were born." Mrs. Murphy heard the refrigerator door open

and close. *"Who would even know about his life before he became a Greyfriar?"*

"Maybe he molested boys and they've killed him." Pewter knew about the troubles in the Catholic Church.

"How? They hardly ever see boys and girls up there, unless a parent brings a child into one of the shops. It's not a destination for kids." Mrs. Murphy kept an ear tuned to the kitchen. *"The only monks who see kids are the two doctor monks, and I could be wrong but I'd bet you ten field mice there's no way either Brother Andrew or Brother John would be abusing children."*

"Maybe they're abusing one another." Pewter relished the sex angle.

"If they are, who would care?" Tucker began listening to the kitchen, too.

"I would!" Pewter stoutly replied.

"No one's abusing you, Pewter." Mrs. Murphy laughed.

"If I were a monk, I'd care."

"Those are grown men. They can defend themselves." Mrs. Murphy didn't believe sex was the issue.

"Not if two ganged up on you."

"She's right about that," Tucker agreed

with the gray kitty, *"but it does seem un-likely."*

"So does murder," Pewter fired back.

"True enough." Mrs. Murphy half-closed her eyes.

"It's either something Brother Thomas did way back when before he was a monk that's caught up with him, you know, like 'vengeance is mine'—" Tucker, having listened to the Bible-quoting Miranda for years, cited this brief sentence fragment from Deuteronomy, Chapter 32, Verse 35.

"Or he knew something, something big." The tiger cat suddenly shot off the wing chair and raced into the kitchen.

Tucker immediately followed.

"Hey!" Pewter yelled at them, then the aroma of beef reached her nostrils. She hightailed it off the wing chair.

Harry placed cooked beef with crunchies and broth in three bowls. Tucker ate a different kind of kibble than the kitties. Dog crunchies usually contain less fat than cat crunchies, which meant if Tucker could filch cat crunchies, she did.

Harry fried herself a small steak while the asparagus heated in a saucepan. Fair wouldn't be coming over tonight. Monday nights he stayed at the clinic, catching up on paperwork. They tried to spend Tuesdays, Saturdays, Sundays, and holidays together.

Late November and December gave him a breather, as Fair's specialty was equine reproduction. In January and February breeders hit high gear and so did Fair. Thoroughbreds' foaling season overlapped part of breeding season. Foals appeared when they felt like it, like human babies, so Fair endured days with little sleep. The season finally stabilized around the end of March.

Tucker finished first, since she gobbled her food. The cats ate with more decorum, although Pewter sported food bits on her whiskers. This would be followed by a grooming routine that would put a cover girl to shame.

"The cardinal is full of himself because he's the state bird of Virginia." Tucker liked the bird despite his attitude. *"Goes to their heads."*

"State dog is the foxhound. I don't think it's gone to their heads." Mrs. Murphy liked foxhounds; she generally liked all types of hounds since they are good problem solvers.

"Should be the corgi." Tucker exhibited a small flash of ego.

"Queen Elizabeth has dibs on that." Mrs. Murphy laughed.

"Yeah, Tucker, you belong in Buckingham Palace or Sandringham or wherever." Pewter bit into a delicious warm bit of beef, the fat still on it making it extra sweet to her tongue.

"I do, don't I?" The sturdy animal smiled. *"Well, you know the only reason the foxhound won out is because Virginia is the center of foxhunting in America. I mean, it's practically the state sport."*

"Yeah," both cats laughed, *"and the fox always wins."*

Pewter quickly hollered, *"Jigs for a bite."* Then she stuck her face in Mrs. Murphy's bowl, grabbing a juicy chunk of beef.

"Damn," Mrs. Murphy cussed.

"Hee hee." Pewter chewed with delight.

"I know. I wished I'd said it first."

"Ever notice how a cardinal's beak changes color?" Tucker, observant, edged closer to Pewter's bowl, some food still inside.

"Hey, I see you. Forget it." Pewter growled.

"In case you're full, I'll help you out."

"Tucker, you liar." The gray cat hunched over her bowl.

"The cardinal's beak is black when he's a juvenile; he's grayish brown with color on his wings then. Sometimes people who don't pay attention to birds confuse the young males with females."

"Oh, how can they do that?" Pewter, mouth full, slurred her words. *"The female has an orange bill, orange on her crest, and pretty orange-red on her wings and tail. And she has a blush of color on her light gray breast. Can't miss her."*

"Sometimes they're yellowish. There's a lot of color variation. One time I was talking to a female cardinal who was poking around in Harry's rhododendrons and I thought she was a cedar waxwing until I realized she didn't have the black mask." Mrs. Murphy finished her delicious dinner.

"I think what they eat affects their color. What we eat affects the gloss on our coats." Pewter finally gobbled the last mouthful, to Tucker's dismay. *"Greedy,"* she said under her breath.

"Fatty," Tucker fired back.

The cat, lightning-fast, swatted the dog, who scooted backward.

"Ugly. I don't expect my friends to be ugly." Harry flipped her steak in the frying pan.

"It's Tucker's fault."

"Sure." Tucker shrugged. *"To change the subject, I think our mother is on the trail again."*

"But how would she know? She can't understand what the cardinal is saying." Pewter had already gotten over being angry at Tucker.

"The tears of blood." Mrs. Murphy cleaned her face.

"Huh?" Pewter began her grooming, too.

"She saw the tears of blood. Originally she wanted to go back and double-check, but Brother Frank cooled her with his phone call. Then Susan called and told her Brother Thomas died in front of the statue. Set her off. You know how her mind works." Mrs. Murphy knew her human very well.

"Or doesn't." Pewter moaned. *"More treks in the cold."*

"You don't have to go," Tucker airily said.

Pewter gave her an icy stare as Harry sat down at the kitchen table.

"We'd better be extra vigilant." Mrs. Murphy leapt onto an empty kitchen chair.

"Is there a state cat of Virginia?" Tucker asked.

"I don't think so." Pewter thought this a terrible oversight.

Virginia license plates carried various messages. Some had a ship with the date 1607, the year Jamestown was founded. Others had a yellow swallowtail butterfly, the state butterfly. Some had a horse on them, others a school logo. Harry's old license plates were simply white with blue letters, but she liked the ones with a cat and dog on them, signifying the driver as an animal lover. Pewter thought there should be a license plate devoted exclusively to cats, using her slimmed-down image, of course.

"How can that be?" Tucker wondered. *"If we have a state butterfly, a state flower, a state tree, how can there not be a state cat?"*

"Certainly it should be a tiger cat." Mrs. Murphy smiled.

"No, it should be a gray cat just like me." Pewter jumped onto another kitchen chair, peeking over the tabletop.

"I see you and you're not getting one morsel off my plate." Harry squinted at Pewter.

"We want you to start a petition so we can be the state cats." Pewter used her sweetest voice.

"And if we don't get selected—good old everyday cats—then I say we call on all alley cats in the state to descend on the state house, shred furniture, pull out computer plugs, and pee on papers!" Mrs. Murphy gleefully imagined the state house overrun by rioting cats.

"Bet the governor would have a fit and fall in it." Pewter laughed.

"He's seen worse, but this would be a first, a first for the whole nation." Tucker liked the idea.

"You all are chatty." Harry glanced at the newspaper. "Hmm, we still haven't gotten all the money the federal government promised us for security."

The animals as well as Virginia's humans knew if anything went wrong, they'd be on the front line. The image, ever-present in their minds, was the Pentagon on September 11, 2001. Also, much of the Revolutionary War was fought in the state as well as sixty percent of the War Between the States.

"Why do people believe their govern-ment?" Pewter asked.

"Because they have to believe in some-thing. They get scared without a system. They'll accept a system that doesn't work rather than create a new one; they're lazy. They're like a pack of hounds that way," Mrs. Murphy, a cat and therefore a free-thinker, remarked.

"I'm a canine." Tucker tilted her head up-ward toward the tiger cat.

"Of course, you are," Pewter said sooth-ingly, *"but you spend your time with us. Our habits have rubbed off on you."*

Mrs. Murphy laughed. *"Maybe. But Tucker, it's like this: if you or I are scared there's a real reason—you know, the bobcat has jumped us behind the barn. We fight or run and then we're over it. They carry their fear all the time. It's what makes humans sick, you see. And it's why they have to believe in things that can't be true."*

"Like a bunch of men sitting on top of a mountain with no women, no children, and thinking a statue of the Virgin Mary is crying tears of blood." Pewter let her tail hang over the edge of the chair.

"You don't believe in miracles?" Tucker hoped that there were miracles.

"Every day you're alive and someone loves you is a miracle," Mrs. Murphy wisely said.

"If Brother Thomas is resurrected, I'll believe in the tears." Pewter giggled.

Brother Thomas had been resurrected in a manner of speaking. The smooth stone with his name, birthdate, and death date beautifully incised marked an empty grave. Who would notice since it was a fresh grave? And it was a grave dug with difficulty since the ground was frozen. A backhoe had been used, and it was still a chore. The earth was replaced and tamped down. The next snow squall would obscure even the lovely stone that Brother Mark had labored to make perfect.

17

On Tuesday, November 29, a crowd of two hundred people gathered before the closed iron gates at the monastery. Brother Handle refused to unlock the tall, wrought-iron barriers. But by Friday, December 2, when the crowd surpassed one thousand people, many of them holding candles while reciting the rosary, he relented. The people walked slowly, in an orderly manner, to the statue of the Blessed Virgin Mother. Many, like the late Brother Thomas had done, fell to their knees. Some people prayed, immobile, for hours in the frigid air. When they tried to rise, they found they could not and other supplicants had to help them. During the afternoon, when the mercury nudged up to thirty-eight degrees Fahrenheit, Mary's tears began to melt and fresh ones slid down her cheeks, dripping onto the folds of her robe, onto the base of the statue. People dabbed handkerchiefs into the blood as it slid onto the base.

Fearing excessive devotions—perhaps a few pilgrims might be unbalanced—Brother Handle hastily organized a watch of brothers. These groups of four men took three-hour posts—one by the statue, the other three at the edges of the crowd. Another monk was stationed down at the open gates should anyone need assistance. In a concession to the cold, Brother Handle allowed them to wear gloves. Brother Mark, a month earlier accompanying Brother Thomas to a plumbing supply store, had cleverly procured heat packs from the mountain sports shop on the east side of Waynesboro. While others experienced shooting pains in their feet and hands, he stayed toasty.

Nordy Elliott tried to get a TV crew up to the statue, but Brother John, down at the gate, adamantly refused. This ultimately worked to Nordy's benefit, because he interviewed the faithful as they returned to their vehicles. Many people cried, others couldn't speak, but all believed that the Virgin Mary had sent them a sign. Nordy's cameraperson, Priscilla Friedberg, used a lens almost as long as she was tall. She shot footage of Mary in the far distance, which made the statue and the crowds appear ethereal in the soft winter light.

The piece, which aired on the six o'clock news, looked terrific. Much as people would like television to transmit news, in essence the medium can't do this. It can only transmit images, with a splattering of words. The fact that millions of Americans believed they were informed because they watched the news was both ludicrous and frightening. To understand any issue or event, a person must take time, time to read well-written, well-argued positions about same.

Pete Osborne knew this. He read magazines and newspapers because he truly cared about government, world affairs, and the arts. To his credit he understood TV, tried to get the best images possible given the budget constraints of his small station. He checked all on-air copy. The material was cogent, concise, and packed with as much information as possible in the proverbial two-minute sound bite.

The tears of blood had a big bite.

Nordy's career kicked into a higher gear, as did Pete Osborne's, since NBC affiliates again took the feed from Channel 29. The difference between the two men was that Pete knew there would be a price to pay. He couldn't, of course, have known how very high, but he did know that success was demanding. There was a reason the great bulk of humanity elected to be mediocre.

That evening at Alicia Palmer's dinner party for the vivacious Maggie Sheraton, this topic was on all lips.

Alicia originally had envisioned a small dinner party where Herb could meet Maggie. BoomBoom brought up the fact that that looked like a setup. What if they didn't take to each other? Better to protect them by having more people.

More people turned into Harry and Fair, Miranda and Tracy, Bo and Nancy Newell, Susan and Ned Tucker, Tazio Chappars and Paul de Silva (now dating), and Big Mim and Jim Sanburne. Little Mim and Blair Bainbridge were in Washington attending the opera. Little Mim still had not told her parents that she was engaged. Her father knew it was coming because Blair, quite properly, had asked him for his daughter's hand, but the handsome male model did not indicate exactly when he would be asking for her hand, her foot, and other parts. The father was a bit nervous, which he prudently did not share with his wife. Big Mim had the skills to run the country, but she couldn't run her daughter. This did not prevent her from trying, nor did it prevent the attendant resentment from Little Mim.

Alicia Palmer would have asked Deputy Cynthia Cooper, for she was a lively dinner guest, but she'd been tied up for weeks helping Sheriff Rick Shaw reorganize the department, top to bottom.

Patterson's created an elegant, low, long centerpiece for Alicia's dinner party. She had requested white, pink, and purple flowers. This was December 2, and Alicia wouldn't decorate with red, green, and gold for a few more days. She thought it vulgar to rush the holidays. The decorations came down on New Year's Day, too, just as Mary Pat Reines had done. Alicia had absorbed most of Mary Pat's ways. Mary Pat was considered a rebel in her family, not because she was a lesbian (most families had gay members; however, they married and then discreetly engaged in affairs) but because she refused to marry and live by Reines standards. Mary Pat's mother and grandmother had a servant behind each chair when they gave dinner parties. Life was grand indeed.

Mary Pat's mother would visit the beautiful farm and gripe, "You live like a peasant."

Alicia simplified life even more, but by most standards, except for those of a Saudi prince, she lived a beautiful and blessed life.

Alicia asked BoomBoom who she wanted as her escort. BoomBoom said Alicia could be her escort. The older woman laughed uproariously at this but was flattered. Alicia had abandoned the idea of an equal number of men and women at the table years ago.

Mary Pat's idea for any party—and this held true for Big Mim and her aunt Tally—was to always have more men than women. Parties almost always had more women than men; changing the ratio ramped up the competition and energy among the men. It never failed. She'd raid the fraternities of the University of Virginia or call up a dear friend of hers who taught at Virginia Military Institute. She'd make a contribution to the group's treasury, not that she told anyone.

Her parties were wildly successful because they overflowed with handsome young men, each of them coached to pay attention to the various ladies regardless of age.

Alicia, when away from her husbands, would have parties of only drop-dead gorgeous young women, many of them hoping for a film career like that of their hostess. The attention lavished on Alicia picked her up better than any combination of alcohol or drugs. She wondered why so many people in Hollywood succumbed to pills, powders, and liquid fire. As time went by and husbands went with it, she changed. Most women become stronger with age. She no longer needed the secret parties away from her husband, or a secret lover or two on the side—usually female, sometimes male—to spice up her life. The older she became, the more she realized that what she wanted was a partner, a true partner. She certainly hoped the woman wouldn't be ugly as a mud fence, but more than anything she wanted a woman in her life with a bubbling sense of humor, of adventure, of warmth and compassion. She would not turn away a gentleman with these qualities, but she found more of them in women than in men, or perhaps that was her illusion. Perhaps just as many men as women harbored these qualities. She leaned toward women intellectually, and her body gravitated toward the smooth skin of a woman. Long ago she realized there is no more reason to be gay than there is to be straight. It's not a choice. It simply is. You are what you are and it's up to you to make the best of it.

She sat at the head of the table, placing Herb at the foot. He protested that he didn't deserve the honor, but she told him how lovely it was to have a man at the table. She put Maggie on his right hand. Technically Maggie should have sat at Alicia's right as her guest of honor, but the hell with technicalities.

She also sat BoomBoom smack in the middle of the table, not considered a favorable place by those who understood that your place was indicated, literally, by your *place.* But BoomBoom knew her place in this community and had no need of visual reinforcement. She wanted the dinner to be a success, so she herself suggested she sit in the middle. In case conversation lagged, she could rekindle it from that position.

Jim Sanburne sat on Alicia's right. As

Mayor of Crozet this made sense. His wife sat on Alicia's left.

She cleverly placed Harry on Herb's left, for Harry could be quite funny, often unintentionally so. She scattered everyone in a manner she thought would bring the best out in them, keep them alert, and she certainly kept Paul de Silva alert when she placed Fair Haristeen next to Tazio. She put Bo on Tazio's other side and placed Nancy Newell next to Fair.

By the second course the table buzzed. First of all, everyone enjoyed everyone else. They hoped a spark might be kindled in Herb and Maggie.

"They'll need the miracle of the fishes and the loaves," Big Mim commented on the crowds at Greyfriars.

"Can't the faithful brown-bag it?" Harry, ever practical, said, which elicited laughter. "Did I put my foot in it again?"

"No, it's just you." Susan smiled, happy that Ned was paying attention to her.

"Well, the Blessed Virgin Mother can bless a ham sandwich as well as fishes and loaves," Harry commented.

A moment passed and Herb said, his voice deep, reassuring, "I called Brother

Handle to see if I could be of service. He thanked me but said they could manage. He did say people are giving the monks money, leaving money at the statue, leaving burning candles in glass votives, leaving contributions in the shops. He mentioned that the order does not seek wealth. I replied that surely there is no injunction against wealth seeking the order."

Maggie, who had done many commercial voice-overs, asked in her distinctive voice, "And what did he say?"

"That he would bow to God's will." Herb smiled broadly.

"Which means: take the money and run." Ned laughed.

"Susan, did Brother Thomas ever talk to you about his life in the order?" BoomBoom asked.

Susan, wearing a forest-green dress that looked good on her, shook her head. "Not much. The only thing he ever said was, people are people, and I never quite knew what he meant."

"That politics is politics and if you have more than three people in a room, you have politics," Jim replied.

"In Virginia you only need one person."

Tazio, originally from St. Louis, laughed. "One Virginian can hold five conflicting opinions simultaneously."

The conversation switched to a state senator from Rockingham County who they felt would run for governor next election.

Herb, tone measured, inclined his head toward Maggie. "Conservative fiscally but quite liberal on what I call personal-choice issues, an interesting mix."

"The mix of the future." Jim Sanburne became enlivened. "This country can't continue with the kind of polarization we have now, a polarization because the extremes of both parties are controlling them. Americans aren't extremists."

"Only in defense of liberty," Herb smoothly said, cribbing from the late Barry Goldwater, earning an admiring smile from Maggie.

"What the extremists have done, which I find very dangerous, is pull the debates away from the center. So the center is now thirty degrees to the right of where it might have been during the presidency of Dwight D. Eisenhower, a president who I feel was far better than he is credited for."

"Isn't that the truth," Big Mim simply said in reply to Alicia's astute observation.

"But all those men, men of that generation, whether Republican or Democrat, were fundamentally centrists," Tracy Raz, retired from a long career in the military and then the CIA, offered. "What we are seeing now is a generation not tempered by World War Two."

Paul de Silva, a South American with his green card—and therefore a lucky man—softly said, "You believe war brings wisdom?"

Herb, Jim, and Tracy had seen combat in World War II or Korea. Ned, a Navy man, just missed Vietnam but worked in the aftermath. Bo was in the fleet during Vietnam.

Herb lifted his chin. "What war teaches you is that you never want to see another one. I think the leaders that came out of World War One and World War Two did have a deep wisdom, a deep respect for human life. If lives must be lost, then the cause must be just and great. To squander an American life is a terrible calamity."

The group was silent for a minute. All agreed with the good reverend.

Harry finally spoke up. "It is strange, though, isn't it, that we can kill someone in a different uniform, but if we do that at home, it's murder."

"But maybe even murder is occasionally justified," Tracy said. He quickly held up his hands. "A wife kills a drunken husband who has their baby by the heels and is threatening to destroy the child. There are no easy answers, I'm afraid."

"And that's a gift." Alicia broadly smiled and brought them back to a lighter mood. "If it were easy, think how bored we'd be. Aren't all the great questions of life irrational, irrational to the human mind but perhaps not irrational to a mind greater than our own or to nature?"

"Like what?" Susan leaned toward Alicia.

"Love, the only fire against which there is no insurance. Intelligence is no guarantee that one will find the right love, shall we say? After all, consider Arthur Miller in love with Marilyn Monroe."

"Do I have to?" Harry popped off.

"Harry, God forbid you consider anything of the sort." Susan teased her.

"Let's pick someone closer to her generation." Miranda looked across the table at Tracy, thinking him the best-looking man for

his age she had ever seen, and he was looking at her thinking the same of her.

"You don't have to give me examples. I
know what you mean."

"Honey, I'll be your Arthur Miller anytime," Fair gallantly promised as the others
applauded him.

"Does that mean I have to wear low-cut
dresses, wiggle, and get a boob job?"

Maggie Sheraton's mouth dropped open
for a second.

"That's our Harry." Herb beamed at Maggie.

"Darling, you don't need breast augmentation." Alicia carefully chose her words.

"You say that to all the girls." Harry
couldn't resist.

"No, only the special ones." Alicia laughed
at herself, which only made her guests all
the more animated.

"Well, now, there's a subject for philoso-
phers." Fair nodded to his hostess. "Beauty
is in the eye of the beholder."

This set them off.

Maxwell, sitting patiently by his mother's
right hand, listened. Humans amused him,
and being a Gordon setter he was more
generous in his assessments than a Jack

Russell terrier might have been. Tucker, Mrs. Murphy, and Pewter hunkered under the table. Tucker hoped for fallen tidbits. Alicia allowed them to attend the party because she loved animals, they were well behaved, and Maxwell and Tucker were fast friends. Resting in the front hall was Brinkley, Tazio's yellow Lab. He liked people well enough but, even though Labs are not known for being guard dogs, he liked watching the door. Brinkley had been saved by Tazio last winter during a nasty storm. His entire life was devoted to Tazio.

"Love stuff." Pewter yawned.

"They'll rattle on all night." Tucker chuckled.

"I had a boyfriend once," Mrs. Murphy said.

"We all know your boyfriend. Worthless, that Paddy." Pewter couldn't abide the black and white cat, who now lived in Keswick, having been rescued by Meredith McLaughlin.

Not only was he rescued by one of Albemarle County's biggest softies, he was doted on by her neighbors, Claudia and Andy Lynn, who loved creatures as much as Meredith did. The result was that Paddy

was insufferable—plus he had a new girl-friend, named Twisted Sister.

"Worthless he may have been, but he was fun." That was all Mrs. Murphy had to say on the subject.

"While they're talking about love, you know Mom is figuring out when she's going back up to the monastery." Tucker thought the main course smelled mouth-watering.

Nordy Elliott was already there, lugging a heavy camera. He thought if he went alone and in the dark, he could shoot the footage he desperately wanted: a close-up of the Virgin Mary's face. And he was certain he could sneak in and not be detected. He was wrong.

18

Sweat poured down Nordy Elliott's face; a line of sweat rolled down the middle of his back. The heavy camera added to his distress. He'd been smart enough to park well away from the iron gates. Footing was treacherous. He'd pitched and fallen flat on his face but managed to keep the camera intact.

Breathing heavily, he approached the statue, which shone with a silver glow in the waxing moonlight. The skies, clear for a change, throbbed deep electric black, a black seen only in winter.

The crunch of his boots frightened Brother Mark at the statue. The men startled each other.

Nordy ordered, "Don't move."

"Don't give me orders," snapped Brother Mark, tucking his rosary in his robe's deep pocket. He stood up as Nordy walked to the front of the statue. He observed closely the look on the reporter's face when he beheld the tears of the Virgin. Rapture. This wasn't the rapture discussed in religious texts. This was the rapture of greed, greed for fame, for a bigger market, a national show. Without hesitation, Nordy swung the camera eyepiece to his own eye, his fingers numb with cold, sweat still running down his back. He held his breath so the camera wouldn't shake, the whirring sound of the motor being his reward. Nordy congratulated himself on shooting for two minutes, stopping, moving, then shooting from a different angle.

"All these shots are up toward her face. I need one where I'm level or shooting down." He spoke as if thinking out loud, not as though speaking directly to Brother Mark. He took a step back, slipped a little, and caught himself. He gingerly picked his way to a tree, put the camera on the ground, and, with difficulty, swung up.

"Her face is beautiful in this light."

Brother Mark slid his hands into the heavy sleeves of his gray woolen robe.

"Mmm, hand me the camera, will you?"

Brother Mark picked up the camera, hoisting it over his head while Nordy leaned down and grabbed it with one hand.

"Heavy."

"I don't know how Priscilla does it."

"Oh, you can get women to do anything. I envied you that when we were in college."

"You tell them they're beautiful, smart, and that you want them. Works ninety percent of the time. You were always to the left of Pluto, Mark. You were out there spinning in your solitary orbit. Still are." Nordy hiked the camera to his eye, getting good footage of the statue. "This is going to look great."

"People need to see the tears." A pious tone informed Brother Mark's voice while he ignored the insult. "They need to feel that the Blessed Virgin Mother is crying for them."

"Uh-huh." Nordy cut the motor. "Here." He handed down the camera, then slid down the tree trunk backward. "I don't believe man is descended from the apes."

Holding the camera, Brother Mark found this observation peculiar. "Of course we aren't descended from the apes. Man is created in God's image."

Nordy laughed. "We aren't descended from apes because we'd climb trees better."

"You know, Nerdy really is the right nickname for you." Brother Mark handed the camera back to Nordy. "You have no feeling for beauty, no faith."

"I do, just not in the same things that you do," the reporter honestly replied with humor in his voice. "If you kneel like when I first walked up here, it would make a great shot."

"No."

"Why not? No one will know it's you; pull the hood over your head."

"No."

"What if I shoot you from the back?"

"In the back is more like it, Nordy. You'll walk over anyone to get ahead. The answer is no. Besides if Brother Handle found out, he'd—" Brother Mark stopped, listened carefully. "You'd better get out of here. Someone's coming."

"Maybe I can get them to let me shoot them praying before Our Lady."

With urgency, Brother Mark said, "And have your camera smashed? Then you've got nothing. You've got your footage of her tears of blood. People will see the miracle. Now get out."

Nordy now heard the footsteps coming closer. He ducked down the back side of the statue, slipping down the slope into the woods, where the sliver of moonlight wouldn't reveal him. He'd worked too hard for this footage to have it destroyed.

Brother Andrew's voice called out, "Who's there?"

"Me. Brother Mark."

As Brother Andrew came into view, he walked faster. "Who were you talking to?"

"No one."

The lanky monk looked down at the footprints, slick in the packed-down snow. There were so many footprints. "Who would be up here at this hour?"

"No one."

"Why are you here?"

"To pray. Why are you here?"

"I don't know." Brother Andrew shivered as a fresh wind rustled the dry oak leaves and pine needles, which wouldn't drop until spring growth. "I needed to think."

"This is the best place to do that. I come here as much as I can."

"Are you sure you were alone? I would've sworn I heard voices. Sound carries on a clear, cold night like tonight."

"Yes," Brother Mark lied.

Brother Andrew stared at him, then quietly said, "I don't believe you. If you know what's good for you, you'll go back to your cell."

19

"Makes me sick." Harry turned up her nose.

"It's supposed to be progress." Susan slowed her station wagon as they passed the brand-new post office, under construction on the southwestern side of the railroad overpass.

"There wasn't one thing wrong with the old building. It's small, but Miranda and I made out okay."

"Miss it?"

"I do and I don't." Harry stared out the window as they drove north toward White Hall. "I miss seeing Miranda every day, and I really miss her orange-glazed cinnamon buns." Harry laughed. "I still see her, but it's not the same as working together. She spends more time with Tracy now." She paused a moment, turned toward Susan. "I expect she'll marry Tracy, don't you?"

"I expect." Susan laughed.

"Know what I miss about the post office?" Harry returned to Susan's original query. "Reading other people's postcards."

Susan smiled. "You were right to leave. It was time. You can do more and you will."

"Thanks for your vote of confidence." Harry meant it. "I alternate between not having a care in the world and dire panic."

"If you would remarry Fair, honey, much of your financial stress would lift."

"Is that why you married Ned?" Harry bit her lip.

"I married Ned because I was nineteen and pregnant with Danny, which you well know."

"Would you have married him anyway— later?"

"Yes." Susan nodded.

"This love stuff is too complicated." Harry sighed.

Susan braked as a squirrel foolishly dashed in front of the station wagon. "It can be."

"Do you love Ned?"

"Where did that come from? Oh, never mind." Susan took her right hand off the steering wheel and waved it dismissively for a second. "I do love him—more than I knew I did. I'm scared to death I'm going to lose him."

"Could you cheat?"

"Anyone could, given the right or wrong circumstances."

The temperature had soared to fifty-four degrees, and the melting snow and ice created flooded ditches, jammed culverts. In some places, creeks had jumped their beds. All one could hear was melting water, running water, water sloshing underfoot or overfoot. Susan slowed on some curves as water flowed over the black asphalt. The road to White Hall was twisty.

"A secret love?" Harry prodded. "Ever have a secret love? One you never told anyone—even me—about?"

"When I look back at how I felt when I was Brooks's age, you know, I can remember the events better than the emotions. When you're feeling powerful emotions for the first time, it's confusing and overpowering. My mind said one thing, my body another. That's not a secret love, but I suffered secret crushes.

"Let's get something to drink. I'm thirsty. I put too much salt on my eggs this morning. I'm on a sea-salt kick, but salt is salt and I've got to cut it from my diet." Susan wearied of reflecting on her past.

They crossed the road. There wasn't much traffic out in White Hall. One other car, a BMW X5, was parked at the white clapboard convenience store.

"Nordy Elliott's car cost a pretty penny. He must be making good money." Harry had a memory for horses and cars. "What's he doing in White Hall?"

The answer was quickly forthcoming when she slid out of the station wagon and glanced across the street. On the southwestern corner of this small crossroads reposed a large, pretty crèche. Nordy was there, microphone in hand, as Priscilla Friedberg held the camera on her shoulder.

"What would you like?" Susan knew Harry would have to go over and find out what he was doing.

"Uh, Co-Cola."

"Food?"

"Mmm, I'll wait until we get to town."

As Susan pushed open the door to the store, Harry walked across the paved two-lane road. She waited behind Priscilla until Nordy finished.

"—the joys of the season. Nordy Elliott. Channel Twenty-nine News." He waited a moment as Priscilla cut off the camera. "Harry, how are you?"

"What are you doing out here?"

"Every day until Christmas I shoot a crèche or Christmas decorations."

"We cover a lot of territory." Priscilla patted the compact professional Panasonic, the latest in equipment. The flat image of video didn't bother her, because she was shooting reportage. Had she been shooting a television film it would have driven her crazy.

"Bet you do. The Virgin Mary story is good for you, Nordy. Everyone's talking about it."

He smiled broadly as he walked with Priscilla back to his car. "National feeds. It's a hell of a good story. Guess I shouldn't say hell."

"The Blessed Virgin Mother isn't revengeful," Harry replied. "However, Brother Handle might be."

"He's not too happy with me," Nordy acknowledged.

Susan emerged from the store with her hands full. Harry started up the wet steps to help Susan before she came down.

"Hi, Nordy. Hi, Priscilla," Susan called as they said their hellos.

Nordy bounded up the steps, passing Harry, stopping before the top one. He held out his hand for Susan to take it.

"It's nice to see you," he said.

"You're doing a great job with the Virgin Mary story." Susan appreciated his chivalry.

Harry, meanwhile, enjoyed her Coke. In her left hand she held the bag containing Susan's sandwich. Nordy carried the cup of coffee Susan had bought.

As they leaned against the car, Nordy asked the two friends, "Is BoomBoom dating anyone?"

Priscilla laughed. "Come on, Nordy. She'll never look at you in a million years."

He ignored his sidekick. "I asked her out and she said she's 'keeping clear of entanglements for a year,' but that doesn't mean she isn't dating."

"She's not." Susan thought the coffee tasted pretty good.

"What's her favorite flower?" he asked.

"Pink roses," Harry answered. "She also likes those big white lilies with the pink throats."

"Thanks." He smiled.

"She really is taking a year off. I know you're keeping count," Susan added.

"After months of no-go, you might look good," Priscilla teased Nordy.

"I always look good." He smiled, flashing strong, straight teeth.

As Nordy and Priscilla drove off to their next location in downtown Charlottesville, Susan and Harry lifted their faces to the warming sun.

"God, that feels good." Harry's cheeks flushed.

"Whenever winter wears me down, I look at the calendar and tell myself, no matter what, the first snowdrops will be up by mid-March and the crocuses soon follow, even if they have to peep up through the snow."

"Yeah. Winter is beautiful." Harry appreciated all those hidden things now visible with the leaves off the trees. "But nothing beats spring here in the foothills."

"Fall."

"Mmm, toss-up." She finished her can of

Coke. "Looks like BoomBoom has another conquest."

"If she had a dollar for every man who tripped over his own feet in her presence, she'd be almost as rich as Big Mim." Susan wondered what it must feel like to have that kind of power.

"They fall in love with her but she doesn't fall in love with them." Harry crossed her arms over her chest.

"She's falling in love now."

"BoomBoom?"

Susan nodded her head in affirmation. "And you know, I think it's for real."

"How could she sneak out on us like that?"

"She hasn't. She's falling right in front of us."

"She is?"

"Alicia," Susan flatly stated.

"Alicia? Oh, never. BoomBoom isn't gay."

"I didn't say she was gay." Susan crumpled the paper bag her sandwich had been in, aimed for the big open garbage can, and sank her shot. "I said she was falling in love."

"In an ideal world you fall in love with the

person, not the wrapping paper. Still. It's hard for me to believe." Harry frowned.

"Why? Makes you nervous?"

"No. Yes. Not because she's in love with a woman, but because I never saw it coming. Because I thought I knew BoomBoom. This changes things. I hate not knowing."

"Harry, she probably didn't know she could feel this way. And it doesn't change anything. She's the person we've always known. BoomBoom's a strong woman. She's endured social censure for her many affairs, for flaunting her beauty. She took it with good grace."

"You're right. I never thought of that."

"Once she figures out that she really is in love with Alicia, she'll be just fine."

"What about Alicia?"

"Alicia? She's crazy about BoomBoom."

"She is?"

"Harry." Susan threw up her hands in despair. "Come on, I'll take you to the John Deere dealer; you'll be in your element."

Harry brightened. "Have you seen the new compact tractors? Susan, they are something else." She stopped. "Oh, you're not going there, are you? You're pulling my leg."

Susan hugged Harry. "Sure. Come on, Skeezits."

Back in the car, heading east toward town, Harry asked, "Is there anything Brother Thomas ever said to you that stuck in your mind?"

"He was such a sweet man. He used to tell me to trust God. And, um . . . well, I do remember once when I was in high school I was upset about something—I don't even remember what it was—and he told me to thank God for my troubles. They're gifts in disguise."

"Do you?"

"No. I haven't learned that lesson." Susan powered up the steep hill near what used to be a farm called Rustling Oaks, owned by a fabulous horseman, Billy Jones. It was a subdivision now. Susan hoped Billy haunted the big, flashy homes.

"Me, neither."

"You're usually the one with the hunches about everything but romance," Susan smiled at her friend, "but this time I have a hunch that there are troubles up ahead. I hope I have the guts to get through them."

"You will." Harry's voice resonated with

conviction. "I have a hunch, too. Brother Thomas did not die a natural death."

"Harry, don't let your imagination run away with you." Susan didn't want to think her great-uncle had been murdered.

"Why go out in that hellish cold? At his age? Remember Dante's *Inferno*? The lowest circle of hell is ice. Why would he go out?"

"He wanted to pray before the tears of blood."

Harry put her hands together, resting her chin on her forefingers. "I don't believe it."

"You know how you get. You eat up any conspiracy theory that you hear or read. Why, the last book you read was about the British poisoning Napoleon by degrees when he was exiled on St. Helena." She sighed, then continued. "G-Uncle Thomas was sweet and gentle. No one would kill him."

"Sweet and kind people are blasted every day all over the world." Harry marveled at the human capacity for evil.

"Why G-Uncle?"

"I don't know. But you feel that Boom-Boom is falling for Alicia. I trust you about those things. You have amazing radar for human relationships. My radar is different. I pick up blips about these kinds of things, about secrets."

"Not my secrets." Susan said this with humor as they passed the left turn to Barracks Stud and the Barracks, two equine facilities.

"Yours aren't big enough." Harry lifted her eyebrow.

"That's what you think," Susan's voice slightly darkened.

"Then you're really, really good."

A long pause followed, traffic increasing. "Why would anyone kill Thomas? Really, Harry, it's incomprehensible."

"People are often killed just because they're inconvenient."

20

Large, round balls studded with pyracantha berries filled an enormous silver bowl that Mary Pat Reines had won at the Pennsylvania National Horse Show in 1962. Ropes of fresh garland hung over every mantelpiece, doorway, and even the front hall mirror. Alicia and BoomBoom were artfully placing oranges, apples, walnuts, and sprays of wheat throughout the garlands. Before the heavy evergreens were embedded with treasures, a thin red ribbon was entwined with a three-inch-wide gold mesh ribbon, and both were then woven through the garlands. The mesh ribbon's sides bolstered with thin wire proved easy to maneuver. The stunning finished effect lightened Alicia's spirits.

The shimmering melancholy veil lifted from Alicia's shoulders as she and Boom-Boom worked this Sunday. She kept up a good front during Christmas, but the holidays made her dwell on those she loved who were no longer living. Bach's *Magnificat* played throughout the house.

"Every culture fights the dark," Alicia noted, selecting a robust red apple and placing it next to a pale green one. "Hmm, think I'll get one equal in size to the green. What do you think?"

"Your eye is better than mine, but balance is everything." BoomBoom's gold fox mask earrings with ruby eyes caught the firelight.

"Takes so long to find it. Balance." Alicia stepped back. "Better. Another half hour and we'll be about as festive as possible— well, except for the tree, and that monster won't get here until Thursday or Friday, a Douglas fir on steroids."

"Did you decorate in California?"

"Mm-hmm. One year I thought I'd use plants native to the great state of California. I used eucalyptus for wreaths. One eucalyptus wreath would have done the trick, but no, I filled the house with them. The place smelled like a spa. When one was greeted at the door, I'm sure they expected me to come out in a bathrobe. Sherry thought it was hysterical, but he had a pungent sense of humor." She smiled slightly.

"The studio head?"

"Driven man. Brilliant, really."

"Ever speak to him?"

"Once or twice a week. We couldn't live together, but once we gave that up, this amazing, supportive friendship flourished in marriage's place. I am a very lucky woman."

"It's not luck. You're good to people and they're good back."

"Thank you. I try, but once sex is in the mix, one becomes irrational. You know, I think men are more irrational about it than women. Women talk about it and are afforded the luxury of acting irrational, but men really are irrational."

"That's been my experience, except for Fair Haristeen."

Alicia sipped hot cider, put the white gold-edged porcelain cup down, and began tying the large gold mesh and thin red ribbon bow that would be the final touch. "Well?"

BoomBoom wedged in the last of the

walnuts, the rough, roundish shell rubbing against her fingertips. She thought whole walnuts brought luck so she had one in the glove compartment of her car, her truck, and her purse. "Alicia, you're supposed to beg for details, not just a 'Well.' " She imitated Alicia's voice.

"Details at eleven." Alicia glanced at her watch. "Do you know, it's ten-thirty. I can't believe it. It feels like we've only been doing this for an hour."

"Time flies when you're having fun."

"It does and I do. With you. You're marvelous company." Alicia smiled. "All right. Details. Really. How was or is Fair not irrational?"

"Scientific mind, I guess. Think of it: a human doctor needs to learn one circulatory system, one set of bones, etc., but the veterinarian has to learn different species. I think vets need to be smarter."

"Debatable but good point. All right, he's logical. Right?"

"Logical. Considerate. Not especially passionate but not a dullard. We enjoyed each other, but I never felt he was mine. You know how men get when they're crazy about you, they can't take their eyes off you, they touch you constantly even in public, they want to sit close and they become territorial. Jealous. All of that."

"Perhaps he was still in love with Harry but didn't know it. A man under other circumstances would kill to be with you."

BoomBoom beamed. "You think so?"

"Oh, now, you know that. We both do. We have the looks they want, and men fall in love with what they see. It takes them longer to find out who you are, and some don't want to know. Then again, I can accuse some women of not wanting to know the man in their life but they'll take his paycheck in a skinny minute."

BoomBoom laughed. "Haven't heard 'skinny minute' in a long time. I've heard 'New York minute,' though."

"Well, were you angry with Fair?"

"No. He's handsome, strong, and very masculine. I suppose when you deal with life and death, you're covered with blood, you're pulling a foal out of a mare, probably you see life differently than someone who sits in front of a computer in a squeaky clean white office."

"Yes. If anything will cut the balls off men,

excuse my bluntness, it will be the computer."

"I wonder about that myself."

"Men—women, too—aren't meant to sit still for hours on end. Oh, companies and commerce dress it up by using words like 'burn,' 'download,' 'firewall,' making anything to do with computers sound butch, but there's nothing masculine about clicking away at keys all day, staring into a blue screen. The body turns to mush and the mind alters, as well. You aren't fighting, you aren't cutting trees, plowing fields, hoisting up a steel girder. You're sitting, sitting, sitting. I suppose sneaking onto a porno site offers scant relief, but that's not real, either. Images. We're a nation duped by images, and I know that better than anyone. I used to be a twenty-foot image on a movie screen in films shot on seventy millimeter. You know, BoomBoom, it frightens me; what we are becoming frightens me because we run counter to nature, and creatures that violate nature die or cause catastrophe and everyone dies."

BoomBoom picked up her cup of cider and sat on the sofa facing the fire. Alicia had affixed the bow, and she sat down, too, beside BoomBoom. "Funny that we're having this discussion, because I think of it, too. I can do a lot of business on the computer. I can contact accounts, keep accounts, keep up with inventory, but my business sells a real product. I have to go to the quarry, and I'm searching for new quarries or relationships with other companies that have a product I don't, like marble. What I do is still real."

"You like business."

"I do. I'll give Fair that, he encouraged me. Most of the other men in my life, like my husband, either disregarded that part of me, patronized me, or, worse, tried to come into the business. Sort of the way nonacting husbands begin managing their wives' careers, I guess."

"Seen a lot of that. Fortunately, neither of my husbands was inclined that way. One ran a studio and the other one refitted 747s and other big flying cows for rich Saudis and rock stars."

"Did you think of Mary Pat as a husband?"

This question took Alicia off guard; she thought a moment, then burst out laughing. "No. God, she'd laugh to hear that. No, I thought of her as an angel. Even when I just had to have my career, I loved her but she knew better than to move kit and caboodle to Los Angeles. It would have killed her. She belonged in the country and, sad to say, that killed her, too, but Boom, when your time is up it's up, even if the agent of your death is another human being."

"Yes, I believe that."

The phone rang and Alicia reached for it. "Hello."

"Alicia, hello, this is Nordy Elliott. I called to tell you to watch the eleven o'clock news. Pete used the story about you and Boom-Boom at the SPCA. I didn't think he'd use it until tomorrow. I tried BoomBoom but she's not home. I made copies of the story if you'd like, a DVD."

"I'd love one, and I'll be sure to watch. Thank you for calling me."

"I know it's late, but like I said, Pete decided to use it tonight. You wouldn't know where BoomBoom might be, would you? I'd like her to see it if she's near a set."

"Hold on." Alicia handed the phone to BoomBoom as she mouthed the name, "Nordy."

BoomBoom listened as Nordy effused

over how the camera liked her; he didn't say he liked her, rather, the camera liked her. She had trouble getting him off the phone. "Yes, I'll be at Jill and Paul Summers's Christmas party. It's always the high point of the season." She listened. "I'll see you there if not before. Thank you for tracking me down." Once she was able to disengage him, she rolled her eyes, dropping her head back on the sofa. "He's such a wimp."

"Handsome."

"Still a wimp. If you want to ask a woman out, then do it."

"Men face a lot more rejection than we do. Each one handles it a bit differently. Don't be too hard on the fellow."

"You're right." BoomBoom handed her the phone. "We'd better watch our debut as the team of Palmer and Craycroft."

They walked into the den, and Alicia picked up the remote, clicking on the huge, flat-screen TV. After teasers and ten minutes of so-called hard news, they were rewarded with the footage of the two of them at the SPCA delivering a truckload of cat and dog food. Alicia was in the bed, handing down sacks of kibble and cat crunchies to BoomBoom. A stream of smiling workers lined up behind BoomBoom to carry sacks.

Nordy cut away to dogs and cats inside the pound, a clean and spacious one. There were also hamsters, one cockatoo, and an aging black goat. Then he cut back to the women, the truck now half full as workers continued to carry sacks of feed. He did a great job, even making a pitch for adoption and singling out some special animals.

BoomBoom started to cry. "I can't stand it."

"Sugar, what's wrong?" Alicia looked around for a hanky or tissue. She stood up. "Let me get you a—"

"I don't care if I have a runny nose and eyes if you don't. I can't stand seeing those animals. I don't know how anyone could abandon an animal."

"They abandon children. There are thousands of irresponsible shits out there. Excuse my foul language. Personally I'd like to bring back the stocks, put them in the town squares, and lock the creeps in. Then I'd show up with a big basket of rotten eggs and tomatoes."

"You're better than I am. I just want to shoot them."

Alicia dashed into the kitchen, returning with a box of Kleenex. "Here. Speaking of shooting, skeet?" She sat back down. "Sometime this week?"

BoomBoom nodded. "Where?"

"There's that wonderful club west of Staunton, or if Patricia's in the mood, we could go up to Albemarle House." She mentioned Patricia Kluge, who along with her husband, Bill Moses, was a good shot.

"If she's in town let's go there, then we can pick up stuff for Harry. Patricia is helping with Harry's wine research. Just look what she's done with Kluge Vineyards."

"Good idea. You know, it speaks well of you that you are friends with Harry. You genuinely like her."

"I always liked Harry, although she didn't like me, even in high school. Then I slept with Fair, and she *loathed* me. They were separated, but I was the focus for her discontent, not that she blabbed about it. Harry really does have class. You know, we didn't become friends until we were trapped together at University Hall."

"Yes. I heard that was quite an adventure." Alicia remained standing. "More cider? Port? Libations?"

"No."

The television again caught their attention. The footage was Nordy back at the monastery, the gates opened. He noted that it was Sunday. The camera panned the cars and trucks parked as far as the eye could see, many teetering on the edge of the road. It wasn't a wide road. He informed the viewers that numbers had steadily increased and that the statue still cried blood. Cut to the statue, tears actually running now that the mercury had climbed. While it was fifty-two degrees in The Valley, it was forty-five at the statue, still warm enough to melt snow and ice, warm enough to thaw Mary's tears. The cardinal flew onto her outstretched hand, tilted his head, unfurled his crest, whistled out his distinctive four long notes followed by many short ones, trebled. Then he flew away. Nordy interviewed people who weren't at the statue, since he had sense enough to keep it reverent. He nabbed them at the shops. The monastery did a big business between Thanksgiving and Christmas. The interviews were touching. Some came to expiate their sins, others came to be healed, many prayed for peace or for someone in need. All interviewed radiated a hope, a peacefulness.

After that segment passed, Alicia turned to BoomBoom. "Nordy's going to get a big career boost out of this. He's improving by leaps and bounds."

"Did it bother you that he didn't refer to you as a movie star?"

"God, no. I'm relieved. That's the past. This is now."

"What are you now?"

"A farmer." She stared at BoomBoom's face. "How about some Badger lip balm? You can rub it on your nose."

"I'm not going to get chapped from a few tears and a runny nose, but thank you."

"I can't live without the stuff." Alicia put a round tin about two inches from a Tiffany's silver box on the coffee table. "Here."

"Thanks." BoomBoom smeared the pleasant concoction of virgin olive oil, castor oil, beeswax, aloe vera, and other emollients on her nose, then also put a sheer film on her lips. "Smells wonderful."

"Comes in Cinnamon Bay, Tangerine Breeze, Highland Mint, Ginger-Lemon. There are other variations. I have a big tin of hand salve, too."

A long pause followed this. BoomBoom knew it was eleven-thirty, late for both of them. "Roads will be icy."

Alicia rose to check the thermometer in the window. "Still forty-two degrees Fahrenheit. You're in luck, although there might be a few places where the road is packed down. It's the black ice that gets you."

BoomBoom blushed. "I'd be in luck if the roads were icy."

Alicia laughed. "You say."

"I don't get it. If you were a man you'd have lunged for me months ago. Maybe I do get it. I'm not your type."

"BoomBoom." Alicia's voice sounded like dark honey. "You are very flattering. You're full of energy and ideas. You're a beautiful woman. I'm not immune to you."

"You're not?" BoomBoom brightened.

Alicia laughed. "Of course not, but you've taken a year off men. And furthermore, you haven't walked down this road before. It's not about gender, it's about learning another person. That takes time. And you're barreling down on your midlife crisis, if you'll indulge me in being older and a tiny bit wiser at this exact moment."

"You aren't part of my midlife crisis. I've

got three years left." She smiled. "But I see it in Harry and Susan and even Little Mim. Forty lurks just over the horizon, so they must see it in me. That shift. That discarding what doesn't work, finding what really matters in life."

"It's only a number, but our culture makes such a to-do about it. I'm not that far from sixty, and you know what, I don't give a fig." She snapped her fingers.

"Does this mean you aren't going to jump my bones? I mean, what do women do? Who makes the first move? You're driving me crazy. I don't know what to do. Am I supposed to hit you with a flying tackle?"

"Bruising." Alicia felt every molecule of air in her lungs, going in, going out.

"Well, what am I supposed to do? I know what to do with men. I haven't a clue what to do with you, but I know that I have felt happier with you, even without sex or declarations of, what, *amor,* than I have ever felt in my life. I feel"—she searched for the word—"connected. Like I know you. Like I've always known you. I just don't know about the romance part of it, and I don't know how you feel. I don't want to wear out my welcome."

"You couldn't wear out your welcome. I never thought I'd feel this way again," Alicia honestly replied. "And I suppose deep down I didn't think I should make a move. I was afraid I might spoil our friendship."

"You mean you didn't know how I felt?"

"I hoped, but I wasn't going to push it."

BoomBoom got up, walking over to the window where Alicia remained. "Alicia, for the first time in my life I can't hide."

Alicia reached for BoomBoom's hand, and the younger woman felt a bolt of lightning blast up her arm.

She wasn't the only person who couldn't hide that night, but for the other one, the circumstances couldn't have been more alarming.

21

Black asphalt glistened as the snow run-off covered the road with a sheen of water. Nordy Elliott, hopes raised by his conversation with BoomBoom, drove too fast past the supermarket and Patterson's Florist. His spirits remained high even though he suffered bouts of irritation at driving into Crozet this late. No sooner had he clicked off with BoomBoom than his cell rang. The voice on the other end demanded that Nordy meet him at the Crozet Post Office.

Irritated though he was, the bright lights of the Amoco station amused him. Clean and well located, the modern station seemed out of place.

Turning left, he dipped beneath the railroad underpass, the senior home immediately to his right on the south side of the tracks. To his left, a series of small shops were strung out, including two restaurants. Ombra, with its booths, was Nordy's favorite. Right now Nordy wasn't hungry. He wanted to get this impromptu meeting over with and hurry back home to write copy for J&J Tire Service.

Being a reporter, he had grown accustomed to strange demands, personal meetings, behavior calculated for airtime. By now most Americans had learned that the more outrageous you looked and talked, the better your chances of getting your face, product, or cause covered. Anyone who appeared sober, reliable, and thoughtful was at an immediate disadvantage. Nordy had learned to puff them up, egg them on, thereby getting even better stories.

Within a hundred yards the new post office construction, set back, was visible. On Nordy's left, a temporary post office had been set up in a brick building, and that's where his contact had asked to meet him. Post offices are unlocked, with the back part shut up but postboxes available to their patrons. Occasionally, Sheriff Shaw of Albemarle County or his deputy, Cynthia

Cooper, responded to a call about a drunk sleeping in the P.O. when the weather was bitter. Apart from that, anyone going into and out of the building, even in the wee hours, would attract scant attention.

Nordy pulled to the back and parked. His mind returned to BoomBoom. Every single woman in his viewing area thought he was hot. A young, single man, he took advantage of that, but the one he really wanted was the tall, cool blonde. There was something about her, not just her obvious physical attributes, that pulled him toward her. He knew her reputation as a heartbreaker. He could turn the tables. After all, he was handsome, slick as an eel, and on the way up.

He walked around to the front of the post office, opened the door. As the door was closing, his attacker leapt at him so quickly Nordy didn't have time to step back. He threw up his left hand, too late. He dropped like a stone from a ballpoint pen driven up through his left eyeball clean into his brain. Not a drop of blood fell on the floor.

The killer calmly took a chamois cloth to wipe the footprints where he had stood, flattened against the wall. Then he wiped up prints as he backed out the front door.

When Amy Wade entered the back door at seven A.M., she hung up her coat, then unlocked the thin corrugated metal pull-down, which came down to the countertop like a garage door, and pushed it up over her head. It took a moment for her to realize a dead man lay on the floor. She flipped up the divider, hurried over, and beheld the grisly sight. She sucked in her breath, holding it, and raced for the telephone.

Cynthia Cooper happened to be cruising through town, and when she arrived minutes later, she noted the position of the body and saw that the small muscles had gone into rigor. She'd never seen anyone killed with a ballpoint pen. She wasn't an unfeeling woman but one who, like every other law-enforcement officer who has to witness brutal things, had developed a balancing sense of humor. When her boss, Sheriff Rick Shaw, pushed open the door, she gave him a moment to assess the situation, then said, "The pen is mightier than the sword."

22

The orange cordon around the area where Nordy's body had been discovered stopped everyone walking into the post office. Human nature being what it is, plenty of people who didn't rent a postbox in Crozet filed through the door.

Harry and Miranda feverishly worked to sort the mail, deal with people who truly did wish to buy stamps, fend off inquiries, and smile at their friends.

Amy Wade, undone by the horrible sight, had asked to go home for the day. The postmaster called Harry and she immediately filled in, as did Mrs. Murphy, Pewter, and Tucker. Miranda, always a port in a storm, hurried from her home across the alleyway to help.

The two friends worked like a well-oiled machine.

Big Mim strode in, removed her Robin Hood hat with the pheasant feather with one hand as she supported her ancient aunt Tally with her other. Aunt Tally used an ebony cane, elegant with a silver hound's head for the handle, but Big Mim liked to keep close when sidewalks were slick or steps wet.

"Incomprehensible!" the queen of Crozet pronounced judgment.

"Mimsy, it's perfectly comprehensible." Aunt Tally gently shook off her niece's hand to study the outline of the body chalked on the worn wooden floor. "He was uncommonly handsome, a little cock of the walk."

"Roosters are stupid." Pewter lounged on the counter, the better to see everyone.

Mrs. Murphy, next to her, agreed.

Tucker, sitting patiently by the table in the back, called out, *"Yeah, but they're fun to chase."*

" *'Til they hit you up with those spurs."* As a kitten, Mrs. Murphy learned the hard way that even the lowly rooster had survival tools.

"What has that got to do with a gruesome

end?" Big Mim didn't at first follow her aunt's line of thought.

Harry, slipping mail into the boxes, listened, as did Miranda, who sorted through the mail that arrived in canvas bags and was then dumped into a rolling cart.

"Couldn't keep it in his pants."

"Oh, Aunt Tally!"

"Sex. He jumped the paddock and mounted the wrong mare. Bet you even money." The old lady, still quite attractive although thin as a blade, tapped her cane on the floor.

"Doesn't murder usually come down to sex, money, or power?" Harry peeked out from around the back of the brass mailboxes.

"That's what they say." Miranda paused for a moment. "But such an end. So violent."

"And clever." Mrs. Murphy spread open her toes, unleashed her claws, then retracted them.

"What's so clever about jamming a ballpoint pen in someone's eye?" Pewter wondered.

"Simple. Nothing to trace. The pen was left in the eye, and I guarantee you—in fact,

I'll give you my catnip if I'm wrong—there won't be one print on that ballpoint pen, no fibers or anything, either."

Tucker, interested now, padded over to sit beneath the kitties. *"And cheap. Everyone in the universe has ballpoint pens."*

The very tip of Pewter's fat, thick tail moved to and fro as she thought about this angle. *"Because the weapon was a pen, does that mean the killer was opportunistic or thought it out? I mean, anyone could grab a ballpoint pen, right?"*

"Thought out. Well executed." Mrs. Murphy watched the nonagenarian. Aunt Tally reminded her of a twenty-four-year-old cat that she had known years ago. The fire of life burned brightly, more brightly with age. The gift of any animal that old is they know a lot and they no longer care much what other cats or people think.

"Has anyone spoken to Rick?" Big Mim asked Harry and Miranda, who both knew that Big Mim had nabbed him the instant she heard of the death.

"No. What did he say?" Miranda, being Big Mim's contemporary, could let her know they were on to her question.

"Well"—the elegant lady made no attempt to explain her asking them first—"he said there was no blood. Of course, when they remove the pen there will be blood, I guess." Big Mim stopped herself, because the image was too gross. "Sorry. Anyway, he said they will go over Nordy's clothing and an autopsy will be performed, naturally. But he warned me that there wasn't one footprint by the body and the runoff of the melting snows took care of any hopes for one outside the building."

"This killer is too smart to leave a foot-print," Mrs. Murphy offered her opinion.

Aunt Tally walked over to pet the cats, while Big Mim retrieved the mail, then joined her aunt at the counter.

The door opened. BoomBoom and Alicia came in.

"We just left Amy," BoomBoom said.

"How is she?" Harry liked Amy Wade, as did everyone in town.

"Shaken." BoomBoom's face reflected concern.

"But not stirred," Alicia said, then added, "She'll be back to work tomorrow."

"She sends her thanks." BoomBoom studied the chalk outline. "Dropped like a deer."

"Between the eyes or, in this case, in the eye." Aunt Tally ran her forefinger under Pewter's chin, then repeated the pleasing stroke for Mrs. Murphy. "These cats have big motors."

"Purr machines." Harry loved her cats. She flipped up the divider as well as opened the half door so Tucker could visit the people.

Big Mim told BoomBoom and Alicia what Sheriff Shaw had told her.

Alicia remarked, "Whoever committed the murder has to be quick as a cat."

"Why do you say that, darlin'?" Boom-Boom casually called her "darlin'," but then, Southern women rained "sugar," "honey," "honey pie," and other sweet names upon their friends.

"Didn't Rick say there was no struggle? That Nordy's body crumpled?"

"Yes," Big Mim replied.

"Then the killer literally struck like a cat and Nordy had no time to react," Alicia said.

"If it was someone he knew, he might not have reacted quickly." A vague notion was forming in Harry's mind, something disquieting, still unfocused.

"True." BoomBoom nodded. "But even if

he knew his killer, that person hit fast and hard. It takes a lot of force to drive an object into the human body."

"He didn't hit the socket, either. If he'd hit the bone it would have been a real mess." Aunt Tally allowed the cats to rub against her offered cheek. "Think about it. This killer knew what he or she was doing."

"What an awful thought." Miranda shuddered.

"You know, I spoke to him last night." BoomBoom stepped back from the cordoned area. "Like most men, he was tragically transparent."

Alicia smiled. "That he was not, Boom. He may have been transparent sexually, but he could be opaque about other things or he wouldn't be dead. The man was hiding something."

"Hard to believe." Harry folded her hands on the counter, then remembered she had a lot more mail to put in the boxes. The disruption had put them hours behind. "He was arrogant. I didn't like him, but I'm sorry he died like this."

"It is pretty awful." BoomBoom walked behind the counter. "Do you two need help? I'm happy to stay here."

Miranda smiled warmly. "Boom, if you really want to help, we will use you." She pointed to the overflowing mail cart. "Magazines."

"Boom, you are sweet." Alicia walked behind the counter, too. "Many hands make light work."

Aunt Tally glared at her niece for a moment, since this wasn't the type of labor Big Mim was likely to do. "Mimsy, I think we should at least help for half an hour."

"Quite right." Big Mim sighed, removed her lush silver fox short-cropped jacket, walked behind the counter, and draped the jacket over the chair in the back.

The six women worked well together, chatting, going over the dreadful event and then drifting away to other subjects like the college basketball season about to begin. They all followed the University of Virginia men's and women's teams.

Susan blew through the door, stopped cold when she beheld the outline, then walked to the counter and, without a word, flipped up the divider, took off her coat, and attacked the large packages that had to be on industrial shelving. The shelves bore letters of the alphabet. If a person's last name began with "A," their large package would go on the "A" section.

"Sorry I'm late. Brooks's car died, so I had to run her to school. Took the opportunity to talk to her physics teacher." She picked up a package to go to the "T" section. "Nordy's death wasn't on the early-morning edition but it ran as a ticker tape, or whatever you call that underneath the picture, by nine. Good God."

"It will all come out in the wash." Aunt Tally sat at the kitchen table in the back where she sorted mail. "Why don't I toss this junk mail and save someone the trouble?"

"It has occurred to us many times." Miranda rolled the cart over to Harry.

"Thanks," Harry said as she continued to shoot mail into the back of the boxes. She checked the clock on the wall. "We're catching up."

The front door opened. A well-dressed woman who had parked her Mercedes SUV in the front came to the counter. Miranda reached the counter just as the woman placed a small, neatly wrapped package on the counter.

"Would you weigh this please?"

"Certainly." Miranda lifted it, placing it on the stainless-steel scale. "First class?"

"Yes." She glanced around. "What's going on here?"

Since Miranda didn't recognize the woman, she figured she either didn't live here, was visiting for the holidays, or had moved in that second. "We've suffered an unfortunate incident."

"What kind of incident?" She removed one of her gloves to reach into her Bottega Veneta purse for cash.

"The local news reporter, Nordy Elliott, was found dead here this morning."

"What?" Her eyes widened.

"That's all we know."

"Nordy Elliott, that terribly attractive young man who does the news?" She paused a moment. "I'm here visiting my son and daughter-in-law, so I watch the local news. Oh, that can't be."

"I'm afraid it is."

"What's this world coming to?" She fished out the amount, which Miranda told her was $3.20. "Before Christmas."

"Do you want this insured?"

"No." The woman noticed the gang in the

back. Her eyes narrowed as she recognized Alicia Palmer, then they widened with pleasure. She leaned forward, whispering, "Is that Alicia Palmer?" Miranda nodded, and the woman continued, "Never forget her in *War Clouds.*" She snapped up her change.

"No. Might I ask who is your son?"

She smiled. "Dr. Trey Seddons. He's just taken a position in the radiology department at Martha Jefferson, so I've come up to help him and Beth get settled."

As she left, Big Mim muttered, "Carpetbaggers."

"Now, now," Aunt Tally reprimanded her. "Can't be critical because she doesn't speak the King's English with the same perfection and lilt as do we all here. And carpetbaggers bring in money. Always have and always will."

"I don't mind the money, Aunt Tally, what I mind is they come here and want us to be like them. When in Rome, do as the Romans do."

"What's so great about the Romans?" Pewter wondered.

"Empire lasted a thousand years." Mrs. Murphy loved history.

"Because of the work of dogs, horses, cattle, and you cats. How could they have lived off the grains of Egypt if cats hadn't killed the mice? And how could they have had herds of cattle and sheep if we dogs didn't herd them as well as drive off marauders? And do animals get any credit?" Tucker shook her head.

"I don't want credit. I want tuna." Pewter let out a meow.

Harry knew that tone of voice. She handed her fistful of mail to BoomBoom, standing next to her with her own fistful of mail. "All right."

As Harry opened a can for the cats and a small one of beef for Tucker, Alicia and BoomBoom hummed and chatted. Susan talked to Big Mim, Tally, and Miranda as she shuttled packages to the shelves. Harry stopped for a moment and thought what wonderful friends she had, and then she noticed how Alicia and BoomBoom leaned toward each other; they glowed. Susan was right. She blinked, then thought to herself, "Lucky them."

"These tubes roll off the shelf." Susan stood on a small ladder in the "C" section, where Tazio Chappars's blueprints were placed.

"I know. There's a rubber wedge there, an old doorstop. I put one on each side," Harry informed her.

"I would have thought all this was done by computers. Someone would send the blueprints to Tazio's computer, she would print it and blow it up." BoomBoom liked technology.

"Can," Harry replied. "But Tazio says for the clearest blueprints, you have to get them done the old way. Also, this paper, the stuff in the tube here, stands a beating at construction sites. She says printers, laser printers, can't print out on blueprint paper. Anyway, I don't mind dealing with these. Kind of excites me, thinking of buildings going up."

"You have the building gene," Big Mim quipped.

"Your grandfather had it, too." Aunt Tally, long, long ago, had been passionately in love with Harry's handsome grandfather. She was in her late teens and he was married. People didn't divorce in those days.

"Wish I had the money to indulge it." Harry laughed. "But you know, being back here in the post office today is good for me. I know I've done the right thing. It really was time to move on, and I have got to make money."

"You will." Aunt Tally encouraged her. "Set yourself a goal, stick to it. You're smart as a whip."

"Thank you."

"See, she'll listen to you, Aunt Tally. She doesn't listen to me. I tell her how smart she is." Susan placed the rubber wedges on either side of the tubes.

"Ned have his team together?" Aunt Tally inquired.

"He does. Another three weeks and he's sworn in as our state senator and I will be truly married to an elected politician. I can't tell you how many people he interviewed for the jobs. He needs to have the right people, people who know the drill in Richmond. People who can get along. That's the problem, you know, in any office or wherever: can the people who work together get along? I worry about what this will cost us, too. He has an apartment in Richmond; the miles will pile up on the car when he switches back and forth from here to there. I didn't want him to spend money on an apartment, but he reminded me what happened when both houses fought over the state budget: long, long sessions. He really needs a little place there. And like I said, he really needs a team that can get along."

"We always did." Miranda patted Harry's shoulder as she squeezed behind her and BoomBoom.

"Easier when there's two," Big Mim said, then amended the thought. "If it's the right two."

Big Mim and Aunt Tally worked for an hour. Harry and Miranda were grateful to them, because they knew how out of the ordinary this gesture was and the two women really did help.

No sooner had the two climbed into Big Mim's go-through-anything Range Rover, saved for bad weather, than Alicia pulled out her cell phone to call Patterson's Florist.

"More amaryllis?" BoomBoom raised her eyebrows, then turned to Harry. "She's filled one room with red and white amaryllis, arranging them like a tree on this platform she's had built. I'm not explaining this very well. Anyway, she's placed all the pots, wrapped in foil, on the circular levels, and

I've never seen anything quite like it. She's so visually creative."

"You are, too," Harry complimented her.

"Not like Alicia, but thank you."

They overheard Alicia. "Yes, one to Aunt Tally and one to Big Mim. Today, if possible." She paused, smiling at BoomBoom and Harry, then her attention returned to her order. "Yes. Say, 'With thanks from the girls at the P.O.' Uh-huh. Put it on my account. Thank you so much." She hung up.

Miranda said, "We'll divvy that up."

"No, you won't." Alicia waved her hand.

"You think of everything." BoomBoom finished her row of boxes.

"You're prejudiced." Alicia returned to the mail cart.

A beat passed, then Susan simply said, "You two make each other happy."

For a moment no one uttered a word, not even the animals. Then BoomBoom, who thought she'd be scared only to discover she wasn't at all, replied, "We do."

And that was that.

Within the hour they finished the mail. It would have taken Harry and Miranda past closing to do it themselves. Miranda made a fresh pot of coffee, dashed across the alleyway, and soon returned with a large basket filled with chocolate chip cookies, peanut butter cookies, and fresh gingerbread, a thin glaze of vanilla icing on the top.

"Girls, I was in such a hurry to get over here after Pug called me"—she mentioned the postmaster of the area by name—"that I didn't have time to throw together some treats."

An impromptu party followed, with either Miranda or Harry rising to take care of a customer. Miranda even thought to bring dried liver treats for the cats and dog.

Harry bit into her second slice of gingerbread, then stopped mid-chew. Swallowing big, she said, "Know what?" The others looked at her. "The eye. Nordy was killed through the eye. The Virgin Mary is bleeding through the eyes."

The cats and dogs listened to this as they ate the treats brought for them.

"If she could smell, she'd have caught that whiff of lanolin and beeswax when we came to work," Tucker said. *"Don't know about eyes, but I know that lanolin odor."*

"Virgin wool," Mrs. Murphy replied.

"From an unmarried sheep." Pewter giggled.

"From someone wearing a virgin wool sweater, or a robe like a Greyfriar." The tiger ignored Pewter's joke.

23

"It's a strange coincidence. Let that be the end of it." Fair pulled off the thin, long, whitish latex gloves he'd used to check a mare.

The gloves barely made a sound as they dropped into the garbage can in Boom-Boom's stable. At six o'clock in the evening the sun had set an hour ago, and the sky was filled with low, dense, tinted clouds, the remains of one of those sunsets that goes on and on, the last brushstroke of color dying after an hour.

BoomBoom was holding the furry chestnut mare, a well-built animal by Lemon Drop Kid out of Silly Putty, a mare who broke down on the racetrack. BoomBoom, like Harry, Fair, and Big Mim, could pick a horse.

The animal could be underfed, wormy, blowing its coat, or injured, yet she saw the potential. She was highly regarded by other horsemen, all the more so since this particular broodmare was by Lemon Drop Kid, a marvelous stallion who enjoyed a stellar career on the track.

As Fair worked on the mare, BoomBoom and Harry filled him in on conversations at the post office, their ideas, Susan's ideas, Miranda's, and, well, everyone's who flounced into the post office that day— which was everyone who could stand up. If you didn't show up at the post office, it meant you were involved in a flaming seduction or too sick to walk. After recovering from both fevers, one was expected to divulge the details in as amusing a manner as possible.

Harry bristled. "Oh, come on, I'm just tossing out theories."

"Your theories have a way of almost getting you killed."

"True!" the two cats and dog agreed as they sat on the stacked hay bales.

Alicia appeared in the open barn doors, the fading light framing her. Winter sunsets

at this latitude were one more joy of living in central Virginia.

For an instant, seeing Alicia in the doorway, Harry could understand why Boom-Boom had fallen in love with her. Then she looked at Fair washing his hands in the sink in the small tackroom, dirt on his coveralls, his green Wellies half brown with muck, and she thought he didn't need a sunset. He was beautiful to her. A thin pang of desire and even guilt shot through her body. She'd made him pay and pay for his sins. Maybe they weren't really sins. She said she'd forgiven him, and she had. She recognized at that very instant that she needed to forgive herself. She'd held on to the whip hand too long and she'd diminished herself in the process, as well as hurt a man who loved her more than life itself.

"How is she?" Alicia turned up the collar of her bomber jacket; the mercury was dropping faster than the New Year's ball in Times Square.

"Healthy. The infection cleared up." Fair turned to BoomBoom. "I'd ship her out to Kentucky after Christmas. They're so efficient and responsible at Payson Stud. They'll put her under lights and, when she's ready, she'll have multiple covers by St. Jovite." He mentioned one of the good studs standing at the farm. "I know those board bills ratchet up, but, BoomBoom, that's the stallion you want for this mare. He raced for years and retired sound. You want that hardy blood. After she's caught, ship her back. I'll take it from there. If you breed your other mare, go to Tom Newton's stud, Harbor Dean. But send this girl to Kentucky."

"You're right."

"Are you breeding her for the track?" Harry liked the mare; she had clean legs but was retiring because she'd suffered a cracked vertebra in an accident in the shedrows.

"Well, I know that's better for Payson Stud, but, no, I'm breeding her for foxhunting. One of the great things about the people at Payson Stud is that Mrs. Payson runs steeplechase horses, so she understands about jumping and, even more importantly, staying power. Peggy Augustus is another true horseman who cares about going the distance. Everyone these days seems to breed for sprint races. The good old distance bloodlines are thinning out. Remember, Husband, Peggy's stallion, was the sire of my best hunter. I'll be taking one of my other mares to Husband in January."

Horsemen, like golfers, could talk for hours, days, weeks about horses, bloodlines, great chasers and racers, great hunt horses.

Alicia, a horseman herself—although her knowledge was interrupted by the time she'd spent acting in California—said, "Why don't we continue this at the kitchen table? There's potpie waiting for you all, if you don't mind simple fare." She paused a moment. "Not referring to you, Fair."

At the massive farmer's table, the conversation bounced between recent events, horses, and politics, especially Wendell Ordman's career.

Fair cut into his pie, through crusty layers of perfection. "How did Maggie Sheraton like Herb?"

Alicia answered, "Karma. Her words." She imitated Maggie's delivery. "Alicia Palmer, darlin' girl, when I shook his hand I felt a karmic bond. Many lives. Then we spoke and I found in this life a courteous gentle Virginia gentleman."

"Which means?" Harry lifted one eyebrow.

"Means she's coming down from New York for New Year's. She'll stay here, of course. They're going to the dance at Farmington Country Club. She's bought three gowns from Bergdorf Goodman. One of them is bound to be right."

"Wonder what Herb thinks?" Harry thought Herb looked good in a tuxedo. It helped to hide his paunch, which he was now exercising to remove.

"He invited her, so he must like her," Fair reflected.

Fair got up and refilled everyone's coffee cup. He noticed a pair of headlights coming down the drive. "Boom, are you expecting anyone?"

"No."

In the country, dear friends don't feel compelled to call first, so an unannounced visitor wasn't that out of the ordinary.

The car pulled into the drive, the lights cut off. In the darkness BoomBoom couldn't tell the make of the vehicle. The back door swung open and a teary Susan walked in.

"Susan, what's the matter?" Harry asked.

"Well, I drove to your house, then I re-

membered you said at the post office that
Fair was checking Boom's mare and . . ."
Susan rambled on before she got to the
point. "Ned's staying in Richmond tonight.
He said he has so much to do he needs to
stay over, but when I called him back on his
cell he didn't pick up."

Alicia got up and pulled another chair to
the table, as BoomBoom fetched another
plate and table setting. "Susan, sit down.
Please join us."

"I can't eat. I'm too fat. That's why he's
sleeping with other women."

"Susan, you don't know that. Now, come
on. And he needs to stay in Richmond
sometimes, but especially now." Harry led
her to the table.

Fair, upset for Susan, poured a cup of
coffee for her. "She's right, Susan. Don't
worry about him not answering his cell. I
mean, he might be in a meeting or the battery could need a recharge. Don't worry."

Susan wiped her eyes as Alicia placed a
hot potpie in front of her.

"What am I going to do?" Susan asked in
a flat tone.

"You're going to relax with your friends,

enjoy this potpie, and we'll figure this out together." Alicia took charge.

"You'll feel better if you eat this." Boom-Boom encouraged Susan. "Your blood sugar drops and everything looks much worse."

Reluctantly Susan pierced the pie, the enticing aroma curling up to her nostrils. She gingerly took a bite, then another. "It is good."

"The goddess herself made it," Boom-Boom teased.

"Will you stop?" Alicia rolled her eyes.

"Susan, I don't think Ned is having an affair. Really. I'm not just saying that to make you feel better, but I think I'd know," Fair said.

"Would he tell you?"

Fair was reassuring. "Maybe. Look, he's never been in politics before. He probably feels he's over his head."

"I haven't heard a breath of scandal about Ned. If he were up to something I'd know by now." BoomBoom soothed her.

"I've been married to the man since I was nineteen. I know him. He's up to something. He's distant." Susan's lower lip quivered anew.

"Has it occurred to you that perhaps

you're distant?" Alicia reached over to pat Susan's left hand.

"How's his health?" BoomBoom inquired.

"Healthy as a horse," Susan responded, then turned to Alicia. "Maybe I have been weird."

Harry asked as she cut into a spice cake with thick icing, "Susan, you said Ned is healthy as a horse. Wasn't Great-Uncle Thomas healthy as a horse?"

"He was. Why?"

"Why assume he died of a heart attack just because he was eighty-two?" Harry said as she passed a piece of moist cake to Fair.

"It's not an unreasonable assumption," Fair replied.

"But he had no history of heart disease, am I right?" Harry persisted.

Susan thought for a moment. "The Bland Wades live forever. He was worried about his heart. He'd been experiencing irregular heartbeats. But still, at his age that's to be expected. Like I said, the Bland Wades are tough. Brooks takes after that side."

"Danny looks a little like a Bland Wade," Fair said.

"I always thought he resembled his father," Susan hastily replied.

"He's handsome no matter who he resembles." Alicia thought Susan had lovely children.

Susan repeated, "He looks just like his father."

Harry got back on track. "Do you have any reason to believe Brother Thomas was sick?"

"No," Susan said.

"A major coronary would take him right out. There might not be any indication before the attack." Fair was thinking about the kind monk.

"You didn't ask for an autopsy." Harry was thinking out loud, not asking a question.

Susan answered, though. "Of course not, Harry, he was two years older than God. Let the poor soul be buried with dignity."

"I think you should exhume him and have an autopsy performed."

"Harry, we're eating," BoomBoom chided her.

24

On December 9, Friday, the few lovely days of the temperature climbing to the forties ended. Clouds, steel gray, unfurled from the west, winds led the clouds onward, and a low-pressure system made animals and humans tired. The temperature headed down, down.

A small crew stood around Brother Thomas's grave as Travis Critzer sank the big claw of the front-end loader into the earth, aided by Stuart Tapscott. Travis could operate anything with a motor in it. Skilled as he was, he was glad to be digging up the coffin before the hard frost returned, and he was glad to have his father with him. Although not his blood father, Stuart was the man who had raised him, taught him his trade.

Brother Frank and Brother Prescott stood, faces sour. As it was Friday, the day of public execution for centuries, it became considered the devil's day. It was devil's work disturbing what was left of a good and godly man. As the number-two man in the monastery, Brother Prescott volunteered to oversee this disgusting task. Brother Handle, overwhelmed with the response to the statue, gratefully accepted this offer. Dealing with the hordes of people, with unrest among the brothers themselves, made Brother Handle wonder why he ever thought becoming a monk would steer him clear of the world's follies. In fact, the pressures increased to the point where he offered no protest at the exhumation. Once a grave was consecrated, Brother Handle believed it should not be touched. However, Brother Thomas's family, under the leadership of Susan Tucker, was insistent. Brother Handle knew Ned Tucker had been elected to the state senate in November. Best to keep a Tucker happy.

Susan, Harry, and Deputy Cooper also watched the yellow claw dig into the flinty earth. A thin cover of soil was quickly stripped away; the subsequent layers were poor. That's why this corner of the monastery held the mortal remains of the brothers. No sense in wasting good soil.

The county coroner, Tom Yancy, waited, too, glad for a chance to escape the lab. He and Cooper had worked together over the years, a healthy respect developing between them.

Although it was Coop's day off, she accompanied Harry and Susan. She'd seen enough exhumations to know that they can be disturbing to next of kin or friends of the departed. Also, Harry had promised that afterward they'd drive up Interstate 81 to Dayton's furniture store, just south of Harrisonburg. Coop had saved enough for a sleigh bed, her Christmas present to herself, and Harry said Dayton's would have the best—not the cheapest, but the best.

Susan tightened the scarf around her neck. "Wind's come up."

"An ill wind that blows no good," Harry quoted the old saying.

"You're full of Christmas spirit," Tom said.

"Sorry. Kind of hard to be cheery at an exhumation."

"Look at it this way." The coroner grinned. "If the old fellow died a natural death, that will be good news. I know you two ladies haven't witnessed an exhumation. Brother Thomas won't be in that bad a shape; he hasn't been in there long enough. His nose might have crumbled a little, his cuticles might have receded, which will make it look as though his fingernails are still growing, but it won't be all that bad."

"What about the stench?" Harry wasn't one to mince on reality.

He waved his hand. "He won't smell like Chanel Number Five, but remember, it's been cold up here, and even though he's below the frost line, it's plenty cold down there. Might be blowing up some, but just step back and hold your nose. That way you won't get a blast and if you faint you won't fall into the coffin."

"I'm not going to faint." Harry's pride flared up.

"Might puke, though," he genially replied.

"Good God, this is so gross." Susan's eyes misted over. "I feel like I'm violating him."

"I don't know about that, but Susan, if he was murdered then we have to find his killer.

Brother Thomas deserves that, at least. An eye for an eye and a tooth for a tooth."

"There's a lot to be said for simple justice." The lanky deputy took a long draw on a Camel, then gratefully exhaled a plume of blue smoke.

"Cooper, might I bum a cigarette off you?" Susan implored.

"Of course." Coop reached in her parka pocket and fetched out the familiar white pack covered with thin cellophane, the camel, facing left, dutifully standing at the ready.

"Cheater," Harry teased Susan.

"Can't help it."

"Kills the smell," Tom cheerfully added.

"Uh, Coop, give me one, too. I'll buy you a pack." Harry reached for the offered cigarette.

The three women drew on their cigarettes. Nicotine, calming in most circumstances, worked for Cooper and Harry, who rarely smoked. Susan, however, remained nervous and wished she was inhaling a mentholated cigarette.

The claw scratched the top of the pine coffin.

Within minutes, Travis carefully dug around the edges of the handmade coffin.

Brother Prescott and Brother Frank stepped up to the grave site. They dropped two stout ropes down into the pit. Travis, being much younger than the two monks, hopped down, slid the ropes with a little wriggling under the coffin. Stuart Tapscott grabbed the ropes on the edge of the grave to keep them from sliding back into the pit.

The coroner and Brother Frank took opposite ends of one rope, Brother Prescott and Travis the other. Stuart stood well back. He didn't want to see the body.

"All right, one, two, pull," Travis commanded as the coffin lifted up with relative ease.

Travis and Brother Prescott pried the lid. Before the coroner picked the lid off the coffin, he said, "You might want to stand back and let me look first, ladies."

Harry, belligerently, stepped right up to the coffin; Susan stepped back.

Tom looked up at Harry and half-smiled. He picked up the lid.

"Holy shit!" Harry exclaimed.

The coffin contained three fifty-pound bags of potting soil.

Shock registered on Tom's face as well as those of the two brothers. Susan plucked up her courage to look inside.

Coop was already on her cell phone, punching in Sheriff Shaw. "Rick, we've got a real problem."

Susan's nervousness, then anger, focused on Brother Frank and Brother Prescott. "What's the meaning of this? What have you done with my great-uncle!"

Brother Frank, face white as the snow still folded in the deepest tucks of the ravines, stuttered, "Mrs. Tucker, I swear to you with God as my witness, your great-uncle was in this coffin when the lid was nailed shut."

"One more miracle for the mountain," Harry cracked.

"What?" Brother Prescott was deeply upset.

"You've got a statue crying bloody tears, and now you've got a resurrection." Harry, at that moment, didn't trust either of the brothers any further than she could throw her lit cigarette.

25

The clutter on Sheriff Rick Shaw's desk didn't reflect his mind, which was clear and concise in its workings. An avalanche of flyers and bulletins from the county, the state, and the federal government rolled over his desk.

He carefully sifted through the mail, smiling each time junk mail hit the large round metal wastebasket. Anything pertinent he stacked in a steel mesh file box, a gift from Cooper last Christmas.

Now this Christmas pressed on him. He hadn't bought one present. His wife, whom he dearly loved, shouldered much of that burden, but he wanted to buy her something special and hadn't one idea.

Three people had missed work today because of the flu, one being the receptionist, who sifted people like Rick sifted mail. Deputy Cooper had some days coming to her. She hadn't taken any vacation time this year, but he was shorthanded and Coop, being Coop, pitched in. She had one day off, today, and that turned into work. She never made it to Dayton's.

Rick pushed his chair back when she walked into the office.

"Here." She tossed a carton of Camels on his desk. Another carton was tucked under her arm.

"Living large. Thank you." He slid the carton into his long middle desk drawer. "Really."

"They're from Harry."

"Harry?"

"She bummed a fag off me, so she bought me a carton and then one for you. She sends her regards and she's sorry to hear everyone is flat on their backs with this damned new strain of flu. Jeez, hope we don't get it."

"I'm chewing so much vitamin C, I'm about to turn orange. And echinacea. My wife stuffs it down my throat, God bless her."

"Helen's a good woman. Everyone needs a wife—even a wife." Cooper pulled up the wooden chair, an old office chair from the 1940s. "I'd settle for one husband, though."

"He'd be a lucky man." Rick had learned to cherish his deputy over the years, although initially he resented a woman in law enforcement and gave her every crappy job that came along. Her upbeat personality, meticulousness, and steadiness in a crisis changed his mind. He fretted that she wouldn't find the right guy. Many men think a woman cop is gay, and Cooper wasn't. She wasn't movie-star beautiful, although she was attractive. She was, however, shy with men who attracted her.

"Thanks, boss." She opened a fresh pack of Camels. "You won't believe this—on top of the coffin with bags of potting soil, I mean—but Harry actually smoked half a cigarette. She gagged, but she puffed like a chimney."

"Did she, now?" He laughed.

"She thought when the lid came off the coffin she'd be puked out by the stench, so she lit up. Not a bad tactic, since smoking compromises your sense of smell. Sticking a gob of Vick's Vapo-Rub up your nose is better." Cooper pulled a small jar out of her coat pocket. "Didn't use it since I figured Brother Thomas would be frozen."

Rick grunted. "Maybe they intended to plant him and misplaced the body."

"Very funny." She tapped the end of the fresh cigarette on the desk. "Anything on Nordy?"

"Pete Osborne copied the last year of Nordy's assignments. We viewed those segments that Pete thought could possibly inflame someone to murder." Rick accepted the cigarette Cooper offered him. He sniffed the distinctive rich aroma of unsmoked tobacco, then struck a kitchen match on the large red matchbox. Rick didn't like lighters. He thought the gas odor filtered into the cigarette. "He made us copies." He held up a DVD in a blue cardboard envelope, which bore Pete's distinctive scrawl. "Can't believe the technology."

"If I have a good Christmas I'll buy myself a DVD player. Still have a year of car payments left." She paused. "Prices keep coming down. Eventually I'll be able to afford one. Didn't mean to get off the subject. What do you think about what you saw?"

"The segment where Nordy was outside

a supposed drug dealer's house was vola-
tile. Jamaicans ran out and hit him. The one
where he broke the story on the check-
kiting scheme shook up people. The trials
on that start in March. People have killed for
less. There are the usual interviews with victims' families, with murderers—emotional
but not the same payoff."

"How do you mean?"

"Emotions run high, and Nordy's footage
creates sympathy for the victim. However,
that's not the same as pointing the finger
and accusing someone of guilt. Murder usually isn't a thought-out crime; most of what
we see is spur-of-the-moment. But the
check-kiting schemes, mmm, that kind of
crime demands thought. It's usually committed by someone with a higher education,
someone who might get off with a good
lawyer. To save their own neck, that kind of
criminal might murder."

"But a white-collar criminal wouldn't kill
Nordy. He'd hire a dog's body, don't you
think?" She used the phrase "dog's body,"
meaning someone who lived for odd or
onerous chores.

"Exactly." Rick swung his feet up to rest
on his desk. "Nordy was going to see the

check-kiting story to its bitter conclusion. As for the Jamaican drug dealers, again, there's a lot of money at stake. This is a wealthy county, and people want their cocaine, Oxycontin, and whatever, you know? They'll get it. There's motive there and cunning."

"You're not convinced."

He exhaled. "No."

"It's the pen in the eye, isn't it?"

His eyebrows lifted in appreciation. She knew how his mind worked, which was a comfort. "In all my years I have never seen that. I've seen torture, I've seen infants raped, which is about the sickest goddamned thing I have ever seen, but I've never seen this. It's so simple."

"Yeah, how do you trace a ballpoint pen? Harry thinks it might have something to do with eyes. That's a message, the eyes."

He pursed his lips together. "The carton of cigarettes is a bribe. She's going to get stuck right in the middle of this. Incorrigible! The empty coffin, so to speak, must have sent her into the stratosphere."

"It was a jolt."

He swiveled to face her better but didn't move his legs much. "Damned queer."

"Harry is convinced this is linked to Nordy's murder. Linked to the Virgin Mary's bleeding eyes. In fact, she said, 'The eyes have it.' "

"These inspirations spare her the legwork, don't they?"

"She's not averse to legwork, boss, but she isn't a professional. She misses things. She gets to third base without touching first or second, but you have to admit, she gets a hit at bat."

He exhaled in a sort of agreement, "Well, I guess that's better than being born on third base and thinking you've hit a triple."

His first concern was protecting the public. His next concern was procedure. If he didn't touch each base on his way to home plate, a lawyer, not even a clever one, would blow all that hard work to smithereens. Harry worried him with her meddling because she endangered herself and others and because she could muck up a carefully built case.

They smoked in silence, then Cooper broke it. "How's Pete holding up?"

"Good. He's a strong man. The other on-air reporters are nervous. He's doing a lot of hand-holding and he's interviewing for a replacement. He said he feels ghoulish but it's necessary. The station is understaffed as it is. I can sure appreciate that problem."

"At least that's a profitable business."

"Yeah, right. We're public servants, and some days I really feel the servant part."

"Think there is any connection between Nordy's death and the statue, the monastery?"

"I can't disregard any possibility. Nordy was making a big name for himself with that story. Pete and I watched everything Nordy did up there, as well as the footage he didn't use. He didn't come out and say the tears were false, only that they were an unexplained phenomenon. He was respectful. I can't disregard the Virgin Mary angle, but for the life of me, I can't find one thing that computes."

"I can't, either. A man in his eighties dies while praying before a statue on a night so bitterly cold even Satan with his built-in heating unit wouldn't be walking around. Andrew, Mark, and Prescott thaw him out, wash the body, prepare him for burial. They put him in the coffin, nail down the lid—all this is testimony." She held up her small notebook that she kept in her purse. "He's afforded a simple service in keeping with the order. Susan and her family attend. They throw earth on the grave and that's that. I also talked with Brother Handle, the head honcho. He said Brother Thomas was well loved. 'So why would someone steal his body?' I asked." She drew in another long drag. "He did say that the body was possibly sold to a medical school. But who would do such a thing? Surely not one of the brothers. He didn't believe so, either, but selling to a medical school was his one idea. He's wound tighter than a piano wire, by the way, and the whole place is overrun by people crying, praying in front of the statue. You wouldn't believe it."

"Is she really crying blood?"

"I took a sample and sent it off to the lab. Shouldn't take long even with all they have to do."

Coop heard a rat-a-tat on the windowpanes outside Rick's office. She stood up to look. "Damn. It's going to be another long day."

He swung his legs down, got up, peered out his office window. "Where'd that come from? I watched the Weather Channel this morning as well as the weatherman on Channel Twenty-nine."

"Who knows." Her voice was mournful as the ice pellets struck the window harder.

He sat back down. "If we find Brother Thomas's body, that will tell us something."

"The dead tell all their secrets if you know how to ask."

26

Knowing that a woman in a position of authority might be disquieting to the Greyfriars, Rick briefly interviewed each brother.

Brother Handle agreed to this because Brothers Frank and Prescott impressed on him how bad it would look if he didn't cooperate. It would appear that the Greyfriars had something to hide.

Rick made the questions brief. He knew from many years of experience that he had to piece together this case, each bit of evidence, each person questioned, a tiny square of information in what would become an intelligible mosaic. He had queried Brother Mark about the last time he saw Thomas's body then switched gears, asking him about Nordy.

Brother Mark, head down, sat opposite him. "I loathed him. I tried to like him. I prayed. Still hated him."

"Even at Michigan State?"

"Especially. He swaggered, humiliated me in front of my dates. We were in the same fraternity but he was a year ahead of me."

"I see. What about printing and selling fake I.D.s?" Rick surprised him with this information.

Mark raised his head. "His idea. I was weak and went along with it."

"Made a lot of money?"

"Yes." He brightened, although wary of the Sheriff. He wondered just why Rick had dug so deep into his own past. "We made over fifteen thousand dollars in one semester. One semester!"

"And you got busted. He didn't."

"Nordy's father could pull strings. Mine could only pull on the bottle," he said with rancor.

"That's when you, uh, took a nosedive."

"Puree." Mark used an expression for a total loss.

"That's a good one. Puree is worse than toast?"

"Yeah."

"Tell me what happened next."

"Drugs. Couldn't hold a job. If I hadn't found God I'd be in jail or dead. I was this far"—he held up his thumb and forefinger close together—"from becoming a career criminal."

"What happened?"

"I woke up in the middle of Beverly Street in Staunton on a cold night. A doctor was dragging me out of the road and she said, 'Son, you can go into rehab or you can find God. I'll help you either way.' "

"And she did?"

"I went to a clinic in North Carolina, not expensive or anything. I detoxed. I found God and I found the Greyfriars. But every day I have to work on myself."

"Could you have killed Nordy?"

Mark half-smiled. "The thought occurred to me. I suppose I could have, but even though I couldn't stand him, nah." He shrugged. "I pray harder."

Rick checked his watch. "You've been helpful. One last question. Do you fit in here? Is this the place for you?"

"Yeah. I'm surrounded by dinosaurs. I know they make fun of me behind my back, but," he shrugged again, "I ignore them. I miss Brother Thomas. He taught me stuff. I could talk to him, and even though he was eighty-two he could use the computer as easily as I can. He said if he made it to eighty-three he was going to build his own computer. He even knew he could specify what he wanted from ASUS, the company in California."

"You lost me." Rick closed his notebook.

"ASUS. They build motherboards. Brother Thomas really was going to build his own computer with a motherboard he helped design."

"I can see why you miss him."

"No one here even knows what a motherboard is."

"Bet Nordy did."

"Yeah, but he'd kind of have to know. Every now and then I'd use one of the computers here and fire him an e-mail." He cupped his chin in his hand. "Funny, he really pissed me off, but I'm going to miss him. I never thought someone my age would die, you know?"

"Well, Brother Mark, you've had the great good fortune not to be in a war. Your generation has been spared. If it were 1943 or

1970, a lot of your running buddies would be dead. You might be dead. When you say your prayers, pray for them, for those that went before."

Mark blinked. "I will. And I know the Blessed Virgin Mother weeps for them."

27

Harry remarked to Susan as they drove the rig back from a foxhunt, "I am in the best mood. The best mood."

"Good, because when you get home you know those two cats will have shredded something." Susan smiled. The bracing day had improved her spirits, too.

She was right. When Susan dropped her off she walked inside to behold two silk lamp shades slit open, shredded. Then Harry went down to the basement to fetch a jar of orange marmalade and found the birdseed bags that Mrs. Murphy and Pewter had ripped open when she last left them alone in the house.

Tucker, quick to defend herself, told Harry in no uncertain terms that she would never shred silk lamp shades, nor would she spill seed upon the ground like the Biblical Onan although Onan wasn't spilling birdseed.

"Brownnoser," Mrs. Murphy growled at the dog.

"No impulse control." Tucker walked away from the cat, her claws clicking on the kitchen heart-pine boards.

"Why are you so happy? You got left behind today, too," Pewter complained.

"We are not supposed to go to foxhunts. Sometimes Mom will let me sleep in the cab of the truck but we really aren't supposed to go. You know that."

"Tucker, I might know it but I don't agree with it." The tiger cat swatted at the corgi.

The phone rang. Miranda informed Harry that Big Mim had just been told by her daughter that Blair Bainbridge proposed to her on Thanksgiving Day. Big Mim had mixed emotions but put a good face on it. Mim called Miranda to talk it out.

Then the phone rang again.

"Susan, you must have just gotten to the house. What's up?"

"Harry, you and I are both country girls. Today's hunt pulled me out of my torpor. My mind's working again and I'm ready to fight the world."

"I'm ready, too." Harry liked hearing the energy in Susan's voice.

"Here's what I think. G-Uncle Thomas is laid in the coffin, three brothers see him. According to Brother Mark, the lid was nailed down, he's buried. Right?"

"Right."

"All the brothers attend the brief entombment, as do I."

"Right."

"The coffin is heavy. No suspicions. Still with me?"

"Always and ever."

"All right, then. Either Brother Andrew and Mark are lying through their teeth, which I don't discount, or someone removes the body before everyone gets to the cemetery, putting in three bags of potting soil. Something was in his coffin."

"You're right." Harry had already considered this.

"So what do they do with him? None of the brothers left the grounds that night. At least not that anyone knows. No car was taken, and only a few brothers have access to the keys. G-Uncle Thomas was taken somewhere and dumped or reburied. It would be a hard job to rebury him. I figure all this happened within one night, in darkness. He can't be far. How far can you drag a body in bitter cold and snow? I'm willing to bet my great-uncle is within a mile's radius of his grave, or should I say his intended grave."

"Susan, you're on to something." Harry encouraged her, glad that her friend didn't sound as anxious or troubled as she had been in the last few weeks.

"If we find him, maybe we can find out what happened to him."

"We're country girls. If anyone can find him, we can. The cats and dogs can help. We have to be careful. We can't blow through the joint, know what I mean? We'll have to work up from the ravines."

"Thought of that, too. I say we go in from behind the Inn at Afton Mountain just before dawn. Work up to within sight of the Virgin Mary, then work around in a southwest arc. Since it's Sunday the brothers will be in service and prayer, at least early in the morning. We have a shot at it, and we can be out of there before attracting notice. We'll have to work in sections. We can't do it all in one day."

"Great idea." Harry paused a moment. "But, Susan, if we do find him, do you really want to see old Uncle Thomas like, well, like however we find him?"

"I tell myself the soul has left the body. Whatever we find is a husk. And I tell myself that he deserves better. He deserves a decent Christian burial after a lifetime of service to the best of Jesus' teachings."

"You're right," Harry agreed.

"I feel this foreboding. Harry, I feel like he's calling to me. I have a debt to clear, but I don't know what it is."

28

Looking east from the top of the Blue Ridge Mountains, a thin gray line separated the horizon from the frozen earth. The band expanded until the faintest touch of rose diffused the bottom to cast a pinkish glow on the dark earth.

Harry, Susan, Mrs. Murphy, Pewter, Tucker, and Owen, Susan's corgi, paused to watch the blush of dawn before they plunged into the ravine behind the monastery.

The early morning, still as the tomb and clear, promised a cold day but a bright one. The winter solstice, ten days ahead, brought soft light.

Harry marveled at how the light changed with each season. Winter's light, soft and alluring, offered a contrast to the cold.

The two dogs scrambled down the ravine. The cats picked their way over the fallen branches and the jutting rocks. Pewter, never one for vigorous exercise, grumbled with each obstacle.

"You could have stayed in the car up at Afton Inn." Mrs. Murphy tired of the stream of complaints.

"And miss everything! If we find Brother Thomas you'll need my powers of observation."

"If we find Brother Thomas, you'll throw up. It will be like one big hairball," Mrs. Murphy said as she leapt over a large oak branch, the place where it had torn from the tree a different color.

"I will not." Pewter elected to go around the tree branch. *"I don't rejoice in these things. Not like the dogs. Carrion eaters. They love it."*

"Dogs can be gross." Mrs. Murphy couldn't imagine eating anything decayed or rolling in it.

"And Tucker brags about her nose." Pewter wrinkled hers.

"She has a good nose. Rot smells like an enticing dinner to her. I don't get it, either. I mean, you and I have good noses, but that's

one scent we don't like. Humans, either. I guess buzzards like it, though."

"Ever notice how birds who tear flesh have upper beaks that curve down—sort of? Think of Flatface, not just buzzards." Pewter mentioned the large horned owl living in the barn at home.

"Yes. Ever notice how buzzards don't have feathers on their necks?" Mrs. Murphy answered her own question. *"They can stick their entire head inside some really dead animal, but their necks won't get sticky, weighted down. They can keep clean that way, I suppose, and they can fly, too. If a buzzard was pasted over with goo, it'd be harder to fly."*

"Practical. Crabs are carrion eaters, too. So why do they have eyes on stalks?" Pewter liked crabmeat, so long as she didn't think about what the crab had eaten.

"To look goofy." The tiger laughed.

Harry's eyes followed the dogs. On the one hand, she hoped they did find Brother Thomas. On the other, she didn't. She had a strong stomach, but still.

Susan, silent, trudged along. The snow shone deep blue in the boulder cracks and fissures. The rim of the sun crested the horizon, but down in the deepest part of the ravine neither she nor Harry could see it.

"*How upset is she?*" Tucker asked her brother.

"*Pretty upset, but once she made up her mind to do something about it, she settled down,*" Owen replied. "*She can't understand why he would disappear. She fears the worst, too.*"

"*Murder,*" Tucker flatly said, as she slid down an icy bank, then nimbly jumped over a narrow rivulet feeding into a strong running creek.

"*Ever notice how humans have to find reasons for things? They can't relax unless they invent a reason. Susan couldn't accept that one human kills another just to kill. Has to be a reason.*"

"*Usually is. In civilian life. War's different. A human gets used to killing then, I guess.*" Tucker hoped she'd never face a war. "*They get used to killing and it doesn't matter. If it's a religious war, then they really want to kill one another.*" She sighed. "*If this thinned the herd it might be good, but all they do is turn around and breed in more and more numbers. They don't learn much.*"

"Don't learn much from their own history and don't learn doodley-squat from us."

"I don't care. I care about Harry, but since there's nothing I can do for the rest of them, they'll hang on their own hook."

"It's strange to love an animal that's so stupid, isn't it?" Owen stopped, lifting his nose. *"Mmm."*

"Could be deer. Far away." Tucker, too, inhaled the faint, very faint, sweet odor of decay.

The cats joined them as Mrs. Murphy, feeling full of herself, dashed along, zig-zagging, leaning over anything in her path, sending ground-nester birds and little finches in bushes skyward.

Pewter, not to be outdone, also hurried down the slopes. She jumped over the rivulet and bounded up the steep side of the ravine.

Within minutes the four animals reached the top.

Tucker lifted her head, her nose skyward, then dropped it, facing southeast. *"Down there."*

Owen repeated his sister's motions. *"Stronger now."*

Pewter hesitated a moment, looked at

Mrs. Murphy, who giggled at her. Without one peep, she followed the dogs. Damned if she was going to be called a wimp.

The two humans lagged a quarter of a mile behind, the rough terrain more difficult for them to negotiate. Both women sweated although the mercury clung to twenty-eight degrees in the ravines, nudging upward on the ridges as the sun was climbing. The eastern horizon was a flare of pink, peach, and scarlet, quickly fanning out westward. The colors of sunrise never seemed to linger as did those of sunset, or so Harry thought.

As Harry and Susan reached the top of the ridge, they heard the two dogs barking. Startled buzzards flew overhead.

"Hope no one hears that," Susan fretted.

"We're far enough away from the monastery," Harry reassured her. "And they're in services, so hopefully they'll be chanting or singing or doing whatever monks do." Harry swept her eyes along the line of the ridge, then down. The sight of Tucker and Owen gleefully pulling on a dismembered arm stopped her cold. "Susan, you might want to stay up here."

Susan, reaching her, saw the same spectacle. "No."

"Mine!" Tucker raced with Brother Thomas's arm, which she'd found behind a large boulder.

"You didn't find it, I did." Owen raced after her, both dogs enjoying the game, oblivious to how awful this appeared to the humans. The cats didn't much like it, either.

"One arm. Where's the rest of him?" Pewter asked.

"Mmm." Mrs. Murphy sat, watching the dogs carry on, one at each end of the arm now. Tucker had the hand; Owen, growling, pulled on the bone sticking out from the other end where the forearm once connected to the elbow.

"Coyote?" Pewter noticed that what remained of the flesh was gray.

"Or dogs. Wild or domestic. Chances are they've torn poor old Brother Thomas all to hell. Buzzards got at him, too. We'll be picking up pieces until the cows come home."

"Be funny if someone's beloved golden retriever brought home a foot, wouldn't it? That's one human who would pass out." Pewter couldn't resist thinking of the shocked person.

"Best foot forward." Mrs. Murphy trotted past the dogs, who continued to tug at the

arm. *"Come on, Pewter. Let's keep moving. We'll find more of him."*

As Harry reached the dogs she sharply said, "Leave it!"

Obediently, Tucker dropped her end. *"Spoilsport."*

Hearing Susan shout at him, Owen also dropped the arm. *"I was only playing."*

"Don't touch it, Susan. No prints." Harry was glad the morning had proved so cold. The arm, thawed and frozen a few times during the last days, would become more pungent once the temperature climbed.

"I won't. I suppose it's my great-uncle's arm, but I can't say for sure." She wasn't as disgusted by the sight as she thought she would be. At least not yet.

"Over here," Mrs. Murphy yowled as she pushed down into a large boulder crevice where Brother Thomas's head and most of his torso had been stuffed. Coyotes or dogs had pulled off the limbs, but whoever wedged the old man in the crevice jammed him in there, placing large stones on the torso.

Harry reached the body first. "Goddammit!" she exploded.

Birds had plucked out Brother Thomas's

eyes. They'd also been pulling at his hair, for birds like long hair—human, horsehair, the hair from the end of a cow's tail—to weave into their nests.

Susan stopped. She could take seeing her great-uncle's arm, but this was pretty bad. "Oh, Harry."

"Don't look. It's him, all right."

"We found him." Pewter puffed out her gray chest, although she was disgusted at the sight.

"Why not leave him in his pine box?" Tucker joined the cats.

"Because someone was smart enough not to take the chance he'd be exhumed. Obviously, Tucker, there's something to find in the body," Mrs. Murphy replied.

Owen, leaving the treasure, walked over to the cats. *"So tasty."*

"Whoever is behind this knows something about bodies. If the corpse is exposed, maybe the method of murder will evaporate. I don't know. The coroner has his work cut out for him, but there has to be a reason why Brother Thomas wasn't left in his box. Think about it." Mrs. Murphy ignored the "so tasty" remark.

"I am. I don't like any of this, and I really

don't like that Harry's smack in the middle of it." Pewter wanted to go home now.

"She's not patient. She acts on impulse," Tucker observed, wanting to tug at Brother Thomas's remains. *"She thinks about these things. She gets part of the answer, but she rushes in, you know?"*

"They're both in it." Owen's big brown eyes looked at Susan, who was white as a sheet.

"You going to puke?" Harry also noticed Susan's pallor.

"No," Susan snapped. "It's horrible. For God's sake, Harry, how can you be so cold-blooded?"

Harry backed away from the body, going to her friend and putting her arm around Susan's shoulders. "The soul is with his Maker. This isn't really your great-uncle. It's like an old corn husk, Susan. We attach importance to it, but Thomas is gone."

A light lingering scent lured Tucker and Owen to the back of the large boulders. They sniffed around where coyotes had marked.

"They'll be back." Owen hated coyotes.

"Yes, but we'll be out of here and so will what's left of the human." Tucker, like Mrs.

Murphy, was trying to think things through. *"And when whoever is behind this learns that we've found the body, it will be dangerous."* The strong, small dog sat down. *"I'm trying to put the pieces together, no pun intended."*

Owen chuckled. *"Some of these pieces aren't going to be found. They're in coyote and buzzard bellies."*

"Can't talk to the coyotes, even if we found the ones that did this." Tucker watched as Harry punched numbers on her cell phone.

"If all four of us were together we might could." Mrs. Murphy used the old Southern expression.

"Only way I'm talking to a coyote is if I'm high up in a tree." Pewter spit out the word "coyote."

"You've got a point there, Pewter. They'd kill us the minute we turned our backs." Mrs. Murphy hated the marauders as much as her gray feline companion did.

"Can't get a signal. Susan, I'll try from the top of the ridge. Come on with me. We aren't going to forget this site."

Once on the ridge, Harry reached Cynthia

Cooper, who told Harry to mark a trail but to get out of there.

"Why?"

"Because neither you nor Susan is armed. Because you're probably safe, but what if whoever dumped Brother Thomas were to come back? It's a long shot, but I want you and Susan out of there. You've got your pocketknife on you, don't you?"

"Always do," Harry answered.

"Make slash marks where you can, bend twigs. We'll meet you at the parking lot. I mean it, Harry."

"All right, Coop. All right."

Back at the parking lot, the humans and animals waited.

"Prove all things; hold fast that which is good." Susan burst into tears as she quoted First Thessalonians, Chapter 5, Verse 21.

"What makes you think of that? It's usually Miranda who quotes the Bible."

"When I spoke to Thomas about my fears—you know, about Ned—that's what he said to me. I don't even know why I blabbed it. Not his business."

"He was wise and loving. You probably made him feel good by confiding in him."

Later, when Harry called Miranda, Miranda did, in fact, quote scripture. "Thou art of purer eyes than to behold evil and canst not look on iniquity."

Gave Harry a shiver to hear the quote from Habakkuk, Chapter 1, Verse 13.

Gave Cooper and Rick a shiver when the law called back on the sample Coop had dropped off from the statue. Type O human blood.

29

Meticulously laid out on the stainless-steel table, with channels along the sides to capture any fluids should they escape the corpse, were the pieces of Brother Thomas.

Sheriff Shaw and Deputy Cooper watched Tom Yancy and his assistant, Marshall Wells, inspect the remains. Tom used long tweezers to pluck out a fiber or a bone splinter.

"What we're seeing, Rick, is consistent with animals ripping over a body." He pointed with the tweezers to part of the femur still attached to the hip socket. "The bone is cracked open, chewed. You can clearly see the teeth marks here."

"Dogs, coyotes, most all carnivores love bone marrow," Marshall said.

"What about vultures?" Rick viewed sights like Brother Thomas as a matter of course.

Didn't mean he liked it, though.

"Yes. They've been at him."

Coop remarked, "Tom, any idea if he suffered trauma before death?"

"Well, his skull is intact. Upper jaw still attached. Lower one gone. No broken bones around the shoulder. Too late to tell about the arms, of course. There's just enough left of his liver and a scrap of kidney here that I can get a sample. If he was poisoned there might be a trace, depending on the poison."

Rick cracked his knuckles. "Sorry. Bad habit."

"Not as bad as smoking." Tom reached into the body cavity to lift up a tiny piece of kidney, which Marshall snipped.

"No signs of stabbing?" Coop couldn't imagine why his body had been dragged into the ravine and stuffed between and under large rocks.

"No."

"If he'd been hit up with a hypodermic needle, something to put him down, too late for the mark?" Rick wondered.

Tom touched some fragments of one arm; the other hadn't been found. "Not much chance. If the body had been intact, possibly, Rick, because the cold helped us. Yes, we've had a few warm days, enough for him to blow up and give off scent, which brought in nature's garbage collectors, but the cold returned with a vengeance. I don't have much arm here. Most of the flesh has been chewed off. Marshall and I examined the torso, used magnifiers; no obvious puncture except for fang marks. Some of those needles barely leave a trace."

"Hmm, let's say something appears in the kidney tissues or the liver. What would be your first choice?" Rick asked.

"You mean to kill him?" Yancy put down the long tweezers on a stainless-steel tray. "First of all, Rick, he may not have been killed where he was found. That's one possibility. He could have been, say, poisoned at another location, taken to the statue, placed in a kneeling position. His body would be losing warmth and it was colder than a witch's tit; he'd freeze up in less than three hours. Not much body fat on him. I'd estimate about nine percent, given his age and what I know of his people. The Bland Wades get painfully thin starting in their sixties. He was quite thin. Of course, he could have been praying, hard as it is for me to believe, on that bitter night. He could have just let himself go. People can will themselves to die."

"No. I don't think he willed it." Rick shook his head.

"All right, then. Let's say he did go to pray." Tom Yancy shrugged. "He's lost in communion with the Lord, and someone comes up behind him. He's down on his knees. Now, if his neck were broken this would be an easy call. It's not. So either someone reached around and knocked him out with, say, chloroform, or they shot him with the same stuff the vet uses to put down old Rover when his time has come. There's always morphine and heroin, too. Or, my last thought here, he was smothered." Tom moved up toward the head and neck. "There would be bruising on the neck, even now. There isn't. But if he were smothered, at this point I wouldn't know, because the eyeballs are gone." He paused, then continued, "If someone is choked to death or smothered in a less violent way, the eyeballs are bloodshot, red." He pressed his lips together. "I don't have much to go on, but we've got pieces of a body. That's a start, and we will invite poor old Brother Thomas to tell us as much as possible."

"Any idea how long it will be before we hear from Richmond?" Rick hoped the state lab, one of the nation's best, would be quick.

Tom shook his head. "Rick, it's less than two weeks before Christmas. People are killing themselves in greater numbers than usual or they're flaming out on the highway. There's always some damned fool who drinks himself to death and the family won't believe what the county coroner tells them, so off goes John Whiskey Doe to the state's pathology lab. Christmas is a nightmare. I'll do what I can to push them along."

"You knew Brother Thomas; what did you think of him?" Coop asked.

Tom folded his arms over his lab coat. "I'd see the old fellow occasionally at the hardware store, sometimes at the huge nursery over there in Waynesboro, the one where Jimmy Binns used to do such good work. Now, that man could design anything."

Yancy mentioned a retired gentleman who had a gift for landscaping.

"Ever see him, mmm, at the bank?" Rick picked up on Coop's direction of thought.

"No. Can the brothers have personal money?" Tom wondered.

Marshall, a Catholic, said, "Depends on the order. For the Greyfriars, if the money is family money it can be in a trust. The order can't touch it, but the brother can still have use of it. Trusts and wills can be both creative and binding." He added, "Had to study the monastic orders in parochial school. Always liked the Cistercians."

"Coop, check with Susan about this, will you?" Rick turned to his favorite officer.

"Okay."

Rick returned to Tom. "I'd see him at Jeffrey Howe's nursery, Mostly Maples. You couldn't help but notice him in his gray robe with the white hood. Unfailingly pleasant."

"I never heard him even say 'darn.' " Tom gazed down on the pieces of what had been a good man. "Rick, why anyone would harm him, I don't know. That's your job. Mine is to find out what I can from what's left."

"While I'm here," Rick glanced at the large wall clock, "anything else come back on Nordy Elliott?"

"Alcohol in the bloodstream. Not above

the legal limit. A healthy male. Death was straightforward."

"And painful." Coop grimaced.

"Extremely, but it was swift. One blinding pain, and I mean blinding, and it was over." Tom Yancy sighed. "Nordy wasn't on earth nearly as long as Brother Thomas, but he certainly piled up the enemies. And here's Brother Thomas, who, as far as we know, didn't have any."

"He had one," Rick said.

"A lethal one," Coop added.

30

Lips white, face purple with rage, Brother Handle strained for self-control. "He walked out of the coffin!"

"Your angina, Brother, remember your angina," Brother Andrew softly spoke as Brothers Prescott and Mark trembled on either side of him.

"Damn my angina. You put him in his coffin and you nailed shut the lid."

"I nailed shut the lid," Brother Mark squeaked.

"Well, you did a damned poor job of it." Brother Handle ran his right hand over his head, feeling his tonsure.

"Brother, this is painful and difficult for all of us, but we will get to the bottom of it." Brother Prescott, as second in command, knew how to handle the boss, but he'd never seen the boss this distressed.

Brother Handle paced in front of the three standing men. As he did, the knotted rope at his waist swayed with each step. "In all my years, *all my years,* not just as a brother, I have never encountered anything so disgusting, so bizarre, so vile, so disgusting." He stopped, since he was repeating himself.

Brother Handle veered close to out of control, but he still weighed his words.

"It's beyond imagining." Brother Prescott's voice sounded more soothing than usual.

"Things happen for a reason. This is the will of God," Brother Mark stupidly whined.

"This has nothing to do with the will of God, you impertinent young pup. This is an effort on someone's part to destroy our order!" He stopped in front of the slight young man, almost nose to nose. "Destroy our order! First we have a statue bleeding from the eyes. Every half-wit, every fool disappointed in love, every person suffering from illness has dragged themselves up this mountain to pray before the statue. Nordy

Elliott, that insufferable reporter, hung around like a blowfly. He's dead and now this!"

"The tears of Our Lady are a sign." Brother Mark's lower lip quivered.

"Oh, they're a sign, all right," Brother Handle glowered. "A sign that your mental wattage is about fifteen. Fifteen-watt Mark." He smacked his hands together. "Weeping icons and statues have been part of Catholic lore for centuries, whether they're found in Carpathia or California!".

The loud clap made Brother Mark jump back and Brother Andrew wince.

"It is possible those tears are—"

Before Brother Prescott could finish, Brother Handle said, "Manufactured? That is what you were going to say, isn't it?"

"No," Brother Prescott responded with some heat, which surprised the others. "No, I wasn't going to say that. They truly might be a sign."

"Oh, bullshit! You're as weak-minded as this idiot." Brother Handle turned, striding toward the large open fireplace in his office, the main source of heat. A small radiator rested under the window, but Brother Handle kept expenses down by utilizing the fireplace. "In Brisbane, Australia, a small statue has been weeping blood and rose-scented oil. In 1992, a six-inch statue of porcelain wept type O blood in Santiago, Chile. All hoaxes, whether proven or not." He pointed his forefinger at Brother Mark. "A true believer does not need physical manifestation of God. And that's the end of it."

Brother Andrew, in his former life, dealt with extreme emotions regularly. One can't be a physician without seeing the best and worst of people. He didn't like seeing Brother Mark browbeaten by the Prior. He didn't fear Brother Handle. "I, too, doubt the miraculous aspect of the tears, Brother Handle. I'm sure if we tore apart the statue we'd find some simple explanation."

"You can't do that!" Brother Mark cried, tears surging down his face. "She weeps out of sympathy for our sins and suffering. She weeps to bring us back to faith. People need signs."

Brother Andrew turned to him. "She'll never run out of things to weep about, the world being what it is." He turned back to Brother Handle. "This event has brought a most welcome boost to our treasury. Brother Frank has been almost jolly of late—for him." Brother Handle turned, his back to the fire, to fully face the doctor as Andrew continued. "It's not just the offerings that visitors have given us; the sales in the shops have skyrocketed. People mail in donations. If anything, we should perhaps be more organized as to how we present this economic—if not truly spiritual—miracle. Tearing apart the statue, even if we could do so without destroying it, serves no useful purpose. Let sleeping dogs lie."

A long silence followed, then the head of the order spoke, voice lower, less emotional. "I take your point. However, if it hasn't occurred to you, it certainly has occurred to me that if these tears *are* exposed as a fake, a ploy to bring more money into the order, heads will roll. Even though I knew nothing, should this prove a hoax I will be held accountable. The order will be discredited. The buck stops here. I have to take responsibility." He paused again, then spoke, an edge to his voice rarely heard by the others. "I've called you here hoping for an explanation of the desecration of Brother Thomas. I lost my temper. I'm sorry. If any of you removed that body, tell me now. I will forgive you if you tell me the truth." He looked searchingly from face to face. No one responded. "Then I have to conclude that either one or all three of you are lying to me, or that someone in our order has something very big to hide. Big enough to toss away a corpse, big enough to kill."

"Brother Handle," Brother Prescott was scandalized, "what would anyone have to hide? And what would Brother Thomas have to do with it if there were something to hide?"

Brother Handle stepped toward them, silhouetted by the huge fireplace, the glow of the fire enlarging him. "Haven't you asked yourselves what is it that Brother Thomas did?"

"Fixed everything. I miss him already." Brother Andrew sadly smiled.

"He was an example of what we should be." Brother Mark finally found his voice again after being harangued. "He was gentle, forbearing, ready to help. He was patient. He taught me so much. He loved our Blessed Virgin Mother with all his heart and soul."

"Hmm." Brother Handle just wanted to smack this kid. Instead, he all said was "Hmm." He looked to Brother Prescott.

"He knew this place before any of us

climbed Afton Mountain. He knew the grounds, the physical plant, the people who went before us," Brother Prescott thoughtfully remarked.

"Exactly." Brother Handle's eyes burned into the three men.

"What do you mean?" Brother Andrew, middle-aged although still younger than both Brother Handle and Brother Prescott, inquired.

"I mean if something had happened before any of us came to this place, Brother Thomas would have known. Secrets. He knew every inch of plumbing, every part of the buildings that had been repaired. It's safe to say, really, he knew every joint and joist."

"But that was his job, his gift." Brother Andrew shrugged.

"Indeed it was. And if Our Lady of the Blue Ridge had been jimmy-rigged to cry bloody tears, I think it's safe to say that Brother Thomas would have figured out how it was done—if he hadn't done it himself."

"No!" Brother Mark cried anew. "He would never do anything like that."

"You're young," Brother Handle acidly replied.

"Why?" Brother Mark sobbed.

"I don't know." Brother Handle's jaw was set hard.

"Well, maybe he thought he could bring in more money, he could lift us out of our struggle." Brother Prescott folded his hands behind his back. "He would create something to provide a steady income, more or less."

"Yes, I've thought of that, too." Brother Handle half-turned toward the fire. "Yet that wasn't really his way." He laughed for a moment. "Now, Brother Frank, yes, I could see that. Not that he would, but as our treasurer he bears a great burden. Brother Thomas belonged to the 'consider the lilies of the field' school of finance."

"Consider the lilies of the field, how they grow," Brother Prescott began to quote the famous lines from the Bible, which indicate that the lilies neither toil nor sweat nor fret about the Internal Revenue Service demolishing their gains.

"We know the passage." Brother Andrew allowed himself a flash of anger.

"While we are quoting, allow me to mention Psalm One Hundred Twenty." Brother Handle opened his hand, his fingers together as he pointed at the three men. "Save me, Lord, from liars and deceivers."

"I resent that." Brother Prescott stood up for himself at last. "I have served this order and I have served you for nearly twenty years. I am not a liar. I am not a deceiver. I want to get to the bottom of this as badly as you do."

Unmoved, Brother Handle again clasped his hands together in front of him. "I hope that is so, Brother Prescott, I hope that is so. But you three last touched the body of Brother Thomas. So to you I must look for answers."

"He was in the chapel." Brother Mark's voice rose. "Anyone could have come in if they were careful, pried open the lid, and taken him."

"Not anyone. A brother. A member of this order!" Brother Handle remarked. "Now that Brother Thomas has been found, perhaps modern science will discover what happened to him while he prayed before the statue." But Brother Handle's voice filled with anger. "I will find and punish any and all involved."

"Vengeance is mine, sayeth the Lord."
Brother Mark was very close to being disrespectful.

Brother Handle advanced on him, enun-
ciating with clarity, " 'Vengeance is mine,
and recompense for the time when their
foot shall slip; for the day of their calamity is
at hand, and their doom comes swiftly.' Remember your Deuteronomy? Well, I am the
instrument of that vengeance."

"Harry, I'm putting you to a lot of trouble," Susan apologized as she fumed in stop-and-go traffic around Virginia Common-wealth University.

The closer they approached the area of Richmond known as the Fan, the heavier the traffic became, as did the pelting rain just this side of ice.

The cats and dogs slept in the sheepskin beds in the back of the station wagon.

"You'd do the same for me."

Susan, eyes glued to traffic, growled as a Subaru WRX Sti skidded in front of her. "Idiot! Ever notice how the people in the smallest cars drive the worst?"

"That's a great car for the money. One second slower than a Porsche Boxster from zero to sixty. However, it's pretty much a kid's car, as are most little cars." Harry shrugged. "Kids are always in a hurry."

"In this weather!"

"You're sounding middle-aged and we aren't forty yet," Harry admonished her with a grin.

"Damned close. Boy, I hope Danny and Brooks don't drive like this when I'm not in the car."

"Who knows what they do or who they do it with—but whatever, if the Fates are kind, they'll live. As it is, they have pretty good sense. I attribute that to you, of course."

"Of course." Susan turned right onto a tree-lined street of lovely old town houses. "Here we are."

"Where's here?" Pewter opened her eyes.

"The Fan," Owen obligingly answered as the motor cut off.

"That tells me a whole hell of a lot," Pewter grumbled.

Mrs. Murphy stretched, as did Tucker, both hoping they'd be allowed to go with the two women.

"Come on." Susan opened the door.

Harry reached behind her seat, pulling

out a towel. When they stepped through the front door of the house, which had been divided into rental flats, Harry knelt down to wipe off each set of paws.

Pewter pulled hers back, shaking them after being wiped off. *"I can do it myself."*

The carpeted stairs muffled their footsteps as they climbed four flights to the top floor. Susan opened the lock.

"What a pretty room," Harry exclaimed.

The animals immediately inspected the place.

"It is. The rents they get, though." Susan dropped the key back in her jeans pocket. "I'll give you the tour. Two bedrooms. You can see this one is his office." She paused a minute. "Where did he get that etched-glass table? That must have cost a fortune. He didn't tell me about that."

"Susan, it didn't cost five hundred dollars. Places like Pottery Barn carry stuff like this. Actually, the way he's pulled this together surprises me. I never thought of Ned as a particularly aesthetic kind of person. I guess I think of him as a fishing buddy for Herb." She smiled.

"Considering we had a budget of six thousand dollars for everything, and I squeezed to get that, the place isn't bad. I put together the living room, faux Parish-Hadley"—she smiled as she mentioned the famous, conservative New York interior design firm—"but the rest of it really reflects what he wants. I haven't been down here in two weeks. He's gotten a lot done. I guess I'm a little surprised, too, at how modern it is. Lots of glass and chrome, or what passes for chrome."

"Now don't you feel better?"

"Sort of."

"Susan, use your head. If the man were having an affair, or contemplating an affair, would he give you a key to his Richmond apartment?" Harry pointed to the law books and research papers already piling up on the industrial shelving. "He's hitting the tarmac running. He has to hire a staff, he has to get up to speed on all the issues before the Senate. And he has to be available to folks back home or he'll be a one-term guy."

"Well, dammit, Harry, something's not right."

"Maybe so, but I'm telling you, this isn't some kind of love nest."

"Doesn't mean it won't turn into one."

Harry threw up her hands in defeat to Susan's stubbornness. "Show me the rest of the apartment."

The bedroom, simple, also had books stacked next to the bed and a good reading lamp on the black lacquer nightstand. The kitchen, though small, boasted Corian countertops, one with a large inset butcher block for chopping. The place exuded a charm, aided by the light—what there was of it today—flooding through the large skylight over the living room and a smaller one over the kitchen. The glass–paned windows fronting the street helped, too, and the ones in the back overlooked a small garden.

"No women have been here," Tucker pronounced after a thorough search, nose touching furniture.

"Only Ned's scent," Owen concurred. *"Danny's, too; he came down yesterday to help his dad. He had his finals early so he could come home. Danny has a four-point-oh, you know. They're supposed to be Christmas shopping today."*

Pewter giggled, humor restored, *"A present for Dad, a present for Mom, a present for Brooks, a present for me, hmm, another present for me."*

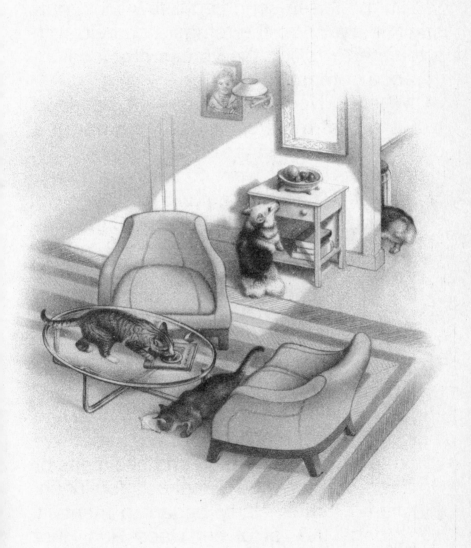

"Want to leave Ned a note?" Harry suggested.

"Sure." Susan scribbled a few lines, putting the paper on the refrigerator, held with a magnet extolling the virtues of a local insurance company.

"Where's Ned's computer?" It occurred to Harry that the etched desk, set up for a computer, lacked same.

"He and Danny went to buy one today. Ned said he's not doing it without Danny."

"Smart. Do you want to do any Christmas shopping while we're in Richmond?"

"No. Do you?"

"No. Can't believe you're passing up a shop-a-thon."

"I've done enough spending."

"How about stopping at the tack shop in Manakin-Sabot? There're actually two tack shops there. The one we always go to and a kind of Western one across the street. We could call Mary Robertson and see if she or Ronnie Thornton could make it for lunch. Or Ginny Perrin." Harry began to mentally go through the list of her Deep Run Hunt friends who lived in the area.

"It's Tuesday. They're hunting," Susan said.

"They may have started out, but I bet they're coming back in. Getting nasty out there. By the time we reach them they'll be in the stables cleaning up."

"Let's call them when we can all relax and enjoy one another's company," Susan suggested.

"Hey, there's another tack shop in Manakin-Sabot. Makes it three. We can go to the first two, and then there's the one around the corner from Mary Robertson's farm."

"Harry, what do you need? What's the tack shop kick?"

"A new martingale. We could hit up the shops in Manakin-Sabot, then go up to Horse Country in Warrenton, then on to Marshall and then Middleburg and—"

"Sure. I'd burn a tank of gas while you grieved in each shop about how expensive everything is. You'd compare all the martingales, buy none, then after Christmas go buy one. Harry, you need to change your attitude about money just like I guess I need to change my attitude about Ned. If you say he isn't cheating, I reckon he isn't." She stopped, staring up at the rain on the skylight. "Still, something's . . . mmm." She shrugged.

"I don't have any money."

"And whose fault is that?" Susan, as only an old friend who has watched for years can do, let her have it. "You farted around in the post office. You never tried to develop outside income. You really took an economic nosedive when you divorced Fair, and now you have a chance to work together and you're tanking that."

Harry stiffened. "I don't want to work for him. It would be different if I were a vet."

As their voices became stronger, the animals filed in to watch.

"I understand that, but if you don't have money, that's your choice. You were born with many advantages, as was I. Neither of us was born rich but we weren't poor, we received excellent educations, we're white—which is still an advantage in this world—and, okay, we're women, that's a hurdle to overcome in some situations but a real plus in others. What's your excuse?"

Furious, Harry's face flushed. "I don't need an excuse. I never made money the center of my life."

"The hell you didn't. All you talk about is

not having it. That's like an alcoholic in Alcoholics Anonymous. No, they aren't drinking anymore, but alcohol, its absence, is central to their life. Wake up and smell the coffee."

"Damn you!" Harry's lips compressed, she sputtered, then controlled herself. "At least make me a cup of coffee if you're going to be a pure-D bitch."

"Gladly." Susan poured water into the coffeemaker. She ground whole beans kept in the freezer. As the brew percolated, she leaned against the counter, arms crossed over her chest. "Who else is going to tell you the truth?"

"No one. Even Miranda will sugarcoat it," Harry admitted. "I hate it when you're right. I just hate it."

"I love you. You're my sister, the sister I never had. I want you to be happy and you can only be happy if you're productive. That's your nature. Other people need love. I'm not saying you don't need love, but you need to be doing something, you need a task, a goal."

"That's true." Harry opened the fridge. "Least Ned has half-and-half. If I'm going to drink coffee I need real cream or half-and-half."

"Almost ready."

The reassuring aroma of coffee filled the kitchen. Susan poured them each a large mug. They perched on stools at the counter between the living room and the small kitchen.

"I've been an ass."

"No, you haven't. You've been avoiding the big issues, and you know why I can recognize it? I have, too."

"Susan, you've raised two children, worked nonstop for every good cause in the county and the state. You're perfect. Almost." Harry wryly smiled.

"Don't you feel sometimes like you're looking in a pair of binoculars? Pretend the binoculars see into the future. I look and it's blank."

A long sigh escaped Harry. "Yeah."

"But I have a good life. I know I have a good life, but I feel . . ." Susan couldn't find the words; she turned her hands palms upward.

"I know. That's why I like solving problems. I've done something. I guess I've held the blankness off."

"Do you regret not having children?"

"When I see you with your children, I do.

When I see other people with those little consumer parasites, no." Harry laughed.

"What do we do now?"

"I don't know. I guess we grow old disgracefully."

"I don't want to grow old. I don't even want to turn forty." Susan tried to sound funny, but she meant it down to her bones.

"You know, Susan, it's funny, but I don't give a rat's ass. It's not the age thing, it's exactly what you said: I don't have a purpose. And I didn't take money seriously, which I truly believe is a woman's fault. We aren't raised to be responsible that way. We're raised to take care of other people, not the pocketbook."

"Lot of truth to that."

They drank their coffee, sat quietly, and then Harry said, "Since we found Great-Uncle Thomas, I've been reading about the Carmelite order on which the Afton monastery is modeled. Back in the seventeenth and eighteenth centuries, people, including the Carmelites themselves, believed in a mythology about the order. They believed that the sons of the prophets, the Old Testament prophets, belonged to the Essenes one thousand years before Christ. They lived on Mt. Carmel. One thousand years later, some of these holy men were present at St. Peter's first sermon on Pentecost. He converted them to Christianity and they built a chapel on Mt. Carmel in honor of the Blessed Virgin Mary.

"According to the myth, the Virgin Mary and the Apostles enrolled in the order.

"Clearly this is all made up, but that didn't prevent people from believing it. Over the centuries the order would relax, then suffer a cleaning paroxysm. Discipline would be restored. But throughout, many believed the story about Mary. My point is twofold." She smiled. "Do I sound like a lawyer?"

"More like a professor."

"Ah, well, anyway, here's where I'm going: this order has a long and rich history, and the Blessed Virgin Mary is at the center of it. My other thought is, what do we believe now that is as patently false as the stories about the Essenes, the sons of the prophets, Mary, and the Apostles? That's where we're coming a cropper, see? We can't see what's real. We literally can't see what's in front of our eyes."

"As in your life and my life?"

"Right."

"As in my great-uncle Thomas and Nordy Elliott meeting their Maker?"

"Right. It's in front of our eyes, but our belief system is so strong, we are so invested in it, that we can't see."

"I see," Susan replied, then had to laugh. "I mean, I get your point but I don't see. Not yet."

"Another thing. I didn't tell you. I didn't tell anyone if that will make you feel better. You've been worried. Crazy things are happening all around us."

"And?"

"Fair has given me until Christmas Eve to answer with a yes or no concerning his often-repeated marriage proposal." She stared down at the coffee cup.

Susan straightened in the chair. "That is news!"

32

A cavern of snow faced Harry, Mrs. Murphy, Pewter, and Tucker at the soapstone quarry in the northeastern corner of Nelson County. The quarry was so deep that snow in the bottom didn't completely melt until the end of April. In the mid-eighteenth century the quarry brought prosperity to the small community of Schuyler. Like everything else in Virginia, the profits disappeared after 1865. Two generations after the war, the quarry boomed. Its fortunes shot upward and plunged down many times over the twentieth century. Despite the varying demand for soapstone and other types of stone, the quality of the product remained what it had always been: high.

"Imagine digging stone with pickaxes,"

Iggy Monroe said as he walked alongside Harry, the animals, and Bo Newell, who had introduced her to Iggy. "Before white men, the Indians didn't even have iron picks and shovels. Harder work for them." His beat-up work boots sank into the snow as he led Harry to the main road down into the open mines. "This stone is so special because it makes the best wood-burning stoves in the world. Perfect material."

"It conducts heat," Bo added. "Evenly."

"This grade of soapstone conducts it in an even manner without cracking," Iggy added. "You don't get the exterior heat that an iron stove throws off. An iron stove can turn red-hot on you. Not going to happen with this."

"You can carve it?" Harry inquired.

"Yeah, better in slabs, though."

"But you can carve it into statues and stuff, you can cut into it to make signs?"

"Kind of a waste. If you want to make signs, use slate."

"Isn't soapstone a little oily?" Bo inquired.

"Yes."

"Could it leak liquid?"

"No, not if the stove is properly built."

"I'm not being very clear. When I mean, Mr. Monroe, is, if there were a vein of iron ore inside the stone, might the stone ooze iron ore—you know, a rusty liquid coming out of a crack?"

He shook his head. "No. There's no iron ore in this. We'd have hit a seam by now, and you can see"—he swept his hand toward the cavern—"there haven't been any iron seams for over two hundred and fifty years."

"Would it be possible to drill up through the stone and run liquid through it?"

"Sure, but you can do that with most any stone, even marble, which is dense and tight. The soapstone isn't a good candidate for that."

After chatting a few more minutes with Mr. Monroe and saying good-bye to Bo, Harry and the animals returned to her truck. As she drove the winding asphalt road back toward Route 29, she turned on the old radio, frowned at the static, then clicked it off.

"Babies, someone has worked on the statue of Our Blessed Virgin Mother. There's not one doubt in my mind. And whoever did it was smart. They knew enough to bury their little line beneath the frost line." She thought longer. "It'll freeze above the frost line when it's bitterly cold. Hmm."

"If someone planned a miracle, you can bet they considered that and figured it out, too," Tucker sagely noted.

"If she's right. It's still possible this is a miracle." Pewter sat next to the dog. *"Not that I think it is, but you need an argument."*

"Can't believe you admit being contentious." Mrs. Murphy was jubilant.

"I admit a lot of things." Pewter slightly tossed her head, then laughed. *"On rare occasions."*

Harry had the bit between her teeth. "Heat tape? Oh, that would take too much room. Could someone keep a pipe warm off a battery? Wonder if there's another way to create tears without drilling up through Mary." She absentmindedly reached for Mrs. Murphy, sitting closest to her. "And how could someone work on that statue without being detected? If my idea is right, drilling up through her, that would take time. How would someone get away with it? And it would have to be done in the summer. Damn."

"She's about to go into a tizzy." Pewter

listened to the note of frustration in Harry's alto voice.

"If she's right, about the drilling, it points in one direction, doesn't it?" Mrs. Murphy didn't like the direction.

"Brother Thomas." Harry said what Mrs. Murphy was thinking. "It's not possible. Why would he do something like that? I can't believe it." She exhaled a blast of air from her nostrils.

Unable to contain herself, she drove to Susan's just as Susan was coming out her driveway. She stopped as Harry pulled alongside her, pressing a button. The automatic window whined as it slid down.

Harry rolled down her window.

"Harry, I'm going up to Afton."

"Why?"

"The report just came in from the lab in Richmond. My g-uncle had traces of chloroform in his body and," she paused, her anger rising, her voice trembling, "morphine. He was killed with an overdose of morphine."

"Oh, Susan." Harry's eyes widened. "But wait. Wait. Don't go up there, Susan. Not yet. It's not safe. Come on, turn around, let me tell you what I've dug up"—she didn't think about that being a pun—"and we can formulate a plan."

"Why isn't it safe? I'm going up there to tear that goddamned Prior a new one!"

"No. Don't. Calm down. Uncle Thomas is dead, and so is Nordy Elliott. Okay. We didn't care about Nordy like we cared about Uncle Thomas, but, Susan, those deaths were connected. I know it. I just know it. You don't want your name on the list."

Susan felt the cold air on her left cheek. "All right."

Once in Susan's kitchen, the two sat down at the wooden table. Susan poured a cup of tea for each of them.

"Look, Susan, I have no idea what's going on up there. The usual motivations for murder don't seem to apply, or if they do, I haven't figured them out. Love, sex, and money seem in short supply."

"I'm not sure about the money." Susan stared into Harry's eyes. "When G-Uncle was here for Thanksgiving, he told me he had willed me the Bland Wade tract, all fifteen hundred acres of it."

"Jeez Louise."

"Worth a great deal of money both as real estate and for timber."

"I'll say." Harry, like most Southerners, loved the land and felt one could never own enough.

"He said that the monastery life was dying. But I don't know as he would have given it to the Greyfriars anyway. In his way, he had a sense of family, even though he was separate from us much of the time."

"Who knows?"

"Ned. Brooks. Danny. The will hasn't been read yet, so I don't know if Brother Handle knows."

"Fifteen hundred acres in Albemarle County might be pretty good motivation to kill someone—if you thought it was coming to you."

"Me?" Susan's hand flew to her heart.

"No, silly, Brother Handle."

"Now I'm doubly upset. Rick is going to ask me all kinds of questions. I'll be a suspect."

"That's his job. He's been sheriff a long time. He's got a sense of who kills and who doesn't, according to the circumstances."

"That's reassuring," Susan said sarcastically.

"Relax."

"Easy for you to say."

"Look, something is going on on top of that mountain. We need to find out what the hell it is."

"Look what happened to Nordy. Maybe he found out."

33

"When Nordy Elliott got up that morning, he didn't know he was going to die." Herb Jones's deep voice filled his office, a simple, beautiful room, windows overlooking the exquisite quad of St. Luke's Lutheran Church.

His two cats, Elocution and Cazenovia, lounged on the back of the leather sofa, eyes open, appearing to drink in every word.

"Keep going, Poppy, it's good," Cazenovia, the long-haired calico, encouraged him.

"He rose, as do we all, filled the time with the daily chores, then drove to work. How could any of—no, wait, that's not right." He stopped, scribbled on his papers.

"Yo ho."

"I'm in the office, Harry. Come on in."

She trooped in, shedding her coat as she walked down the hallway, hanging it on a peg just outside his door. Mrs. Murphy, Pewter, and Tucker accompanied her.

"Rev, you look divine in your spectacles."

"Very funny." He removed his glasses, got up from his chair, and walked to the sofa. "Before I sit down, coffee, tea, sherry?"

"Nothing for me."

"Well, I need fortification. This service for Nordy—" He shook his head. "Can't find the right tone."

"Didn't his parents ship his body back to, where was it, Michigan?"

Herb poured himself a small glass of port, then joined Harry. The four cats squeezed around the two humans, while Tucker plopped in front of the fireplace filled with crackling applewood.

"I think so. Pete thought we should have a small service for those who knew him. But I hardly knew the man. A pushy sort." Herb shrugged. "I don't want to stand up there and mouth platitudes."

"You could never do that," Elocution praised him.

"He's the only reason Mom comes to church. She wants to hear Herb's sermons." Mrs. Murphy noted the large walnut trees outside the window. The birds fluttered on the branches, because Herb had placed a large bird feeder in the tree nearest the window.

"Maybe Pete can help," Harry suggested.

"Pete wasn't overfond of him." Herb smiled slightly.

"Everyone was a launching pad for Nordy's career, especially Pete, I guess."

"I suppose a reporter needs to be aggressive, have a big ego, but I think Pete thought Nordy wasn't half as smart as Nordy thought he was." Herb sipped the delicious fortified spirits. "God bless the people who invented port."

"Dionysus."

"Wine."

"Well, isn't port fortified wine?"

"It's a balance of wine, which is fruit, after all, and brandy. Port, at its best, is regal," Herb answered.

"You feel about port the way I feel about orange pekoe tea." She smiled. "When it's right, it lifts me right up." She snuggled down in the deep leather cushions, where many a rear end had parked over the decades. "Aren't you going to ask me why I've come calling?"

"You'll tell me when you're ready, but I know it isn't about any issues before the vestry board."

"How do you know that?"

"You're usually armed with papers or you're in tandem with Tazio Chappars."

"Don't you want to worm it out of me?" she teased him. "Take your mind off the eulogy."

"Nordy." He leaned on the large curved arm, a needlepoint pillow behind his back. "Pete may have sold him short. Nordy was like a terrier, he wouldn't give up. I suppose I could comment on his persistence. Persistent in more areas than his career, too, so I've heard."

"True enough, but he was barking up the wrong tree with BoomBoom—to continue your terrier image."

"Terriers are mental," Tucker flatly stated.

"They're just scrappy, Tucker, not considered and reasonable like you," Elocution purred.

"But some have tails." Pewter giggled.

"The good ones don't." Tucker barked.

"Tucker, you're not part of this discussion," Harry reprimanded her corgi.

"You don't have to listen to Pewter's insults," the dog said.

"A simple observation isn't an insult." Pewter's voice was syrupy.

"You all can talk all you want, but if any cat opens the closet containing the communion wafers, there will be a serious blessing," Herb's voice rumbled.

Harry laughed. "People will be telling the story of the cats eating the communion wafers when we're all resting in the graveyard." She stopped as the word "graveyard" prompted her toward her subject. "The real reason I'm here, apart from enjoying your company, is to ask you about the Greyfriars. You probably know the men up there better than the rest of us do."

"Some."

"Over the years you've formed an opinion of the Prior, of Brother Prescott and Andrew and poor old Thomas."

"I have."

"And?"

He sipped the deep red liquid, Cockburn 1987, a decent enough year, although Herb had laid away a case of 1983 and was just waiting for 2010, when he thought it would peak. "The religious life, on the surface, appears benign, noncompetitive. Factor in a group of men who have retreated from the world, and it would seem an easy life. It isn't. A ministry is difficult, because if you truly tend to your flock, if a priest, pastor, reverend has a church, you deal with birth, death, marriage, divorce, disappointments, betrayals, the whole human range of emotions. You have financial woes, as you know from serving on the vestry board. You have politics." He inhaled. "You get two human beings together, honey chile, and you got politics. So the brothers have many of the same problems the rest of us do, and in a funny way I think that makes it all the harder for them."

"Why?"

"Because they withdraw to the contemplative life believing it will succor them. At least, that's what I think. And because they have no women. Women sweeten life." He held up his hand. "I don't mean that in a loose way. I mean female energy changes a man. Look at how we work together on that vestry."

"Sometimes I think it's a lot of hot air."

"It is, but if half the board weren't women, we men would waste time over pecking order, who's on top."

"You."

He laughed. "Yes and no. But men are different. Women make men work better together, and if a man finds the right woman, life is richer."

"You must feel so alone sometimes, Herb. I'm sorry I haven't been more sensitive to you. I know you grieved and all that, but I don't know what it's like to lose a life partner. Forgive me for not being a better friend."

He reached over for her hand. "Sweetie, you're young. And you are a good friend. I was a lucky man to have a good wife, and I'm starting to go out in the world again. It takes time."

"What becomes of men without women? Straight men, I mean."

"Gay men need them, too. I reckon three things happen: a man becomes bitter and hates women, blaming them for his failings; a man becomes morose and withdraws from the world, he thinks he can't win a woman or he's not worthy; or, the third possibility, a man looks inward and recognizes he'd better change. Naturally, the third possibility is the one I see the least. People are amazingly resistant to change, even when it's in their best interests." He finished his port.

"The Greyfriars aren't a mystical order. Whatever their reasons for withdrawing, for living without women, creating a false miracle is out of keeping. I mean, that's my conclusion after a cursory study of the monastic life," Harry said.

Herb shifted his weight. "By virtue of being a force in Western life for over two thousand years, the Catholic Church has witnessed its share of frauds, forgeries, hoaxes. The shroud of Turin is one of the better fake reliquaries. It was painted sometime between 1260 and 1390. The bishop reported to Pope Clement that the artist who did it was cunning, clever."

"People want to believe these things. The more downtrodden they are as a group or as individuals, the more they have need of miracles, seems to me."

"My favorite is the preserved bodies of saints. Some have been tampered with, others dried out into mummies, and those buried in limestone soil fool everyone. The limestone turns the body fat into hand soap, which doesn't decay. Presto! A miracle."

"Maybe something like a noncorrupted corpse would inspire an individual to change his life, dedicate himself to God. Personally, I'd run in the other direction. I don't want to be around dead bodies regardless of condition! I mean, I have, but I want to get away as soon as I can!" Harry shuddered.

"Few of us look our best." Rev. Jones chuckled.

"So you don't believe in the Miracle of the Blue Ridge?"

"No."

"Me, neither."

"That's a given." He smiled.

"For whatever reason, I think Brother Thomas—a believer, most likely—and Nordy are connected to the tears, the statue."

"It's possible. Killed by . . ." He paused, holding his palms upward.

"Killed by a brother," Harry said with assurance. "Both of them. I don't think Brother Thomas was killed for his land. He willed Susan the Bland Wade tract. She told me yesterday, and I expect she's with Sheriff Shaw even as we speak. Given that we now know her great-uncle was killed with a morphine injection—I'd guess it was shot into him—she figured Rick should know she stood to gain by his death."

"She told me the day after Thanksgiving. Susan"—he paused—"is circumspect. She thinks long and hard about moral issues. Many people see only her social side. You and I see that she's really a thinking person."

"She'll be a suspect, she thinks. Anyway, I caught her yesterday right after she'd gotten the news and she was going to go up to Afton to raise holy hell, excuse the expression."

"Not wise."

"No. But she was upset. It's understandable. Anyway, I hauled her back to her kitchen. She finally calmed down. We talked things through. The killer is one of the brothers, I just know it. I don't know why."

He drummed the arm of the sofa with his fingers. "No one is going to kill over the Bland Wade tract no matter how lucrative a sale might be. For one thing, Harry, it's too obvious."

"That's what I think, too."

"Brother Thomas, over his long life, saw

many things, heard many things. As for Nordy, I expect he stuck his nose in it."

"I keep thinking this has something to do with eyes. I guess because of the statue and the way Nordy died."

"Literal."

"What?"

"You're literal. What do eyes do but bear witness?"

Harry's cell rang. She picked it out of her fishing-gear bag. "Susan. Maybe I better take it."

"Go on," he said indulgently.

"Hi. I'm with Herb."

"Harry, Rick sent someone to take another blood sample from the statue. Coop took one, and, well, hers came back type O. This one has come back type A."

"Jesus!" Harry exclaimed.

34

A thin blue plume of smoke curled upward as Sheriff Shaw sat opposite Brother Andrew. He offered the monk a cigarette; Brother Andrew refused. Rick offered not to smoke, but the physician monk told him to please go ahead; after all it was the Sheriff's office. He could do as he pleased.

As Rick gratefully drew on the unfiltered cigarette, Brother Andrew inhaled the secondary smoke.

"Are you sure you don't want one? I can call out for filters if you'd prefer?"

"No. It's an indulgence I understand only too well, but I can luxuriate in your smoking."

"No one smokes up there?" Rick was incredulous.

"Uh, in theory, no. In practice, yes." Brother Andrew folded his hands on the small metal table, which rattled with each touch.

"Must be like high school, sneaking cigarettes." Rick smiled, remembering his days at old Lane High School, when he and his friends would duck behind a car in the parking lot to light up.

"Yes. Those of us in thrall to nicotine would usually hide our stashes where we worked. For instance, I locked mine in the medicine cabinet in the infirmary. Brother Prescott—well, I shouldn't rat on a brother, should I?"

"Stays here."

"He keeps his on a thin ledge behind a bookshelf. It's funny, really."

"Booze?"

"Oh, yes." Brother Andrew nodded. "We aren't in prison, Sheriff. We can go to town."

"I thought you took a vow of poverty."

Brother Andrew held up his palms. "We do, but one earns a little pocket money here and there. Some have access to family money. We have few earthly pleasures, if you will, although watching the sun rise from the top of the mountain is certainly a large one."

A knock at the door diverted the conversation for a moment.

"Coop?"

"Yes," came the voice on the other side of the door. "May I come in?"

"Do you mind if Deputy Cooper takes notes? She's much better at it than I am."

"No, not at all." Brother Andrew welcomed the opportunity to be in a woman's company, even if the circumstances were strained.

"Come on in."

"Hello." Coop entered, took a seat slightly behind Rick so she wasn't right up at the table. She carried a stenographer's notebook.

"It's nice to see you again, Deputy." Brother Andrew liked Coop.

"You know, it's nice to see you, too, and I regret the circumstances."

"Yes," he quietly replied.

"Did Brother Thomas smoke?" Rick questioned.

"He did up until his eightieth birthday, and then he gave it up. Cold turkey. I teased him about that." Brother Andrew gestured with his right hand. "Why renounce something that soothed his nerves at eighty? He said, 'I want to see if I can do it.' That was a challenge, so I bid the weed good-bye myself. We became quite close after that."

"Did Brother Thomas have enemies?"

"No."

Rick leaned forward, the bottom of the chair legs scraping the floor. "Brother Andrew, you know that Brother Thomas had both chloroform and morphine in his body, the latter killing him. You and Brother John are the only two people with access to those substances." Rick stubbed out his cigarette. "Legally."

"Correct. Why am I here and not Brother John?"

"We grilled Brother John rigorously. He said a bottle of morphine is missing from the locked medicine cabinet, along with needles." Rick stopped and thought for a long time.

"Needles can bend. Whoever killed Brother Thomas probably took extras for insurance. They'd be ridiculously easy to hide."

"Like cigarettes and booze."

"Yes." Brother Andrew kept calm about

the news of the missing morphine and needles.

"Might I say something, Boss?" Coop
glanced over her notebook.

"Do you mind?" Rick asked Brother Andrew.

"No."

"Did you know the needles and morphine
were missing?" the deputy asked the
brother.

He sat still, breathed a few times, then
answered her. "Yes."

"Morphine is not something you'd want
to find missing from your medicine cabinet."
Rick sounded surprised.

"No, it isn't."

"Why didn't you report it?" Cooper asked.

"I thought I could find out who took it on
my own. If I told Brother Handle or you it
wouldn't help. I thought it better to lull the
killer."

"Convenient explanation," Rick flatly replied.

"Brothers live in silence much of the time.
I really believed I could uncover the thief."
Brother Andrew lifted his eyes slightly. "Bet-
ter this be done among our own. You all,

forgive me, wouldn't help. You'd hinder. You don't understand the order."

Rick, voice calm, said, "You know exactly how to use chloroform. You know how much to put on gauze to knock out a person. Morphine is there for your taking. You would know exactly how to drive an object through the eyeball into the brain. You're tall enough, strong enough to do it."

A moment of silence followed, then Cooper asked, "What was your relationship with Brother Thomas?"

"I loved him."

"We often kill the ones we love," Rick stated.

"Yes." Brother Andrew flashed back on giving his suffering wife the injection that ended her wretched pain. "Yes, I suppose we do, but you are thinking in different terms than I am. You are thinking of murder. I am trained as a physician. My job is to save lives, not take them. My job is to lessen suffering. Why would I kill Brother Thomas?"

"That's what we want to know," Rick said. "For instance, perhaps he was terminally ill and no one knew it but you. You gave him a safe and quick exit."

Brother Andrew blanched, then composed himself. "No, and if I did I wouldn't prop him up against the statue of Our Blessed Virgin Mother."

"I imagine the brothers hide many secrets. The little secrets like smoking and drinking," he paused, "and drugs, no doubt. Little secrets. Then there are perhaps bigger secrets about why each man is there."

"Your assumption is that we are there because of something we did wrong, we are there to expiate a sin. It is possible, Sheriff, for a man to choose such a life because he feels it will bring him closer to God."

"Has it?"

"Yes, and"—Brother Andrew swallowed hard—"no. Christianity is a hard path." He allowed himself a slow smile. "When I hear pundits say that we are now embarked on a crusade, the final war with the Muslims, which is always justified by saying that the Muslim wishes to kill every Christian, I think to myself, no worry here. There are no Christians in America, just hypocrites."

"Surely there are some." Coop's voice exuded a warm quality.

"Oh, I'm cynical, but I know from my experience that Christianity is difficult. Didn't

Christ tell us that it will be easier for a camel to pass through the eye of a needle than for a rich man to enter the kingdom of heaven? What do we do but lay up riches? We have preachers telling their flocks that Jesus didn't really mean that. In fact, the richer they are, the more this is a sign of God's favor."

"Calvinism." Coop read her history.

"Indeed. And then I tell myself that my job isn't to save anyone's soul but my own."

"Brother Andrew, you surprise me," Rick said.

"You thought I'd come in here and mouth pieties or beg forgiveness or confess to a crime I didn't commit?"

"Give me some reason why you didn't," Rick pressed.

"I told you. I loved Brother Thomas. I had no quarrel with him about anything. He was as close to a Christian man as I have ever seen. He was devoid of vanity, of falsity, of cunning. He took delight in his tasks, whether they involved horticulture, his favorite, or plumbing, not quite his favorite. He gladly helped when needed and he had an uncanny knack of knowing when one needed help. I would never have killed him."

"Who would?"

"I don't know."

"But if you did, would you tell? Is your first priority to protect the monastery?"

"If I thought one of the brothers killed Brother Thomas and I knew who, I hope I would have the courage to come to you."

"Well, that monastery sits on top of the mountain, hardly two miles from Interstate 64 and only a half hour, at most, from the interchange of Interstate 81 and 64. It would be a perfect cover for drug distribution— not sales, distribution. And not necessarily street drugs, but the hard drugs. How easy to leave kilos of marijuana? Or Oxycontin? Percodan? Viagra and Levitra?"

"Given our vow of chastity, the latter two would be rather cruel."

Rick smiled. "I didn't say you all were taking these drugs, just distributing them."

"I'd know."

"Why would you know? You don't know who got into your locked medicine cabinet."

"No, I don't."

"I'm going on my hunch that you supplied the morphine."

"I did not," Brother Andrew protested.

"Brother, you *are* the most likely suspect,

unless you can point me in a better direction."

"I can't." Brother Andrew threw up his hands.

"You put the body in the coffin."

"After he thawed out, yes."

"You nailed shut the coffin."

"No, Brother Mark did that. Brother Prescott and I dressed the body, laid him in the coffin. Brother Frank put in an appearance, but he didn't do much. We put the lid on and Brother Mark nailed it shut. I saw him do it."

Rick's voice grew stronger. "And you carried him to his grave."

"I was one of his pallbearers, and if the coffin had been empty, I would have known. Of course, now I know three fifty-pound sacks were in the coffin, not Brother Thomas."

Rick switched tactics. "Nordy Elliott must have known the secret. Maybe he was in on it, a distribution ring, for example."

"He was ambitious, Sheriff, that doesn't mean he was selling drugs," Brother Andrew coolly answered.

"He must have known something."

"If he did, it's gone with him. And with

Brother Thomas, as well, if he knew something. But what could he have known? If
there is a drug ring, if the old man had stum-
bled upon it, he would have gone straight to
the Prior. Straight to him."

"What if Brother Handle is in on it?" Rick
paused as this sank in. "Did you tell Brother
Thomas your secrets?"

"He saw me smoke. Occasionally, I took
a drink."

"You were a successful physician in your
other life. You made a great deal of money.
Rarely does a man walk away from something like that."

"I did."

"Why?" Rick bluntly kept at him.

"My wife was dying of cancer. I couldn't
save her and she was in terrible pain. When
she finally died, I—there's no other way to
put it, I broke down. If I hadn't chosen this
life, to retreat and pray, I think I would have
committed suicide or drunk myself to death.
She wouldn't have wanted that."

Rick was silent for a long time, then said,
"No, she wouldn't." He reached for the pack
of cigarettes on the table, then thought better of it. "You check your medical supplies
daily?"

"I should but sometimes I let it slide. I figure Brother John has done it for me."

"Wouldn't Brother John report the missing morphine?"

"Not necessarily," Brother Andrew said. "I thought he'd have more sense. I thought I'd get to him before he talked, *if* he talked."

"He ran right to Brother Handle. How long did you know?"

"Hours." Brother Andrew put his head in his hands. "The cabinet is locked. So I naturally thought that it was John who took the bottle, see? I wanted to ease my way toward him on this. I thought he was the killer."

"A clever fellow could pick the lock. I'd be willing to bet anyone could have picked that lock. It might not have been John who took the bottle."

Cooper interjected. "Why would you think Brother John would kill Brother Thomas?"

"That's just it. I couldn't fathom it. I wanted time."

"Let me ask you this: the tears of blood from the statue of the Virgin Mary. Do you think this is a hoax?" Rick pressed.

"Hoax is a strong word. I think it's a natural phenomenon."

"One bringing in money, much needed money."

"If Brother Handle were unscrupulous, it could bring in more."

"How do you know he isn't?"

A shocked look passed over Brother Andrew's face. "I would know. Brother Frank gives a treasurer's report."

"What if Brother Handle and Brother Frank are in collusion and keeping the money for themselves?" Rick pressed.

"Never."

"Maybe Brother Thomas found out and tipped off Nordy Elliott. Brother Thomas probably wouldn't go to an outside authority, but Nordy was a reporter, not a cop. If the story got out it might pressure the schemers. Brother Thomas thought like that."

"He could have come to you," Rick said.

"I doubt he would," Brother Andrew replied.

"He found out you were in on the cut of the fake miracle," Rick stung him.

"I am not. I would never do something like that."

"You're here because you're a suspect

for murder. What's a little fakery and ill-gotten gains compared to that?"

"I didn't kill anyone." Brother Andrew folded his hands together.

"Then perhaps you can explain this to me." Rick spoke as to a slow-witted child. "You keep your medical certification current. Right?"

"I do."

"And how do you do that?"

The monk resented this question because he knew that Rick had the answer, had done the legwork. "To maintain my license I must take thirty hours of study, updating my knowledge, every year."

"Required by the Board of Medicine and the Medical Society of Virginia, correct?"

"Correct. These requirements can be satisfied by lectures, conferences out of state so long as the board recognizes them. If I were to fall behind, my license would be yanked out from under me."

"I'm glad that you know the law in your profession, I mean so far as your certification goes. Tell me then why you keep a blood and plasma supply in the infirmary when you know it is against state regulations? A private physician cannot harbor a blood supply. If I read the law correctly, both nationally and for the great state of Virginia, you aren't even allowed to give a transfusion in a private home."

A pause followed this as Brother Andrew sat stock still.

Clearing his throat, the lean monk replied, "That is the letter of the law, Sheriff, but the spirit of the law, if you will, may be more flexible."

"Not in my business," Rick flatly said.

"We both save lives at our best but in different ways." Brother Andrew leaned forward. "I have no doubt you've bent the rules to save someone."

"Brother Andrew, you're the one being questioned, not me. But I'm listening and I like to think I'm fair about things."

"Driving rains, the outskirts of a hurricane, or a howling blizzard, make it impossible to get up Afton Mountain or down. Have you, in your detective work, looked at the average age of the brotherhood? The average is fifty-nine. I need to have blood and plasma on hand just in case disaster should befall someone. So yes, I have violated the letter of the law and I would do so again to spare a life. I simply must be able to give someone a transfusion in extremis."

"I understand that but I also understand that the blood supply is tightly monitored. How do you get it?"

"I won't tell."

"Do you steal it?"

"Of course not," was the indignant response.

"Do you have your own blood drives?" Rick slyly smiled.

"No. Look, Sheriff, I am not going to put someone else in jeopardy. All I will say is one can get blood from a blood bank, a hospital, or an ambulatory clinic, usually run by a nurse but with a physician overseer. Obviously, you know that."

"I do. I also know that if you wanted to kill someone it would be awfully easy to do it with tainted blood, shall we say."

"Blissfully easy. I don't even have to have infected blood. I can pump too much potassium in the blood and that's it. And being the presiding physician, I'm the one to sign the death certificate. It's so easy to kill someone and make it natural, literally of natural causes, if one is a doctor or nurse. But did I kill Brother Thomas? No. Besides, he didn't need transfusions on a regular basis. Brother Sidney is the one who needs those."

"You're a cool customer, Brother Andrew."

"A doctor has to be cool or he can't function."

"All right, let's consider something else. I would guess it's no huge secret that you gave Brother Sidney a transfusion. And no one has questioned the practice?"

"Why would they? Medicine is a different world. There's no reason that anyone up on that mountain would wonder about Brother John and I keeping a blood supply. The other thing is, as long as people are healthy they pay no attention to their doctors."

"Tell me, then, how would you bring up the supply?" Rick held up his hand. "I'm not grilling you on your source, just want to know if anyone would go with you."

"Brother John if we both could be spared, of course. Brother Thomas would occasionally go with me and we'd run all the errands he needed and pick up the blood last. He stayed in the car while I ran in and picked up the container. It's a blue container which can hold dry ice. But again, I'm sure you know that because your research must have told you how quickly the hemoglobin can break down if warm."

"Yes. Anyone else?"

"Uh, no."

"Think. Have you ever sent anyone to pick up blood without you or Brother John?"

"Never."

"No one else ever went with you?"

"No. Just Brother Thomas."

"Would Brother Thomas ever have reason to steal a packet of blood?"

"No." Brother Andrew shrugged. "I can't think of any reason."

"Well, I can if the Blessed Virgin Mother is crying tears of blood."

This stopped Brother Andrew breathing for a moment. "Good Lord!"

"Seems obvious to me. And really, it should be obvious to you. Your surprise doesn't convince me or let me put it this way, it's a good thing you went into medicine and not acting."

"I resent that."

"Thought you might." Rick smiled. "You do confess that you have broken the law by keeping blood and administering transfusions?"

"I do," was the terse answer.

"Well, if you are willing to bend the rules in one area, I expect you would bend or break them in another area."

"Sheriff Shaw, I try to follow a narrow path. But sometimes one must break the rules."

A long silence followed this. Rick finally said, "I'm arresting you for the murder of Brother Thomas. You have the right to a lawyer. You waived it earlier. Would you like to reconsider?"

"Yes, but I don't know where to turn. And I only have one phone call, right?"

"Don't worry about that." Rick rubbed his forehead. "The state will appoint a lawyer if you don't have one. Or you can call someone you trust to find one. I'm not going to stick to one phone call. Your situation is unique because you have withdrawn from the world for the most part. Perhaps there's someone you treated whom you would trust."

"I trust Ned Tucker."

"Why Ned?"

"Brother Thomas. Susan would visit from

time to time. Brother Thomas loved her and thought highly of Ned."

"Mmm. You can try. He might decline since you are accused of killing his wife's great-uncle."

"Are you going to lock me up?"

"Yes."

Brother Andrew's face registered his uneasiness. "I see. Will I be in a cell with other men?"

"No. I'll put you in your own cell. But remember, Jesus died with criminals. I would think being with the fallen would be an opportunity for you."

Brother Andrew dropped his head a moment, then looked up. "I will do my best, but I wish you wouldn't lock me up."

"Brother Andrew, you're my best suspect at this point." Rick lowered his voice. "And if you didn't kill Brother Thomas and Nordy Elliott, being in jail may just save your life."

35

"We cannot but speak of what we have seen and heard." Miranda quoted Acts, Chapter 4, Verse 20.

"Miranda, what have I seen?" Harry bent over the large dining-room table at Miranda's house, where Miranda had spread the plans for her expanded garden and the blueprints for a small gardening shed. "Wow, this thing has running water, slanting windowpanes for forcing bulbs, staggered shelves, even long sinks for potting, watering, and replanting. You've thought of everything."

"Tazio was a great help to me. What a mind that young woman has; she can see things in three dimensions."

"That's why she's an architect." Harry

admired the clapboard structure, a small weathervane on top. "What kind of weather-vane will you buy?"

"Have to think about that final touch." Miranda put her hands on her hips. "This is a lifetime dream. Harry, I am so excited."

"You deserve it. I'm good with a hammer and nails, you know."

"You'll be called." Miranda hugged her.

"Now, about this quote, seeing and hear-ing. That's witnessing, right?"

"Yes, but witnessing isn't talking as much as it's living the Lord's word. You bear wit-ness, you don't talk witness."

"I understand, but Herb said something to me and I can't get it out of my mind. It's this eye stuff. The tears, Nordy's death. I don't know, I'm fixated on eyes, and Herb said, 'What do eyes do but bear witness?' "

"It's a moot point, Harry. Brother Andrew is in custody."

"Circumstantial evidence, I say. Until we know why, well, let me put it this way: even if Rick has enough for a conviction, I can't rest until I know why."

"It's the Hepworth in you." Miranda men-tioned her maternal line. "Curious as cats, every one. That's why your mother spent so

much time in the library. Kept her from meddling, but she satisfied her curiosity."

"Well, that's a nice way of saying I'm
nosy."

The older woman smiled. "You are wonderful as you are. Nothing wrong with being
curious."

"Don't even think of it!" Harry snapped
at Mrs. Murphy, who was wiggling her
haunches, ready to spring onto the table.
"Pawprints on your plans."

"Spoilsport." Mrs. Murphy complained
but didn't jump up.

"Gets crabby when she hits a dead end,"
Pewter observed.

*"That's what worries me. What if it is a
dead end? A man's in jail. She should leave
it be."*

*"When she stops poking around we'll
know she's ready to die. She wouldn't be
herself."* The tiger sauntered into the kitchen,
the others following.

"Give me another example of witnessing."

Miranda rubbed her chin with her forefinger, then quoted. "So we are ambassadors
for Christ, God making His appeal through

us. We beseech you on behalf of Christ, be reconciled to God."

"New Testament, right?"

"Second Corinthians, Chapter Five, Verse Twenty. We aren't being asked to go around and preach so much as we are charged with living Christ's teaching. Of course, some are called. They go out and preach. I couldn't do it."

"Why not?"

"I'm afraid of speaking in public." She laughed.

The door flew open and Susan, madder than a wet hen, blew through it, shaking in her hand an expensive fly-fishing rod and reel. "Another mystery solved! I will kill him. He promised me he wouldn't buy this. I'm scrimping to paint the inside of the house. Do you know what this cost?" She answered her own question. "A thousand dollars. There isn't a fish in the James River worth a thousand dollars. I will strangle him."

"Susan, he's had that since summer." Harry opened her big mouth.

"Oops." Mrs. Murphy giggled in the kitchen, turning on her heels to better watch the show.

"Someone better pour Susan a drink. She's stressed out," Pewter sensibly suggested.

"You knew!" Susan's eyes widened. "You knew and you didn't tell me. I ought to strangle you, too."

"Now, wait a minute, Susan—"

Susan threw the rod on the table, saw that it plopped on blueprints and plans, and quickly picked it up. "I'm sorry, Miranda."

"Girls, a late-afternoon sherry might be in order."

"Thank God." Pewter rubbed against Miranda's legs.

"I'll take a baseball bat, thank you." Susan's eyes burned.

"Oh, Suz, come on. Take a drink. Sit down. I can explain, really, I can."

Once settled in the living room, Miranda handed each woman a sherry glass. Harry wasn't a drinker, but a sip of sherry on a cold day can provide a touch of warmth.

"You two sort this out and I'll bring in scones and tea. A bit of hot tea with sherry works wonders."

As Miranda bustled in the kitchen, the animals with her because she tossed them treats, Harry started in, "It's like this: Herb borrowed the new rod and reel. He made a bet with Ned last summer and, I don't remember what it was, but anyway, he won, so he got to use Ned's fancy rod and reel for a fishing trip over in Monterey on the Jackson River. Ned feared your wrath, so Herb kept the rod and reel at his house. Guess Ned took it back. Where did you find it?"

"In his clothes closet in the back. I usually don't go in there, but I wanted one of his Brooks Brothers shirts. How could you keep this from me?"

"Everyone needs their secrets. It seemed harmless enough. And isn't it better to know this than to think he's having an affair?"

"He could still be doing that."

"He probably has a guilty conscience about this. He knows how much you want to get those rooms painted. It's so much money."

"For just two rooms, seven thousand dollars." Susan slumped back in the chair. "The whole house needs it. I guess I could try to do it myself, but I just hate painting. The fumes make me woozy. And we just spent all that money on the apartment in Richmond. How could he!"

"Look, I'm not working. It's winter, so I

can't put in any crops. I'll do it for you. Let that be my Christmas present to you. You buy the paint. I'll do the work."

Susan burst into tears, got up, threw her arms around Harry. "I love you!"

Harry, surprised, hugged Susan back, although she had to get out of the chair to do it. Susan was so overcome, they both fell back into the chair just as Miranda walked into the room.

"Girls, don't you dare hurt each other!" She put the tray down.

Susan, tears rolling down her cheeks, extracted herself from Harry, who was wedged in the big chair. "We fell over. Really, Miranda, I wasn't hurting her."

"Child, what is wrong?"

"Harry is going to paint the inside of my house for a Christmas present." Susan bawled all over again.

"What a special gift. That is the best Christmas present ever." Miranda put her arm around Susan's waist. "Now sit down. I'm going to serve you scones and tea while you sip your sherry." When Susan sat back down, Miranda brought over the large tray, placing it on the graceful old coffee table. "Honey, you've been under quite a bit of heavy weather. You've been so troubled about Ned and you loved Thomas. It's been a very hard time. It's in God's hands. You relax and let's enjoy one another's company." She then served Harry, and Harry had to shoo away Pewter, who was perishing of lust for the clotted cream.

"If I beg like George Packard, that long-haired red tabby, think she'll give me cream?" Pewter mentioned a local cat who imitated the dogs.

"Here." Miranda put down a little bowl of the rich cream as Pewter's new trick worked.

"If she gets any fatter I'm going to have to get her one of those children's car seats where you strap them in." Harry laughed at her cat, whose dark gray whiskers now had a cream coating.

Mrs. Murphy stuck her face in there, too, while Tucker contented herself with a large Milk-Bone.

"I spoke to Coop this morning," Susan said. "Andrew did not confess."

"Not surprising," Harry replied.

"You'd think a monk would be truthful." Susan thought the scone, with little currants in it, was the most delicious thing she had ever eaten.

"Guess that's why the different orders of monks have had cleanup periods over the centuries. They become corrupt." Harry broke open a scone, the aroma and heat within rising.

"The question is, Susan, are you satisfied? Do you think justice is being served?" Miranda drove straight to the point.

"I don't know. I told Harry right around Thanksgiving that I had this odd sense of foreboding. I still have it."

"What we need to do is crawl over the Virgin Mary."

"With all those praying people?" Susan's eyebrows shot upward. "Can't, and you can't do it at night. Also, its snowing again on the mountains. If she has been tampered with you aren't going to find it in the snow."

"If she's been tampered with it will be up through the middle, a line buried from underneath. We won't see it. Wish we had one of those heat-imaging things. If the line is wrapped in heat tape, we'd know."

"God, I never even thought of such a thing." Susan was dismayed.

"Has to keep the line warm somehow or it will burst." Harry munched, paused, then said, "Unless the line is drained each night."

"Now, there's a thought. If the line comes out far enough away from the statue, someone could sneak out and drain it. But it would still be under the snow, don't you think?" Susan pondered this.

Harry got up, brought Miranda's plans back to the coffee table. "See how Tazio's laid out her water lines?"

Miranda and Susan studied the gardening shed. "Yes," they said in unison.

"Miranda is going to install leaky pipe. All she has to do for her gardens is turn on the spigot, set it to a timer. She doesn't have to turn it off if she forgets or is busy. The pipes will drain out. Now, granted this is a leaky pipe, has those little holes so it will drain, but the regular water line here into the gardening shed is regular pipe, copper pipe. She's got the pipe packed in PVC up from the frost line, and between that and the copper it's going to be wrapped in heavy-duty insulation, the kind that won't blow up if it gets wet. The insulation runs into the gardening shed, so in theory, those pipes should never freeze. And the gardening shed is heated. Now, she didn't set those pipes up to drain, because it ought to be unnecessary, but if she wanted to, she could set up a small drain field over here, put a runoff pipe to it, and drain it nightly in the cold. See?"

Even the animals studied the plans.

"She's got it." Mrs. Murphy simply said with admiration.

"If the Virgin Mary is rigged," Miranda shook her head, "who could do it without drawing attention to himself?"

"Brother Thomas," Harry replied. "He's the only one with the knowledge."

"Oh, God." Susan sat back down with a thump.

"And he was the one who repaired her last summer."

"With Brother Mark's help. At least, I think so. Brother Mark was his apprentice."

"Girls, I just can't believe, not for a single second, that Thomas would stoop so low to create a false miracle." Miranda's face flushed with emotion.

36

Worn down by questioning, anger, and grief among the brethren, and the press of people worshiping at the base of the statue of the Blessed Virgin Mother, Brother Handle felt his mind was fraying. He knew his temper was, but he would have to go over the same question, the same info, two or three times before it lodged in his head. Never a sound sleeper anyway, he would lie awake, eyes wide open.

Although the news of Brother Thomas's demise had been given to him only days ago, the time seemed like weeks since so much had been compressed in those days. Badgered by Rick, questioned in a nicer manner by Deputy Cooper, the stony faces of the monks contributed to his wondering if he should step down from his post. On the one hand, he would clear the way for a more vigorous Prior; on the other hand, it would look as though he ran away from trouble. Miserable though he was, he decided to stick it out. He told no one of his inner struggles. Even if Brother Handle had thought someone would be willing to listen, he would not have divulged his torments.

"I know this is the second time I've been in here," Brother Handle stood in the middle of the infirmary examination room, "but show me one more time."

"The morphine?" Brother John raised his bushy eyebrows.

"The routine. Go through the whole routine."

Indulgently, Brother John walked into the large supply closet, with Brother Handle close behind. "Everything is kept here. As I've told you before, the medicines, the needles, the linens, bandages, whatever we might need is kept here. In the examining room, the surgical implements are in a locked drawer. If Brother Andrew or I needed them, they were placed on the stainless-steel tray. Everything sanitized, of course."

Brother Handle pointed to the white metal cabinet, lock prominent by the handle. "It's in there."

"Yes." Brother John pulled a key from a chain around his neck. "Only Brother Andrew and myself have a key."

Brother Handle knelt down, peering at the lock as Brother John slowly opened it so as not to smack him in the face with the door. "Someone with dexterity could pick the lock."

"Yes, if someone were especially dexterous I guess they could get away with it." Brother John pointed to the bottles, most of them dark brown with white labels; a few were in white boxes.

"The morphine is clearly marked. Mmm, flu shots."

"Have you had yours yet? I didn't give it to you? Did Brother Andrew?"

"No, but—"

"Brother Handle, you need the flu shot. You're due and it's going to be a bad year."

"We can do it tomorrow."

"Today. It stings for a second and that's that."

Resigned to his fate, Brother Handle sat in the wooden chair. "Get it over with. I hate these things."

"Do you know anyone who likes them?"

"No."

Brother John took out the bottle. With his thumb he flicked off the hard plastic cap covering the top. He peeled the clear plastic wrapper off the needle, allergy-size, stuck the point into the rubber, and with his left hand turned the bottle upside down, drawing out the liquid with his right hand as he pulled back on the needle plunger. "Simple. Anyone can draw liquid out of a bottle. I know Brother Andrew is under arrest because he didn't report the missing bottle, but it doesn't take specialized knowledge to use a needle. They're being too hard on him." He checked the milligram bars, turned the bottle upside down, and removed the needle. He dabbed alcohol on a cotton ball and rubbed that on Brother Handle's left triceps. Straight as an arrow, he quickly inserted the needle, pressed the plunger with his thumb, removed the needle straight, held the cotton swab on the spot. "You'll live."

"I wonder," Brother Handle pessimistically groaned.

"A flu shot isn't going to do you in."

"Not the flu shot I'm worried about."

"I know. We're all worried."

Brother Handle leaned forward in the chair. "At what temperature does blood freeze?"

"30.99 degrees Fahrenheit. That's why blood is separated from plasma; the water and minerals freeze earlier than the actual blood."

"Who would steal blood?" Brother Handle asked.

"No one. It breaks down quickly. It would be worthless in medical applications." Brother John opened his hands, palms upward. "Unless the thief were a doctor or trained nurse, the blood would be useless rapidly. I can't see any reason for someone to steal blood."

"Do you count the blood packets each day?" Brother Handle's eyes bored into Brother John.

"No. Brother Andrew and I did count them but not every day."

"Did you ever lose any?"

"No." Brother John shut the refrigerator door. "Wait. Yes. September."

"What happened?"

"Brother Thomas and Brother Andrew picked up a container—you know those big blue containers with dry ice—of blood. They parked the car up here and then couldn't find the blood."

"Container."

"The container was in the car."

"I see."

"This is December. What does that have to do with the terrible situation—I know Brother Andrew is under suspicion but I don't see what blood has to do with it nor do I think Brother Andrew would kill Brother Thomas. It's absurd." Brother John's jaw set hard.

"I don't know, anymore. But I do know it took a crane to put Mary back on her boulder, and that was mid-September." Brother Handle raised his voice. "Who? If not Brother Andrew? *Who?*"

Brother John walked over to the Prior. "We live close together here, Brother Handle, yet we don't know about one another on many levels. A man could live his entire adult life here and others would only know of his temperament and his habits. Who is to say what or why?"

"You're certainly sanguine about it, forgive the pun."

"I'm a scientist. A doctor is a scientist. If I remain dispassionate I can help you more readily than if I'm emotionally involved." Brother John noted to himself that Brother Handle did not know about the laws involving the storage of blood by private physicians. He wondered how long before the Prior would begin making queries to outside doctors and learn about what Brother John considered a necessary irregularity.

Brother Mark ran into the infirmary. "Brother Handle!" he called out.

"Speaking of emotions," Brother Handle sourly said. "I'm in the supply room."

Brother Mark hurried to the open door. "Brother Handle, the main boiler broke down."

"Well, fix it."

"I don't know if I can."

"You spent all that time assisting Brother Thomas and you can't fix the boiler?" Brother Handle's hands flew up in the air in disgust.

"I lack his gift," Brother Mark pleaded.

"You'd better find it, because I am not calling j. g. cohen."

"That's an electrical company, Brother," Brother John quietly corrected him.

"All right, then," Brother Handle fumed, "I am not calling a plumbing company. Bunch of damned thieves. The type that set upon St. Paul."

"Setting that aside, it's nineteen degrees outside," Brother John flatly remarked.

To Brother Mark, the Prior sputtered, "Isn't there anyone else in this place who knows some plumbing?"

"Brother Prescott knows a little bit about the boiler. He was with us this summer when we drained the boiler, drained all the radiators, and then restored the pressure."

"Get him, then!" Brother Handle bellowed.

"Yes, sir, but," Brother Mark's voice trembled, "if I can't fix it, you really will have to call a plumber right away, because if the radiators freeze they will blow apart. A big chunk of metal could kill someone."

This stopped Brother Handle. "Let's all go down into the bowels of this place. You, too, Brother John."

Once in the cavernous underground, they stepped down another four feet to the enormous cast-iron furnace built in 1914, installed that same year. It was still heated with coal, the huge pile of dense anthracite, shovel next to it, near the open door of the furnace.

A water gauge—a clear tube one foot tall on iron hinges—was attached to the side of the furnace but far enough away from the metal itself so one would not be burned when reading it. The pressure gauge, face as large as a railroad clock, sat atop a pipe emerging from the box of the furnace itself.

"Pressure's falling fast," Brother Prescott, summoned by Brother Mark, stated the obvious.

"She's full up on coal. I shoveled it in myself," Brother Mark said, his grimy hands proving it.

"You know," Brother Prescott spoke to Brother Handle, "most people alive today have never seen a boiler like this, a furnace this huge. Brother Thomas worked on these kinds of things when he was a boy. If you call a plumber, chances are whoever walks in here will be over his head. All he'll tell you to do is to replace it with a modern furnace or heat pumps."

"I know that!" Brother Handle snapped.

"The only thing I can think of is that one of our water pipes is leaking or burst. Everything here is all right," Brother Mark added.

"You're the smallest; you'll have to get into the crawl space. It has to be down here," Brother Prescott stated. "If a pipe had burst in the kitchen or the bathrooms, we'd know. There'd be water everywhere."

"Here." Brother John handed the young man a powerful flashlight, then gave him a leg up to wiggle into the crawl space, a maze of pipes.

Brother Mark slid along the cold underbelly of the monastery. Cobwebs festooned his robe. The robe itself was an impediment. The occasional rat stared at him, then scurried away. At last, he found the leak at a U-joint where the pipes turned toward the housing side of the building. He was belly-flat in water.

He then had to back out, bumping his head in the process.

Brother Prescott grabbed his feet when they dangled from the crawl space.

A begrimed Brother Mark announced, "I found it. I need a new U-joint, a wrench, and grease. We need to turn off the main water valve. I can fix it in an hour, in less time if one of you will come in with me and hold the light, hand me the tools."

"I'll shut off the water valve," Brother John volunteered.

"Brother Prescott, get in there with him," Brother Handle commanded. "We've got to get this fixed as quickly as possible."

Wordlessly, Brother Prescott walked over to a corridor running from the big room at a right angle. Brother Thomas had kept everything necessary for the furnace there. "How big a U-joint?" he called out.

"I'll get it." Brother Mark, dripping, dashed over to the room.

"Brother John," Brother Handle turned to the physician. "You'd better stay down here to give them a leg up and to pull them out. Also, if anyone should get hurt in there you'll be on the spot. Better safe than sorry."

"Of course."

Then Brother Handle strode out to leave them to it. He reached his office, pulled on an overcloak, grabbed a small high-intensity flashlight from his desk. There was a pump in the forge, one behind the greenhouse, which also served the gardens, and another one in a small building behind the chandler's cottage.

While not a plumber or a particularly handy fellow, he knew the basics. He could spot a split pipe, a worn-out hose. He could read a pressure gauge as easily as the next man. He wanted to get outside despite the cold and he wanted to be alone. Double-checking everything would give him a reason to go out, not that he really needed one.

The chandler's shop was fine, as was the forge. His last stop and the one farthest from the monastery was the pumphouse behind the greenhouse. He could hear, even though he was one hundred yards away and on the ridge, people praying, chanting.

Grimacing, he ducked into the pumphouse, which was about eight feet by six feet, with a seven-foot ceiling. The pump in here, more modern than the one in the monastery, powered the sprinkler system in the greenhouse and the watering system outside. The brothers had long ago given up carrying buckets to the many plants and shrubs as the gardens expanded.

The overhead naked lightbulb, 150 watts,

afforded some light. A standing kerosene heater was lit to provide warmth, to keep the pipes from freezing. The kerosene odor made Brother Handle woozy. He clicked on the flashlight, checking the gauge, the dial, the pipes. Then he got down on his hands and knees, cursing, to check those pipes running out and under the ground. A narrow-gauge copper pipe behind the pump caught his eye. It was tucked behind a large pipe. The copper pipe had been freshly painted black. He scratched it with his thumbnail and was rewarded with the sight of gleaming new copper. A metal box, painted black to blend in with the pipes and the walls of the pumphouse, hung under this pipe.

"He has put my brethren far from me, and my acquaintances are wholly estranged from me. My kinsfolk and my close friends have failed me." Brother Handle, heart sinking, quoted Job, Chapter 19, Verses 13 and 14.

He touched the box, cold to his fingertips. The pipe, too, was cold but not freezing.

He didn't know how long he remained there, cramped under the larger pipe. He blinked and shook his head to clear it, then moved backward before standing up.

He whispered to himself the lament of Job, "My brethren far from me."

37

Staring into the silver bowl, three feet across, engraved with the details of a steeplechase victory by Mim's grandfather, Angus Urquhart, Susan was mesmerized as she stood in the large center hallway, Persian carpets underfoot.

"Ma'am." The short gentleman in livery behind the bowl held up a silver cup, the long, graceful curving ladle in his right hand.

"Hank, I can't get used to seeing you in livery."

"Mizz Big"—he referred to Big Mim by the nickname her staff called her—"does everything tiptop. How do you like Gretchen in her do?"

Gretchen, Big Mim's right hand, the woman who truly ran Dalmally, wore a mobcap with a low-cut eighteenth-century gown in deep maroon. Over that she wore a starched bright white apron. During the mid-eighteenth century it wasn't uncommon for women to be well dressed with an apron over their skirts. This protected the dress while they served or did anything messy. They removed the apron when dining or dancing. What set apart the lady of the house from the servants wasn't so much the fabrics, because a rich household dressed the servants with great care and at great expense. The dividing line for women was jewelry.

Mim, queen of Crozet, mourned the loss of elegance. She would quote Talleyrand: "He who did not live in the years before the Revolution cannot understand the sweetness of living."

Rev. Herb Jones would reply that it depended on one's station. An aristocrat might live very well but then again could be impoverished. A merchant might live like a prince although not be allowed a coat-of-arms or any such distinction. A skilled laborer might also enjoy the fruits of his labors. And then there were the hundreds of thousands who toiled, who sowed but did not reap. What sweetness life held would be found under a woman's petticoats, in the bottle, or perhaps one sunny day when the fellow found a gold coin on the road.

To this Big Mim argued that the century is not that important when it comes to the suffering masses. There will always be millions on the bottom. No amount of social engineering has ever figured out how to truly distribute wealth without either punishing the enterprising, murdering the aristocrats, or burning up resources in wars.

Perhaps she was right. The twenty-first century displayed no signs of a solution, although the leveling tendencies flared up regularly.

When Susan beheld the gargantuan punch bowl, she was overwhelmed with its workmanship, including the perfection of the cursive engraving.

Harry walked up next to her. "Every time I see this bowl, which Mim breaks out for her extravaganzas, I think the damned thing must be worth over a hundred thousand dollars. It's lined in gold, for Christ's sake."

Susan tipped back her head and laughed. "Harry, you are so predictable."

"What did I do now?"

"Not one thing. You're just you." Susan accepted the filled silver cup from Hank with an appreciative nod.

"Mizz Harry?"

"Hank, I need a tonic water with lime. I'll go to the bar for that. Can't drink eggnog."

"Jim mixed it up himself. The first cup will taste ever so delicious." His eyes sparkled. "The second cup will make you roar like a lion. If you drink a third, we'll carry you out of here feetfirst." His deep laugh rumbled.

"Thanks for the warning." Susan peered into her cup, a sprig of fresh mint floating on top along with a little sprinkle of nutmeg. The mint was Jim's special touch when he gave instructions to Hank.

"Now, you know, Mizz Big cooked up her orange blossoms. A little less lethal." Hank winked.

"Thanks. Merry Christmas, Hank."

"You, too, ladies."

As Susan accompanied Harry in her fight to reach the bar, she said, "Did you notice the color of the eggnog in the bowl?"

"Yeah."

"Living room. I want that color in the living room."

"I thought you were only painting two

rooms and that wasn't one of them." Harry snaked through two rotund guests whose stomachs nearly touched.

"I know. I'm getting carried away. But I'll pay you."

"Don't be silly. I actually like painting. But what I'll do is get a large batch mixed up; I don't want to go back and have a second mix. Never quite matches up, I swear it. Anyway, I'll get enough for my living room, too. That can be your Christmas present to me."

"I'm still getting the better deal."

"Actually, I am, because I've got you for my best friend." Harry smiled, her teeth exceptionally white.

After getting a large tonic water with a slice of lime, the two friends pushed through to the living room, a festival of white, red, and gold. Red and gold were Big Mim's stable colors, as well.

In this part of the world, even if a person had one acre with a run-in shed on it, they displayed stable colors, often in a small square on their truck on the driver's side, certainly on the sign to their place. It added color to country already steeped in nature's colorful wardrobe. Even winter greeted the eye with white, all shades of gray, mauve, purple, and brilliant red holly berries set against dark, glossy green. The sky gleamed intense robin's egg blue or true turquoise, at night giving way to pink, salmon, every shade of scarlet to purple.

The living room, indeed every room but those upstairs, bulged with friends, acquaintances, a smattering of nonfriends and a few enemies. The ages ranged from a few months old to Aunt Tally, closing in on one hundred. The net worth spanned less than twenty thousand dollars a year to over seven billion dollars. And there wasn't only one billionaire in the room. There were folks who could neither read nor write and those who made their living with language. The mix, heady, even combustible, represented a true Virginia party, and it was perfect.

Most everything Big Mim did was perfect. She didn't cotton to not being the richest person at the party, but she made certain she was the most charming, elegant, and hospitable. Her legendary aesthetic abilities were much in evidence, and in this department she had hot competition. Again, it was Virginia. Colors had to be subtle, furniture had to be hand-built from exquisite woods, floors, often hundreds of years old, had to glow with the patina of time. If your house looked as though you'd spent a fortune decorating it, you were already off the board. This, of course, made the competition for beautiful homes and inviting interiors much, much harder. Big Mim ran first, although Alicia ran a close second and BoomBoom wasn't far behind: win, place, show.

Then there was Harry, valiantly bringing up the rear. But she was cherished because she knew what was good and because she didn't violate the integrity of her old farmhouse. Then, too, everyone knew she didn't have the money to do it right.

Tazio Chappars, from a wealthy African-American and Italian family in St. Louis, endured an adjustment period when she first moved to Albemarle County. Being an architect, she had definite ideas about design and she loved interior decorating even though it wasn't her profession. Defiantly, she decorated her attractive clapboard house in a minimalist style. After two years she found that bored her. She began to be seduced by Wedgwood blues, putty grays, seaweed greens. The soft curve of the back of a Sheraton sofa sang a siren song. When her two brothers visited her, they teased her but they had to admit, a softness, a welcome comfort, was part of her home and life.

Also part of her life was Paul de Silva, Big Mim's steeplechase trainer. They couldn't keep from touching each other's hands as they spoke to others. BoomBoom, Alicia, Fair, and Ned chatted with them as Harry and Susan joined in.

"Where have you been?" Ned asked.

"Took me forever to get my eggnog."

Ned peeked into the silver cup. "Doesn't look like it took forever to finish it."

"I'm sticking to one. Hank gave me fair warning."

"Every year Jim makes that concoction more potent." Fair laughed.

"Well, Harry, when are your mares due?" Paul asked.

"Mid-February."

"Fair, you'd better party now, because once January is upon us you'll be a busy man." Tazio smiled.

"Every foal is a gift. I never get tired of helping a new life." Fair meant it, too.

"I know all of you have bets on my mare.

Did she get covered by Peggy Augustus's stallion or did she behave like a slut with that donkey down the road?" BoomBoom giggled.

"Girl's gotta have a good time." Harry giggled, too.

"If she gives me a mule I'll make it and ride it in the hunt field."

"BoomBoom, you will, too." Alicia laughed.

"May I have your attention, please," Jim Sanburne called out.

Took a few minutes, but everyone quieted as the band set up in the ballroom.

Big Mim stood alongside her husband. "Merry Christmas," she greeted the guests.

Jim raised his arms, a big smile on his face. "Every Christmas Mim and I love to have you with us. The Urquharts have kept Christmas in these rooms since 1809. Guess before that they celebrated in the log cabin." He paused and smiled. "I like to think of Christmases past; I like to imagine that those guests who danced before us are with us. And I like to think that Christmas brings out the best in each of us. This Christmas is very special to my wife and me, because we are pleased to announce the engagement of our daughter to Blair Bainbridge. Come on up here, honey."

"Daddy," Little Mim demurred, but Blair took her elbow and led her next to her father.

"To the future union of Marilyn Sanburne the Second and Blair Bainbridge." He stopped and held his glass over his head. "To the future!"

"To the future!" the assembled called back.

An eruption of noise followed this, as did the sounds of the band tuning up, then breaking into "The Virginia Reel," to announce that the dancing should commence.

As guests surged forward to congratulate Blair and to wish Little Mim the best, Harry, Fair, Susan, Ned, BoomBoom, Alicia, Tazio, and Paul slowly moved into the line.

Alicia mentioned to Harry, "Have you visited the Greyfriars' Web site?"

"Yes, why?"

"Tepid. Nothing about the tears," Alicia replied.

Harry moved along, hoping Fair wasn't listening to their conversation. He was bending down to listen to Paul, a shorter man than himself—but then, most men were.

Harry motioned toward Fair. BoomBoom winked.

Alicia understood and whispered, "Have you visited Web sites about the Virgin Mary?"

"Yes," Harry said.

Susan squeezed closer to hear.

"I found one mentioning the statue at Afton. Goes through the whole history—you know, the legend of the tears before World War One and World War Two. Tells about the tears now, and the Web master promises to pray for you at the statue, say a rosary if you like."

"No kidding?" Susan raised her voice.

"Susan." Harry elbowed her. "Don't let him hear you."

"Harry," BoomBoom whispered, "he was married to you. He knows you're up to something."

"He doesn't have to know what," she whispered back.

"The Web master—a pseudonym, I'm sure—is called Brother Love." Alicia reached for BoomBoom for balance when a large group of people crowded up behind them. "Brother Love is making a pretty penny."

"I know," Harry replied. "Cooper knows, too. I was playing around one night and found it. I called Coop, but she already knew."

Glorious though the party was, Harry couldn't wait to get home. Fair came home with her, and there was nothing to do but park him in front of the computer, too.

Silently, he read everything.

After they'd gone through it all, the cats on either side of the computer, Fair remarked, "Brother Love will take your Visa card number for a rosary. Extra prayers are available, too. Irritates me."

"That's capitalism." She anticipated his next question. "I didn't mention this to you because you were busy—me, too, and, really, I just found it myself yesterday."

"You should have told me right off the bat, dammit."

Harry squinted, took a deep breath. "Susan said something to me once. She said, 'Sometimes it's not who has the most to gain, it's who has the most to lose.' "

Neither Harry, Fair, nor the animals could have known that as they scrolled through the Bleeding Mary Web site, Brother Handle was suffering the long, dark night of the soul. He knelt on the cold floor of the chapel as he prayed. He knew the killer was in his flock, and he didn't think it was Brother Andrew. If he called in the sheriff, that would warn the killer, who must be relaxing thanks to Brother Andrew's arrest. He hoped he could flush the man out. He still couldn't imagine the reasons for anything so foul. He didn't know about the Web site, but even if he had, it wouldn't have led him to the murderer. He didn't know what to do. He couldn't think of how to set a trap. He couldn't confide in anyone. He didn't trust anyone.

As he prayed, tears falling down his cheeks, he thought this would be the worst night of his life. It was a blessing he couldn't have known what was to follow.

38

A massive lone oak, well over three hundred years old, graced the middle of the family cemetery at Blair Bainbridge's farm, which touched Harry's farm on the western border, a strong-running creek being the dividing line.

This cemetery contained the remains of the Rev. Herbert C. Jones's ancestors. The Rev always considered this farm the old home place, lost by his uncle's frivolous nature. The now departed man had sat under the oak among the hand-carved tombstones and read his life away. Fond of Russian novels, he had learned Russian, but he also devoured literature in French, Italian, and German. Brilliant though he was, the

stout fellow hadn't a grain of common sense.

A parson barely makes enough to keep body and soul together. Herb couldn't step in to repair the outbuildings or the house. When hard necessity dictated the farm must be sold, he was glad a young, well-to-do man bought it. Blair transformed the farm into a tidy, working place, helped by Harry's country wisdom.

A light snow fell on the oak as Harry and Blair stood underneath. At 7:45 A.M. the skies promised even more snow to come, for clouds darkened in the west. In the country, people meet early, since the workday begins by six A.M. In summertime, it often begins at five A.M., so people and animals can beat the heat.

"There you have it." He smiled wanly. "I've poured my heart into this farm." He laughed. "If I'd known how much work these couple of hundred would be!" He whistled. "I would never have made it without you."

"You're a very intelligent man, Blair. You would have figured it out," she demurred.

"What I would have done is hire a consultant who would have charged me an arm and a leg. You did it all because you're a good neighbor. I don't think there's anything you don't know about farming." He sighed deeply. "It's so beautiful in this graveyard, with the wrought-iron fence, this oak, which was a sapling seventy years before the American Revolution. Guess you know why we're here."

"Well, Blair, I have a pretty good idea."

"You asked if I would come to you first if I decided to sell. I love this farm, but Little Mim wants to live at Aunt Tally's. She'll inherit that farm, and I guess both she and Stafford will inherit Dalmally someday."

"Be a cold day in hell, because the Urquharts live forever." Harry laughed.

"I thought of that. I expect that Dalmally will go to Stafford's children and to ours. We hope to have children. Mim's spoken to her brother in New York about all this. They're on the same page. But I hate to leave this place, I really do, even though Rose Hill is only another two miles down the road."

"It's a lovely, lovely place, and you two will make it your own."

"I expect Aunt Tally will drive us both crazy sometimes, but you know, she's a good woman. I'm glad to know her. She's a free thinker. To have that kind of energy at ninety-nine, she really has become one of my heroes."

"Mine, too."

He paused, watching a blue jay fly onto a tombstone, bitch and moan at the cats below, then fly off, dusting them with snow. "Jane Fogleman at Roy Wheeler Realty says I can ask one point two million and probably sell for a million, but—" Harry's face fell. He held up his hand. "You and Herb can't come up with that kind of money. Here's what I propose. You've saved me plenty. You laid out my pastures. Took me to the tractor dealers. Introduced me to the honest workmen and craftsmen in the county. You hauled me over to Art Bushey and got me a deal on two trucks. You even sat down and explained to me what a four-ten axle is compared to a lesser one and why I needed that to haul cattle although it would make for a bouncier ride. You spent weeks with me that one summer showing me the different kinds of cattle, the ratio of meat to bone. You were patient. You're a good friend to me. Let me be a good friend to you. I'll sell the farm to you and Herb for five hundred thousand dollars. I'll write you up a lease-to-buy contract for all my equipment. It will be simple, five thousand dollars a year. You maintain the equipment and you give me the right to borrow it from time to time should Aunt Tally's tractors or implements break down. How does that sound?"

Stunned, Harry opened her mouth, but nothing came out.

"*Yes!*" Mrs. Murphy spoke for her human.

"*But we don't have the money.*" Tucker's brown eyes implored the tiger cat to think of something.

"*You don't pass on a deal like that, Tucker. And she'll get the money. Risk drives people forward. This kind of scramble separates the sheep from the goats.*"

Her mind racing, Harry gulped the cold restorative air. She held out her hand. "Blair, I accept your offer. How much time do I have to raise the money?"

"If you can do it in four months' time, great. If not, a year."

"All right."

He touched a tree limb, low and so old the thickness of it was as big as a man's thigh. "I'm not a poor man. My profession, silly as it is, has made me a lot of money, but I'm a piker compared to the Sanburnes and the Urquharts. They must have triple-digit millions."

"Easily, but they're responsible people. They manage their wealth with wisdom and they're the mainstays of important charities."

"Oh, I know. I admire them but I keep asking myself, how do I raise children in this wealth and teach them that other children are starving?"

"Tally and Big Mim will pass that on. Take your cues from them, and you're good with people, you'll be good with children. Actually, I don't know how anybody does it. I can raise cats, dogs, horses, and cattle, but I don't know how I'd do with the human variety."

He beamed. "You'd do just fine. Probably have them cleaning tack by the time they could walk."

She laughed, a sense of relief and fear bearing on her with equal measure. "Blair, you're probably right."

As she walked back through the snow, passing the ever-growing beaver dam in the creek, she thought about how unpredictable was life. Then she laughed out loud because she was glad of it.

"Happy," Pewter, jumping from human footstep to human footstep, remarked.

"For once, she's taking a big chance. Even if she falls on her face, and I know she won't," Mrs. Murphy said, *"this will be good for her. She'll finally make good in the world, the human world."*

Once beyond the beaver dam, beyond the low hillock at a right angle to the pond the beavers had created, Harry noticed fox tracks heading to the den on the hillock. "Smart," she said to her companions.

"Too smart," Tucker replied.

Harry lifted her head. "Hey, come on." She ran through the snow, breathing heavily. Snow wore you out.

Opening the door from the kitchen was Susan, and Harry reached it just as Susan was leaving. Before she could open her mouth to exclaim her good fortune, Susan grabbed her by the arm, pulling her into her own kitchen. She helped Harry with her coat.

"Susan, I can—"

"Harry, Ned ran a check on the Brother Love site. Ned forgot about it until this morning. He's on overload and gets forgetful. As an elected official Ned can get information from the phone company, from the Internet services that we can't. He can ask the sheriff to get information, too."

"What did you find?"

"Brother Love was Nordy Elliott."

"What?" Harry had one arm in her jacket, the other arm out, the jacket dangling to the floor as the cats attacked it.

"Nordy Elliott set up and ran the Web site." Susan became more clear. She was rattled.

"What a total creep."

"If Nordy set it up and now he's dead, there had to be someone else in on the deal." Pewter stated the obvious.

"I hate this," Mrs. Murphy said. It was all much too clever, almost catlike.

"Susan, we've got to get up on that mountain." Harry slipped her arm back into her jacket.

"Take your thirty-eight, Harry. I left the house in such a fit I forgot mine."

39

"I'm listing to starboard," Harry remarked as she and Susan once again trudged through the snow. The cats and dog walked ahead of the humans since the thin crust on the snow, an eighth of an inch of ice, didn't break under their light weight. Harry and Susan crunched through, sank ankle deep in powder, lifted their boots out again, and kept going. Their thighs felt the effort after twenty minutes. The going was slow.

"I'm just listing," Susan grumbled.

"The gun. It's heavier than i thought," Harry replied. She'd slipped in her coat pocket the Les Baer competition series handgun, a .38 Super that Fair had given her for her birthday. Harry's hand–eye coordination was excellent. Fair knew she'd like target practice with the competition series gun, as it was extremely accurate and reliable.

A gaggle of buzzards turned their long necks to gaze at the five creatures fumbling in the snow. They'd settled on what was left of a deer. One huge bird stretched her wings wide, holding the posture.

"Jeez, that wingspread must be four feet." Susan respected the buzzard's task in life.

"Hope it's not an omen." Harry's right foot sank deeper into the snow than her left.

"*That's a happy thought,*" Pewter, claws gripping the ice, said sarcastically.

"*If these two think they'll be incognito up there, they're lunatics.*" Mrs. Murphy had to laugh.

"*Mother knows she'll be spotted sooner or later. But coming this way at least they didn't pass through the gates. Mother's afraid she'll be stopped since Brother Handle and Brother Frank think she's a pest. And maybe she doesn't want to disturb the people praying at the statue,*" Tucker remarked.

"*Tucker, why get on your knees in the*

snow?" Pewter thought the whole posture ridiculous.

"*Slaves kneel. Freemen stand up,*" Mrs. Murphy commented.

"*Huh?*" Pewter gripped the ice again.

"*In Roman times, a slave knelt before his or her master sometimes. So humans are showing the Virgin Mary they are her slaves. She's the boss,*" Mrs. Murphy deduced.

"*I thought Christians weren't supposed to worship idols.*" Tucker found human religions baffling.

"*They don't consider Mary an idol,*" Mrs. Murphy confidently replied.

"*Wait a minute. Moses pitches a fit because the Hebrews are worshiping a golden calf, but these people can lay down and sob in front of a statue?*" Pewter's tiny nostrils flared when she caught a whiff of the buzzards as the wind shifted.

"*That's why people are what they are, Pewter. They can rationalize anything. Reality is pretty much irrelevant to them. It's what they make up. It's why they suffer so much mental illness. How many alcoholic cats do you know? Cats on Prozac? Because sooner or later in human lives, in the life of their nation, reality intrudes and it's al-*

ways unwelcome, a big, fat shock. They just go off." Mrs. Murphy wobbled her head to make her point.

The other two laughed.

"Can't reconcile reality with illusion or delusion," Tucker noted.

"Tucker, that's almost poetic." Pewter's pink tongue unfurled when she spoke.

As they neared the site of the statue, the animals could hear people saying their rosaries. Harry and Susan couldn't hear it yet.

Harry stopped. Susan collided into her and they fell down.

"Dammit, Harry, you should have given me warning."

"Sorry." Harry sat on the cold frosty snow for a moment to catch her breath.

"Come on." Susan, up first, held out her gloved hand.

Harry scrambled up. "Let's start with the outbuildings closest to the statue."

"The glassed-in greenhouse below, the garden cottage, the chandler's cottage. The other outbuildings and shops fan out all along the back high ridge."

"I wish we could go over the Virgin Mary with a fine-tooth comb." Harry sighed.

"Springtime," Susan answered.

"That will be too late." Harry stayed down on the slope away from the statue.

They passed the pumphouse and the greenhouse, electing to go to the chandler's cottage first since they could see figures inside the greenhouse.

The heavy door to the chandler's cottage was shut against the cold, snow piling by the door. Smoke spiraled out of the chimney, then swooped down low as though a large hand pushed the gray smoke flat.

Harry opened the door.

"Harry." Brother Mark smiled. "I'm glad you're here. Business has been light given all this weather. Hi, Susan. You know, it's not the same around here without Brother Thomas."

"I can well imagine." Susan loved the odor of the different candles. "What are you doing in the candle shop?"

"Brother Frank put me here today since Brother Michael, who usually runs this shop, you know, is coming down with a cold." He watched as Mrs. Murphy and Pewter marched directly to a small hole in a floorboard by the corner. "I knew there were mice in here! Every now and then Brother

Michael complains of a chewed candle—never one of the tallow candles, always beeswax."

"Does Brother Michael make all these candles?" Susan admired a huge taper.

"He has help."

"Do you ever make any?" Harry inquired.

"No. It's a little too artistic for me. I mean, I can pour the wax in the molds, that part is okay, but it's when Brother Michael wants colors. I mess it up." He brightened. "I can collect beeswax with the best of them. They call me when they get stuck."

"Mountain honey." Susan could drink an entire jar of honey and savor every drop. However, the calories would send her right over the edge.

"Brother Prescott has charge of the hives. Funny to think of him in beekeeper's garb. Of course, the hives are in the same places they have been since the nineteenth century. Got 'em at the edge of every meadow."

Harry had sidled up to the computer as Susan and Brother Mark chatted. She noted that the computer was new, sophisticated.

Brother Mark caught her observation out

of the corner of his eye. "Something, isn't it?"

"I thought you all had old stuff." Harry admired the thin flat screen in front of her.

"We did. Brother Prescott and I talked Brother Handle into a new system. Every shop is connected. Brother Frank can sit in his office and call up sales figures when they are transacted."

"What about Brother Handle?" Susan asked with seeming innocence.

"He's got the best." Brother Mark leaned forward and said conspiratorially, "About all he can do is turn it on. Great piece of equipment wasted."

"I would guess a lot of the brothers don't know how to use a computer." Harry couldn't take her eyes from the screen, its resolution crisp and clean.

"Uh, it's an age thing. I mean mostly it's an age thing. The brothers running the shops had to learn, didn't much like it. The others don't use them."

"Did my great-uncle know how to use one?" Susan asked.

"He could do anything. If it had a motor or was wired, Brother Thomas could figure it out."

"He was pretty amazing," Susan agreed.

"I know you're down there," Mrs. Murphy called into the mouse opening.

A high voice called back, *"And down here we'll stay."*

Another voice yelled, *"Hairy brute."*

Mrs. Murphy stuck her paw in the hole.

"Wouldn't you love to grab one!" Pewter's pupils grew large in her chartreuse eyes.

As the cats fiddled with the mouse hole, Tucker sniffed everything. All was in order.

"Do you own a computer?" Harry asked.

"No." Brother Mark pointed out a candle in the shape of a cat.

"Girls." Harry pointed to the candle.

The cats glanced at the object, then returned their focus to the mice between the floorboards and the joists.

"I'll buy this for the kitties." Susan reached into her jeans' pocket for bills. "Brother Mark, do you think you'll remain a monk?"

He paused a long time. "It was easier when I had Brother Thomas to turn to, to work with. Now I feel pretty much alone. I don't know if I'm cut out for the contemplative life."

"Darn." Susan dropped her money, bills fluttering to the floor.

Harry bent down to retrieve them and her .38 gun handle clearly showed in her jacket pocket.

"What are you doing with a gun?" Brother Mark's voice rose to a higher register.

"Forgot to put it away after target practice," she fibbed.

"Stuff it down in your pocket. Everyone's jumpy around here."

"You think Brother Andrew killed my great-uncle?" asked Susan.

"I don't know." Brother Mark accepted the bills, his palm open. "He had the best opportunity for it."

"It is strange," she concurred. "Don't all those people at the statue work on your nerves?"

"No, not really. They need help and comfort. And they're generous. Even the poor ones leave something. I believe that Our Lady will intercede for them. She may not give them what they ask for, but she'll give them what's best."

"Yes," Susan simply said.

"She ought to do something about these mice," Pewter piped up.

Slyly, Harry reached for the keyboard but didn't touch it. "Brother Mark, did you know there's a Web site dedicated to Our Lady of the Blue Ridge? If you send money, the person posing as a brother will pray for you or say a rosary."

"No."

"I'm not kidding." Harry's hands hovered over the keyboard. "Want to see?"

"Uh—well, yes, but if a brother walks in here you'll have to bail. No personal use."

Deftly, Harry typed in the Web site address, Brother Mark hanging over her shoulder. When the photo of the Blessed Virgin Mother, tears bloody on her cheeks, appeared, he gasped.

Harry scrolled up text and Brother Mark read quickly. Then the door opened and she clicked off the computer, stepping back so Brother Mark could step forward as though he was making a sale.

Brother Frank walked in, his face soured at the sight of Harry. "Here to meddle?"

"That's a Christian greeting," she shot back.

He considered this. "Well, what are you doing here?"

"Candles." Susan pointed to the bag into which Brother Mark was placing the cat candle and a fat beeswax candle.

"Are the cats and dog buying, too?" Brother Frank scowled.

"Mice." Brother Mark indicated the hole in the floor.

"Well, put rat poison in it!" Brother Frank commanded.

"I can't do that, Brother. It will kill the mice, but I can't get them out without tearing up the floor, and the shop will stink to high heaven."

"Get a cat," Mrs. Murphy suggested.

"Right," Pewter seconded the motion.

"You've always got an answer." Brother Frank fumed, then abruptly conceded, "You're right in this case."

Susan picked up her bag, smiled at Brother Mark. "Nice to see you."

As Harry, Susan, and the animals left the shop, Brother Frank peered through the window. "She's on a search-and-annoy mission. Ah, heading for the greenhouse. Stopped. Talking to Susan. Going behind the greenhouse. Now, why would she do that?"

Brother Mark shrugged. "I don't know."

"Nothing back there but the pump-house." Brother Frank turned from the window. "I came in here for a reason and I forgot it. Damn that Harry. She made me forget it." He peered out the window again. "There goes Brother Handle. He's going behind the greenhouse, too. Oh, he won't be happy when he finds Harry and Susan." Brother Frank chuckled. "He won't be happy at all. All right, then, I'm going. If I remember why I came here in the first place, I'll tell you."

"Good-bye, Brother." Brother Mark's eyes squinted as the treasurer closed the door with a thud.

Because of the runoff from the greenhouse and garden cottage, the ice crust was thicker behind those buildings. The cats and dog dug in, but Harry and Susan looked like skiers without skis.

Harry hit the side of the stone pumphouse with a thud. She noticed the shoveled-out railroad-tie steps at the rear leading up to the path. "Dammit."

Susan noticed it at the same time and laughed. "Be easier getting out than getting in. Think a monk can use a computer in the middle of the night and get away with it?"

"Yes. What I need to find out is if that information is fed back into Brother Handle's computer. Every time you log on, it's recorded in the computer, right?"

"Right."

"It seems to me, if all the computers are tied in, it wouldn't be that hard to keep track of who is watching what. But even without that, each of these computers will have that stored inside. A whiz will know how to get the traffic pattern out of the motherboard."

"Right." Susan pushed open the door with Harry's help.

The animals dashed in.

"Flip on a light," Susan said, smelling the kerosene.

Harry hit the switch. "Wow, this baby is powerful."

"Why isn't she worried about someone seeing the light?" Pewter wondered.

"At this point she doesn't care if she's yelled at or not. If someone was looking out of the garden cottage or the greenhouse, they'd have seen us all come in here."

Harry and Susan inspected the pump.

"Wish I had a flashlight." Susan could see that a bright focused light would help.

"We can see well enough." Harry squeezed behind the pump. She dropped down on her hands and knees, and Tucker came up, sticking her wet nose in her mother's face. "Tucker, don't."

"You look silly on all fours," the dog rejoined.

"Susan, here it is." Harry found the thin painted copper pipe. "This has to be it."

"Could run to one of the fountains."

"Yeah, it could, but look how new the copper is. See the scratch here? If it had been in service for a while, the copper would be green." She noticed the smallish box, painted black, underneath the copper tube, feeding into it. She fished out her trapper knife, wedging it under a flat cap. "Damn."

"Frozen?"

"It's above freezing in here. If it weren't it'd be Niagara." She pointed to the kerosene heater in the corner. "Does the job." She returned to the small box. "I guess someone has the job of lighting that. Damn, I can't pop this."

"What are you looking for?"

"I think this has liquid or powder in it. Red."

Susan said nothing, then stiffened and

whirled around. Harry was still on her hands and knees.

"Intruder!" Tucker warned as Harry backed out.

Brother Handle opened the door and closed it behind him. "Just what are you doing?"

"Figuring out the miracle." Harry's voice was low, angry. "You knew, didn't you?"

Before he could answer, Susan, her voice trembling slightly, said, "Did you kill Thomas?"

Harry jumped in. "Are you going to kill us?"

The door opened with great force, sending Brother Handle sprawling on the floor.

"He won't kill you, but I will." Brother Mark, knife in hand, leapt for Harry, pinning her so she couldn't reach for her gun.

Tucker sank her fangs into his ankle.

"Climb up the robe," Mrs. Murphy ordered.

The two cats easily climbed up, ripping the heavy wool as they progressed. They reached his shoulders as he kept Harry pinned but tried to shake them off.

Susan leapt onto Brother Mark, as well, grabbing his neck on the right side. The

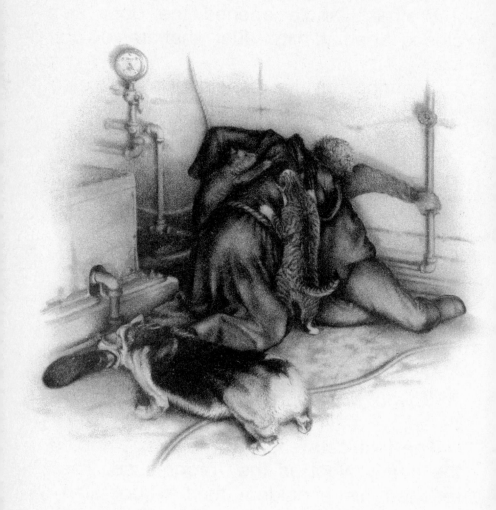

thin, razor-sharp knife was in his left hand. He couldn't reach Susan with it without releasing his hold on Harry.

Brother Handle, on his feet now, lurched toward the melee.

Tucker let go of Brother Mark's ankle, whirling to meet this new threat. To her surprise, the Prior quickly pulled the rope tie from his robe, flipping it over Brother Mark's neck while putting his knee in the young man's back. Susan dropped away.

Choking, Brother Mark released his grasp of Harry, but with his left hand he swung back, stabbing the Prior in the side.

The older man grunted in pain, slightly loosening the rope.

Brother Mark, almost free, swung the knife toward Harry, but she pulled the .38 from her pocket.

"Stay still."

"You wouldn't," he sneered as Brother Handle held his side but didn't let go of the loosening rope.

"I will."

Brother Mark slashed out at Harry. She ducked in the close quarters, firing into his abdomen. He screamed and dropped down on one knee as the cats leapt off his shoulders. "Oh, God," he moaned.

"He's not listening," Susan spat. "You killed my uncle! Kill him, Harry. An eye for an eye and a tooth for a tooth."

"No." Harry steadily held the gun, elbows straight. "Call Rick."

Susan yanked out her tiny cell phone, flipping it open.

"How'd you figure it out?" Brother Mark moaned.

Harry ignored him. "Brother Handle, how bad is it?"

His hand, covered with blood, stayed pressed to his side. "I'll live."

The pain increased for Brother Mark. On first getting hit with a bullet it's a hard thud. As minutes go by the pain intensifies, turning into agony. A wound to the stomach is never good. He curled up in the fetal position.

Susan supported Brother Handle, who was rocking on his feet as she'd gotten off the phone. "Lean on me. Try to relax. I know it's difficult, but the calmer you can be, the deeper your breathing, the better. Honest."

He sagged against her. "God forgive me. I was wrong. I waited one day too long."

Harry never took her eyes or the gun off Brother Mark. "You did what you thought was best, Brother Handle."

"I put the order first." His body was shaking and he was sweating.

"Let's sit down. Can you sit down without a great deal of pain?" Susan gently moved him toward the thick stone wall, slowly doing a deep knee bend against it. His eyes fluttered. She looking imploringly at Harry.

"Is he going to croak?" Pewter was ready to leave if he did. She wasn't big on the moment of death. It was too messy for her fastidious tastes.

"No, he's going into shock. Susan is trying to keep him warm," Mrs. Murphy replied.

"What about him?" Pewter walked over to sniff the groaning Brother Mark.

"Don't know." Mrs. Murphy listened, hearing a siren in the distance. *"Let's hope he lives so we can find out what really happened and why."*

Tucker, firmly planted between Harry and Brother Mark, said, *"I'd be happy to rip his throat out."*

Harry now heard the siren. "I've never

been so happy to hear that sound in my life."

Brother Handle, floating in and out of consciousness, raised his head for a lucid moment. "Hail Mary, Mother of God, full of grace—" He dropped his head again.

40

"It was a simple scam. Straightforward," Coop said to Harry and Susan. "We were closing in, but you two jumped the gun. You know, Harry, sometimes you're too clever by half."

"You said a mouthful." The Rev. Jones smiled.

The four gathered in the St. Luke's rectory office, the fire crackling in the large fireplace.

"How's Brother Handle?" Harry asked Herb, who had been to the hospital that morning.

"He's got a hell of a gash but he was lucky. Just missed his kidney."

Harry watched the four cats play with Tucker and Owen, lots of fake puffing up while the dogs snapped their jaws. It was all very ferocious.

"So the motive was money after all." Susan sighed.

"Yes and no." Coop rubbed her hands on the arms of the club chair. "Mark wanted money. Nordy wanted money and fame. It was his idea in the first place. He'd cover the story; it'd be big news before Christmas, you know, a hopeful, religious story. The story would run as long as he could come up with interesting angles, string it out, which he did. And he was right, the footage was used all over the country by network affiliates. He thought this was his ticket to the big time, a huge metropolitan market."

Harry wondered, "Who would have thought those two would be partners?"

"College. They knew each other at Michigan State, which was no secret. They'd kept in touch. They'd run a little scam in college printing false I.D.s. Neither one was especially honest, obviously. When Nordy started broadcasting from Channel Twenty-nine, Mark, or I should say Brother Mark, the smarter of the two, hooked back up with him. He was disconnected in the monastery. He felt Brother Handle and the other monks disdained him, but he had nowhere to go. He'd burned his bridges behind him. He needed money and he knew from his life outside the brotherhood that he wanted a lot of money. His five years as a brother apparently taught him nothing about the Ten Commandments." Coop wryly smiled.

"Maybe he thought they were the Ten Suggestions." Harry noticed the animals leaving the room.

"Why did he kill G-Uncle?" Susan folded her hands together.

"He cried about that," Coop said flatly.

"Crocodile tears," Susan bitterly replied.

"No, I think he feels some remorse. As you know, he was your great-uncle's apprentice, following him everywhere. Brother Prescott stuck Mark with Brother Thomas because Thomas had such patience. No one else could get along with Mark for very long. Brother Thomas taught him how to keep the plant going, taught him the guts of the place. He learned the wiring and the plumbing. Brother Thomas, pious as he was, suspected the bloody tears. He was going to discover how it was done and he knew the only person, apart from himself, who could rig that up would be Mark."

"But how did Mark do it?" Harry could hear a door down the hall slowly opening.

"When the statue was taken off her base this summer, Brother Mark drilled into her a little each night. First, and this was the easiest part, he hollowed out her head. He painted the inside with a hard sealer to prevent the blood from eventually seeping through the soapstone. He covered the outside hole with epoxy made to look like stone. Special-effects people do this kind of stuff all the time.

"Nordy linked him up with special-effects people he'd met through covering film shoots in Virginia. Mark learned what he needed to know via e-mail.

"Then he drilled a line from the head down to the base. That wasn't so difficult, either, just time-consuming. He ran a copper tube from the head to the base.

"Again he drilled out a big section in the base to hide all that coiled copper until he could dig a narrow ditch down to the pumphouse.

"He had to do that at night. He could work on the statue during the day while she was off her base, since Brother Thomas would come and go. Digging the ditch for the copper line was the hardest part, and he had to do it by hand."

"Then there was blood in the black box behind the pump?" Harry asked.

"No. Water. He'd send a little water up the copper tube, warm water, to meet the blood, and gravity did the rest." Coop admired the plan.

"Ah, that's why he picked winter." Susan got it. "In warm weather she'd cry all the time; he'd have to replace the blood."

"Right. This way he could make the miracle last longer yet be a little unpredictable. He could refill the head. The plug unscrewed once he would scrape off the bonding glue. He only refilled her once, replaced the glue with his special-effects touches—makeup for statues! It was very clever. And remember, he stole one container full of blood types. He didn't know when he could steal another. Sooner or later Brother Andrew or Brother John would have caught him."

"Then why in God's name did he remove Thomas's body? That was so disrespectful!" Susan's face reddened.

He panicked." Coop dropped two perfectly square sugar cubes in her coffee.

Herb's secretary, Linda, had brought a
large silver service, placing it on the coffee
table. Her office was just off Herb's, and the
handy kitchen was next to that.

"Why? Why would he panic?" Harry
thought the procedure grisly.

"You. You have a reputation for ferreting
out secrets. He knew the morphine would
stay in the body for a time, so he thought
he'd get rid of the body in case there was an
exhumation. He also figured that no one
would find the body until springtime and
he'd be long gone. He underestimated you
in that."

"Susan, too," Harry said.

"Actually, we have to give credit to the
cats and dogs." Susan paused. "Coop, give
them credit in your report."

Reaching for a chocolate-dipped shortbread cookie, Herb asked, "Then why did
Mark kill Nordy?"

"Greed. Nordy pushed him. Nordy pushed
everybody. They argued about the fifty–fifty
split. According to Mark, Nordy declared
the money would be a trickle if he hadn't

gotten national coverage and then set up the Web site. There's the ring of truth to it."

"Was my uncle really praying in front of the statue?"

"According to Mark, he was. Perhaps he knelt down out of habit. Mark followed him. All he had to do was reach around and cover his mouth with chloroform. When he passed out, Mark pumped him full of morphine. Those allergy needles barely leave a mark. Thomas had a flashlight; he was intending to look around. He was suspicious. Mark took the flashlight and put it back in the supply room."

"How much money did they make?" Herb, always struggling to balance the budget for St. Luke's, had to ask.

Coop leaned forward. "So far they'd taken in over half a million dollars."

"What!" Harry nearly spit out her tea.

"Religion is big business. Selling cures and hope is even bigger." Coop shrugged. "The Bakkers built an empire on it, as have Jerry Falwell and Pat Robertson. These people or their organizations, if you will, make millions every year. Now, I'm not saying that Falwell and Robertson are crooks, only that we can't even imagine all the ʜoɴely and frightened people sitting watching T.V. who pick up the phone, use their credit card, or write a check."

Herb glanced up at the ceiling. "Don't suppose there's a miracle waiting to happen at St. Luke's Lutheran Church, do you?"

Harry stood up. "I don't know about a miracle, but I believe there's a sacrilege in progress."

"Huh?" Herb's eyes widened.

Harry tiptoed out, peeked down the hallway. The supply door was open, one box of communion wafers was shredded, and she could just make out Elocution, on her hind legs, pulling down another one, egged on by Pewter.

"What are you doing?" Harry shouted.

"Run for your life!" Elocution shot out of the closet so fast she knocked over Pewter, who quickly scrambled to her feet.

The cats hurried up the stairwell, as the closet was underneath it. The dogs, larger, couldn't slip through the stair rails, so they skidded around the end of the stairs, hurrying up to the landing.

Herb joined Harry. "Red-handed!"

Susan, Coop, and Linda, sticking her

head out of her office, looked down the hall-way.

They all walked down the carpet to the closet. Not a crumb of communion wafer remained from the shredded box.

"Well," Herb shook his head, "we know they aren't Muslims."

"Lucy Fur needs to come home from your sister's. She'll keep them in line." Susan mentioned Herb's other cat, who had been visiting his sister.

Once the animals were collected and scolded, Harry and Susan drove back down Route 250, heading west. They'd called Fair and Ned, giving each man the details. Then they called BoomBoom and Alicia, who just couldn't believe Nordy was that devious and smart. Big Mim already knew, since Sheriff Shaw kept both herself and her husband, as mayor of the town, in the pipeline.

As Susan flipped on her turn signal, Harry said, "No. Let's go back up to Afton. I want to see the Blessed Virgin Mary again. I have a prayer."

"Funny, I do, too."

Harry turned to the animals in the back of Susan's station wagon. "If you know what's good for you, you'll have a prayer, as well. I am so ashamed of you. Can't you eat Ritz crackers? Does it have to be communion wafers?"

"The cats made us do it," Tucker whined.

"Shut up, you weenie." Mrs. Murphy clocked him one on the snout, which made Owen crouch down lower in the sheepskin bed.

"Don't be ugly, Murphy," Harry reprimanded her.

"Why eat a Ritz cracker?" Pewter replied. *"They're too salty. Anyway, eating the communion wafers makes a statement."*

"It does?" Owen popped his head up.

"Sure. You know the story about the fishes and the loaves? Well, give me fishes and I won't eat the wafers." Pewter thought herself terribly clever.

The animals giggled. Harry crossed her arms over her chest. "Susan, do you ever get the feeling they're laughing at us?"

"Every day."

This time Susan pulled up to the parking lot at the monastery, which was close to full. The events did not necessarily discredit the powers of Our Lady of the Blue Ridge to the devout or to those deeply in need of spiritual succor.

Harry and Susan, trailed by the animals, walked up the hill, then stopped at a distance from the praying people.

The cardinal flew and sat on Mary's hand. *"Bunch of nits."*

"Good thing no one knows what he's saying but us." Mrs. Murphy fluffed out her fur.

"So much has happened since Thanksgiving, I feel as though I've lived a year," Susan said, her breath escaping like a plume of white smoke.

"Me, too. Herb and I are going to do our best to buy the farm. And this whole thing up here—I couldn't exactly put my finger on Mark, but at least I was in the game. It made me think, made me think about how a life can be snuffed out in a split second and others ruined because of selfishness, greed." She shook her head. "Why? I just don't understand why."

"I don't think we ever will and I don't think it will ever stop, Harry. There will always be humans ready to rape, steal, lie, kill. And they'll either act on impulse or think they have a good reason. I don't think the human animal has advanced emotionally as a species since we've been walking upright."

"Bleak."

⌐usan's lower lip jutted out for a moment. "Maybe we can't do much for the species, but we can change ourselves. We've done what justice we could for my great-uncle. I'm satisfied."

"Good."

"And," she stopped and reached for Harry's hand, "I want to tell you something, something I have carried since I was nineteen years old, since I married Ned. This brush with fate or whatever you want to call it made me realize that it wasn't Ned who was withdrawing, it was me."

"Why?"

"Harry, I've lied to Ned, to you, to everyone since that wild summer."

"What are you talking about?"

She faced Harry directly. "I fell in love with Charlie Ashcraft and I got pregnant. Ned was head over heels for me at the same time. Of course, I never told anyone what was what, and you know how Charlie was. He dumped me like a hot rock. So I told Ned I was pregnant by him and we married. Danny was born eight months later in case you didn't count."

"Susan, why didn't you tell me? How you must have suffered."

"At first," the tears finally came, "I felt lucky. I mean, because I wasn't caught. And Ned is such a good man. Eventually I did fall in love with him. Danny looks so much like Charlie, but—and here's the odd thing— people see what they want to see. Ned has blue eyes, so people would say about Danny, 'He has his father's blue eyes.' I would reply, 'Yes, he's the spitting image of Ned,' all the while lying through my teeth. But what I didn't know is that little by little, I was growing distant. You can't lie to people and not pay for it inside. It's like a drop of poison put in a deep well each day, until one day you can't drink the water."

"Susan, I am sorry. Truly."

"You're my best friend and I've lied to you. Forgive me."

"Of course I do." She thought a few moments. "I can understand why you did what you did. I wish you had trusted me, but I do understand and I love you. You're my sister. I love you no matter what."

Susan choked up for a second, then said, "I told Ned last night."

"You did?"

Susan nodded, sputtering. "It was the hardest thing I have ever done in my life."

God, Susan, what did he do?"

She quietly replied, "He said he always knew."

The two stood there, not moving or speaking.

Harry finally whispered, "That's a big love."

"*Look,*" Tucker barked.

Tears flowed down the Blessed Virgin Mary's face, blood red in the sunlight.

Harry thought for a moment that there was probably some blood left in the statue, and then she thought that it didn't matter. Miracles do happen.

That evening when Fair stopped by, Harry told him, "Yes."

Dear Reader,

Catnip! Tuna! Chipped beef! These are the things that make life wonderful. Of course, I wouldn't mind a bunny with a limp.

The more I write these mysteries, the more I enjoy myself. I don't really need Mother at all except to type, open the canned food, and give me furry toys.

Pewter contributes about as much as the human in the house.

As for the dogs, poor things, they try so hard to read.

I hope you are all well, lots of mice in the cornfields, moles in the ground, and little voles, too.

The old truck finally pooped out at 200,000± miles. I want a big new one with my name emblazoned on the side. Too flash? How about a small S.P.B. on the driver's door? I know Mother is frothing at the mouth to buy one but she has to drag it out, research it to the max. Right now she can't make up her mind between an F-250 4x4 or an F-150 4x4. Personally I deserve an SL 55 AMG, but we are farmers have to be practical. The S.P.B. is a must, though.

You should insist that your human put your initials on the door. After all, they can't put one foot forward without us.

Ta ta,

Sneaky Pie

Dear Reader,

Having just picked up the manuscript, discovering Sneaky Pie's letter, I feel I should set the record straight.

My God, how she flatters herself.

I work just as much on these mysteries as she does. Furthermore, I don't waste time bringing baby copperheads into the house. Nor do I dash after the chickens only to have them turn on me. She's not as smart as she would have you believe.

As for the old truck, I sure got my money's worth. What's wrong with researching thoroughly? A truck or car is a big purchase. I can't just throw the money away so she can ride in comfort. Yes, the star likes to be ferried about in style. Get her? An SL 55 tweaked by AMG. Catitude!

Catitude to the tune of about $119,750 retail base price. I mean, she can't even think about the regular SL 500 at $88,500 retail base price. No, she wants the SL 55 AMG. That's one pussycat that needs to be Number One on the *New York Times* best-seller list, because I'm not buying her orts car. Wait, a sports car with her initials on the door.

I suppose I'll have to put her initials on the truck or she'll shred my shoes. Sneaky Pie practices revenge.

Wish me luck.
Rita Mae

About the Authors

RITA MAE BROWN, bestselling author of over thirty books, loves her work. An Emmy-nominated screenwriter and a poet, she lives in Afton, Virginia. She is The Master of Foxhounds of The Oak Ridge Foxhunt Club.

SNEAKY PIE BROWN, a tiger cat born somewhere in Albemarle County, Virginia, was discovered by Rita Mae at her local SPCA. They have collaborated on twelve previous Mrs. Murphy mysteries: *Wish You Were Here; Rest in Pieces; Murder at Monticello; Pay Dirt; Murder, She Meowed; Murder on the Prowl; Cat on the Scent; Pawing Through the Past; Claws and Effect; Catch as Cat Can; The Tail of the Tip-Off;* and *Whisker of Evil,* in addition to *Sneaky Pie's Cookbook for Mystery Lovers.* She wants everyone to know that the wonderful foxhounds of Oak Ridge are the only hounds in the world supported by a cat.